Beautiful Poison

Michelle Briddock

Copyright © 2023 Michelle Briddock

All rights reserved

The characters and events portrayed in this book are fictitious. Any similarity to real persons, living or dead, is coincidental and not intended by the author.

No part of this book may be reproduced, or stored in a retrieval system, or transmitted in any form or by any means, electronic, mechanical, photocopying, recording, or otherwise, without express written permission of the publisher.

Cover design by: Jay Aheer
ISBN: 9798366503730

To the ones who never felt like they fitted in, a lion never lays with the lambs.

Contents

Title Page

Copyright

Dedication

Official Playlist

A Note From The Author

"We are all made up of an intricate tapestry - infinite combinations of traits and experiences that

Prologue	1
Chapter One	3
Chapter Two	10
Chapter Three	18
Chapter Four	22
Chapter Five	30
Chapter Six	38
Chapter Seven	41
Chapter Eight	51
Chapter Nine	57
Chapter Ten	61
Chapter Eleven	65
Chapter Twelve	77

Chapter Thirteen	82
Chapter Fourteen	96
Chapter Fifteen	104
Chapter Sixteen	115
Chapter Seventeen	127
Chapter Eighteen	137
Chapter Nineteen	146
Chapter Twenty	154
Chapter Twenty One	159
Chapter Twenty Two	166
Chapter Twenty Three	176
Chapter Twenty Four	183
Chapter Twenty Five	194
Chapter Twenty Six	199
Chapter Twenty Seven	210
Chapter Twenty Eight	219
Chapter Twenty Nine	224
Chapter Thirty	231
Chapter Thirty One	237
Chapter Thirty Two	249
Epilogue	254
About The Author	261
Also by Michelle Briddock...	263
Aknowledgements	265
PSSSSTTT...	267
Hey You Lovely Lot...	269

Official Playlist

A list of artists who added inspiration along the way.
Playlist available on SPOTIFY

1. PRISONER - Raphael Lake
2. FROZEN ON FIRE - Madonna & Sickkick
3. IN MY BED - Rotimi feat. Wale
4. DUSK TILL DAWN - Zayn
5. ARCADE - Duncan Laurence
6. I DID SOMETHING BAD - Saphs Story
7. DAISY - Rain Paris
8. CULT LEADER - King Mala
9. GOOD FOR YOU - Selena Gomez
10. LIMBO - Sal3m
11. UNHOLY - Sam Smith
12. HOW VILLAINS ARE MADE - Madalen Duke
13. THE DEVIL - BANKS
14. JEKYLL & HYDE - Bishop Briggs
15. RENEGADE - Aaryan Shah
16. GHOST TOWN - Layto & Neoni
17. MURDER - Mako
18. GASOLINE - Halsey
19. HOME - Machine Gun Kelly
20. MONSTER - Imagine Dragons
21. CLOSE - Nick Jonas
22. TALKING IN YOUR SLEEP - AG
23. IRIS - Valerie Brussard
24. SIX FEET UNDER - Billie Eilish
25. CALL OUT MY NAME - The Weeknd

26. DESIRE - Meg Myers

A Note From The Author

Thank you to you, the reader for taking the time to experience the story of Bennett and Ezra.

Unlike the MMC's from my debut novel Siren, Ezra is very much not your typical morally grey alphahole.
Ezra is an outright villain and although this book is duel POV, I have intentionally given you more of Bennetts point of view so you can watch the mystery unravel at the same time as she does.

Beautiful Poison is a DARK Romance with gothic elements. It is strictly for ages 18+ and features various triggers that could be upsetting to some, graphic violence and explicit sexual scenes.

So buckle up beauties and let me take you on a dark ride...

"We are all made up of an intricate tapestry - infinite combinations of traits and experiences that create the human mind. Every moment matters on a fundamental level. Evil isn't simply born; it's created by the world around us."

— J. ROSE

Prologue

∞∞∞

Then - September 1911

I can't run anymore, oh dear god I can't run anymore.

The chilling nighttime wind beats against the skin of my face as I beg my legs not to give out, my hair whipping across my face, sticking to the sweat that coats my flesh.

The burn in my chest intensifies as if I'm inhaling shards of glass as I slam my back against the splintering bark of the old oak tree, praying the shadows will hide me from my fate.

My quivering hand clutching my stomach, trying desperately to calm my breathing. The erratic pounding of my heart makes it feel like it may break through my rib cage at any second.

All I can hear is the blood rushing through my ears, pain pounding at my temples and nausea rolling in my stomach.

My body is ruined. My gown, torn and soaked in the blood of myself and the one I run from. My feet, naked and almost cut to the bone.

"You can run but you can't hide Theodora."

His laugh is sinister, I try with everything in me to keep silent. I hear his grunting and panting as he passes the tree I stand behind, frozen like a statue.

Oh god, please help me!

The twigs crack and the mud squelches under his large, heavy boots as he powers forward. I briefly glance at his ruthless form, large and muscular, framed by the blackest of shadows. His white shirt, torn from my fingernails and splattered with my blood.

I close my eyes as he passes, merely inches from my face. He hesitates before continuing on.

I silently let out a painful exhale, opening my eyes and scanning my surroundings. The forest is pitch black, laced only with the silver light of the moon. It must certainly be after midnight and the nearest village is miles away. I'll never make it. Never on foot.

Looking up through the trees, their branches twisted and contorted to resemble the fingers of demons, I then glanced back at the house. My only chance is to run back. If I make it to the stables, I can steal a horse.

Oh dear god, oh dear god.

Taking a quick look behind the bark I still cling to, I shuffle to the other side before suddenly making a run for it.

"Found you."

The chilling words are like swords penetrating my stomach as a large hand grabs my hair from the back of my head, yanking me backwards.

Pain flares at my scalp as my eyes squeeze shut. A feral scream leaves my throat as I'm forced backward onto the cold, unforgiving ground, my head slamming against the rocks and into the debris.

The large shadow stands above me, smiling down with bright white teeth. The stench of whiskey and sweat overpowering my senses.

A sob escapes my throat as my hands instinctively fly to my face, a pathetic attempt to protect myself and cancel out the sight of him. The sight of what is to come.

Chapter One

Now - September 2022

<u>Bennett</u>

"Bennett... Bennett, where's my coffee?"
Grabbing my satchel from the bed, I run through to the living room where my dad has parked his ass in front of the television watching 'Spin 2 Win' his favourite game show. His crutches lent against the armchair.

"I'm really late dad, you know I need to be at the club on time tonight or Kano will have my guts."

He scoffs, rubbing his biscuit covered fingers on his shirt.

"Can you just get a normal job, girl? No daughter of mine should be gyrating on a pole for every man to lear at."

I roll my eyes at the words I've heard a million times before.

"Dad, you know we need the money and until you decide to go back to work..."

His exaggerated cough halts my sentence.

"Bennett, you know I'd work if I could but my back has been playing up for years. Ain't nothing left in this old tank ya know."

The exhale leaves my throat louder than I intended.

"Look, here," I grab the coffee pot from the kitchen counter and hand it to him on his little side table with a mug. "I gotta go."

I quickly bend down pressing a light kiss to his cheek.

"I love you."

"Love you too baby."

With that I head out into the evening air, pulling my leather jacket tighter around my body.

Goosebumps pebble across my chest, I suppose that's what you get when you wear nothing but a black, lace bra under your jacket on a chilly, autumn night. My booty shorts and fishnets, doing nothing to keep me warm either, only the *Doc Martens* on my feet resemble anything that should be worn this time of year.

My long, thick, dyed black hair covers my shoulders, serving well as a scarf.

It's natural colour is brunette but I like to use a semi-permanent hair dye as jet black matches my look a lot better. Some call it Goth, I call it matching the colour of your soul. Yep I'm artistic like that!

I don't think I ever left the phase as a teenager, even at the ripe old age of twenty five, I'm still rocking the lip piercing and tiny gold ring in my small pixie nose. I suppose it's just become part of my identity now.

It's only a ten minute walk to Delilah's bar where I've been working for the last two years. My dad has all sorts of health problems so we've relied solely on my income for years.

Jobs I've had in the past have been okay but none have paid as well as Delilah's.

My dad complains but I know he loves the money.

My mum died when I was just a baby. I have a few pictures of her, she looks just like me, and dad has mentioned her a few times over the years, but other than that I don't know much about the beautiful, mysterious woman who gave birth to me.

Dad was left to raise me, and I have to say, regardless of his lack of motivation, he did a pretty good job.

I might have a career most people look down on, but I have strong morals and values and that's all because of him.

The bar looks pretty heaving tonight as I rock up to the front doors.

It's the only strip club in Cedar Cross, the small town I live in, so it attracts pretty much the whole male population for miles around.

Single and married men alike can be found snaking around the chequerboard flooring of old Delilah's.

The interior is pretty sleazy and dated. I would have thought with the amount of money they seem to be clawing in, that they would at least give the joint a little glow up.

It's red lit booths and jukebox that looks like it's been pulled straight out of the movie *Grease* isn't really the most sophisticated decor I've ever come across but hey ho, I just have to keep reminding myself that the men that come here aren't really interested in how pretty the lighting is or how cute the sofas are, they're only interested in how pretty the strippers are and how cute the pussy is.

At the entrance, Jed and Alix, our two security guards, are checking IDs as customers enter.

"Hey guys." I call, arriving at the doors.

"Hey Bennett." Alix gives a small wave while Jed salutes.

"Not you asswipe." Jed grabs some frat boy-looking randomer who's trying to snake his way into the club. He can't be any older than seventeen and looks high as a kite already.

He's with a group of guys who look a little older but not by much and they're egging him on to say something back to Jed, who looks like he's about to dispatch a one way ticket to the local emergency room at any second.

"Alright gorgeous." One of the guys heckles as I pass by to get to the side door. His arm shoots out, grabbing my wrist as Alix ploughs his fist straight into the pretty boy's face.

He instantly releases me with a yelp and I carry on walking, not bothering to look around as I hear the cursing and loud shouting from behind me. *Just another night at the office.*

I enter through the side door, the stench of damp attacking my nostrils and run up the drafty staircase, to the small changing room that the girls and I use to get ready for our performance.

"Bennett, there you are." I hear Kano's voice before I see him. He rushes forward stroking his sandy sideburns and popping a cigarette between his lips. Plumes of smoke cloud his pockmarked face.

"We got a customer for a private dance in an hour, he's loaded, really good for business so I need you on your game tonight babe."

I fake a smile. "Sure thing."

Kano nods before walking out of the room. He's a pretty decent boss but he has no sense of privacy in this place.

"You lucky thing, you're gonna make a killin' tonight." Another dancer, Lacey, nudges me from behind.

"Yeah," I reply, faking a smile. "Let's hope so."

I hang up my coat and pull open the makeup draw at my dressing table.

The changing rooms aren't any more glamorous than the joint itself. All peeling wallpaper and tacky cheap fairy lights. The overwhelming scent of a million different perfumes infusing the air.

Adding a little more eyeliner, I glance at my appearance in the mirror. I hardly recognise the girl staring back at me sometimes.

Tonight my face is caked in heavy makeup with dark eyes and even darker red lips. The black eyeliner makes my jade green eyes pop as I fluff up my long black hair, the ends swishing at my tailbone and spray a few pumps of *Chanel No.5* that one of the girls left laying around.

By the time I've finished prepping, it's time for the private show as Kano whistles into the room in my direction.

Whistles, like I'm a fucking dog!

I say nothing, *although I have the overwhelming urge to kick him in the balls,* swapping my black *Doc Martens* for some six inch, clear perspex heels and heading down the stairwell to the main bar.

Jed leads me through to the back room where a suited and booted, *fairly handsome* customer sits comfortably on the red couch situated across the back of the room. His arms splayed out across the back of his seat, legs crossed in front of him.

Jed closes the door behind me.

"You must be Daniella?" He smiles.

All the girls here have stage names that we choose ourselves, I don't think mine was particularly that creative.

"I am." I reply before waiting for the music to start.

'In my bed' by *Rotimi* begins to play through the speakers, filling the room and I begin to sway my body, letting the lyrics take over as my mind wanders from the room as it always does.

The suited man before me continues to stare, his eyes fixed on my full, round tits as I release the clasp on my bra, tossing it to him. He lifts the flimsy piece of fabric and inhales deeply.

I strut over to where he sits, swaying my hips before turning and giving him full view off my ass still covered in my skin tight bootie shorts.

As I lean forward to touch my toes, I feel a firm hand grasp my ass cheek. Turning, I playfully slap his hand away. *Asshole.*

"No touching, that's the rule." I whisper seductively into his ear and he holds his hands up in mock surrender, a playful grin on his lips.

"Rules are to be broken, gorgeous." He winks. *Creep.*

I turn back around and continue my routine, touching my toes and wiggling my ass tauntingly in his face.

As I stand back up, raising my arms above my head and turn to face him, his hands jolt out grabbing my hips.

What did I just say fuckface?!

I put on my best *I'm not pissed* face and smile at him through gritted teeth.

"Like I said, no touching."

He laughs like he's an exception to the rule.

"Come on baby, you can't say you don't find me attractive."

This guys clearly used to getting what he wants.

I push his hands from my hips as he continues laughing like the smug prick that he is.

"Look asshole, touch me again and I'll have you removed."

He rolls his eyes. *Rolls his fucking eyes*, and stands staring straight at me.

"I paid for your time whore, and I'm gonna get it."

His hand reaches out grabbing me tightly by the wrist, forcing a low wince from my mouth, but before he can bring his other hand anywhere near me, I lean back, swinging my right fist straight into his face. His nose makes a satisfying pop as blood spurts from it.

"You bitch!" He screams and I can't contain the smirk that's desperate to show on my face.

Suddenly the door bursts open and Jed and Alix rush in, Jed's eyes flicking between me and the poor excuse for a man bent over, clutching his bloody pulp of a nose.

"What happened?" asks Alix.

"He wouldn't stop touching, I warned him twice."

Jed grabs the back of the man's collar and escorts him out of the room. "Okay, come on asshole!"

"You okay Bennett?" Alix looks me over like he's searching for a gunshot wound.

"Yeah I'm fine." I force a smile, running my hands over my arms before picking up my bra and hooking it back on.

"BENNETT!"

Fuck here we go!

Kano enters the room. "What the fuck have you been doing?"

I genuinely don't know how to respond to this right now.

"What? He was feeling me up, I asked nicely and the asshole wouldn't get the hint." I cross my arms, staring at the ground, waiting for Kano's response. If there's one thing I've learnt about my boss, it's that he firmly believes the customer is always right.

"Bennett this is the fourth customer you've had issues with in the past two months, I can't keep doing this with you."

I sigh.

"This guy was worth a fortune and he's standing outside at the bar shouting obscenities, holding his nose in a piece of bog roll. Not even my two hundred dollar champagne can help the situation right now."

I stay rooted to the spot, my eyes now leaving the floor, focussing on the sticky piece of pink bubblegum flattened against the tile and turning slightly.

"I'm sorry Bennett but I'm going to have to let you go."

My head immediately snaps up at his words. Horror etched on my face.

"What? No, you can't! Please Kano, I need this job. I'm one of your best dancers."

"Yes B, you are. You're by far the most gorgeous and you're fucking sexy as hell despite this weird goth shit you got going on," he waves his hands up and down my body, "but I can't deal with all the drama Bennett. I need girls who cooperate, girls who..."

"Doormats!" I chip in.

He sighs, running his hands through his sideburns again. "I'm sorry, it's how it is. Grab your stuff, I'll give you double for tonight to help you out, as you've been my best staff."

With that he exits the room, leaving me standing there, with no clothes and now ultimately no job.

Fuck!

Chapter Two

Bennett

How long has that crack been there? I've never noticed it before.

I stare at my bedroom ceiling, the white paint dissolving into a musty yellow.

Our house has never been anything to write home about but it's small and cosy and to be fucking honest, it's all we can afford.

My dad was sleeping in his chair by the time I got home.

I'd headed out to work at eight pm, was unemployed by ten pm and decided to grab a burger from the corner take out before heading back, as explaining what had happened at the bar, to my dad last night, was the last thing I felt like doing.

Maybe I had been a little careless with my job at Delilah's. It was never something I could see myself doing long term and Kano had been ridiculously patient with all the times I'd shown up late or something similar.

Sitting up and swinging my legs around off the bed, I head to our small bathroom and take a quick shower. The water pressure is shocking but I make the most of it, smothering myself in a rich, vanilla body wash.

After showering, I dress myself in some black ripped jeans and a loose white shirt. My long, thick black hair draped over my shoulder in a fishtail braid.

Dad had hobbled over to his living room bed and was watching the news.

This house was in serious need of a clean. If I didn't do it, then it just never got done.

Even if dad was feeling better, I don't think I'd ever seen him with a Hoover or a duster in his hand my whole life. That would have to be a chore for another time.

I grabbed my satchel and headed out the door quietly. Today was the day I needed to get another shitting job.

Cedar Cross was a strange little town. We were this secluded little place, pretty much, it felt, in the middle of nowhere. Sure, it had everything you needed. A doctor. A dentist. A little old bakery that did the best hazelnut croissants but it seemed like if you were born here, you just kinda stayed. For me it just lacked that sense of adventure, that sense of excitement that I was sure existed in some part of the world. It seemed like no one here wanted anything different to the life they had in Cedar Cross but for me, it just wasn't enough.

I craved so much more than this little countryside life.

High in the distance you could see the hefty old forests that framed the fields surrounding us. The same forests we'd make ghost stories up about when we were in school. 'The dark wood' was what we liked to call them as kids. *Original, I know.*

There was so much history and culture here but it was getting more modern by the day.

The appearance of wine bars and little boutiques were popping up all over the place, so it was very different to the town I remember as a kid.

Some residents welcomed the change, others hated the fact that newcomers were tampering with the history of the village.

One place that was always the same though was the little post office run by Mrs Potton.

She was literally the sweetest little old lady you could ever meet. Her pale grey hair swept neatly into a cute chignon.

She would always ask about my dad, offer to bring food round to our house, even after reassuring her that I wasn't a small child and could actually cook surprisingly well. I think she just liked to feel needed.

Every Wednesday, she would update the job search board in the post office. It would be filled with basic recruitment from waitressing to bartending, and I knew whatever was on there would definitely not be making me a millionaire anytime soon, but I needed to eat and so did my dad.

I always thought after school I'd move on, go to uni, build a new and exciting life for myself, but the nearest university was seventy miles away and seeing how much my dad needed me, I couldn't leave. He'd never survive without me, so I stayed.

As I reached the door, it suddenly opened, the little bell jangling from the frame.

"Bennett."

Out walked Hunter Jackson, a look of surprise on his face. His messy man bun and sculpted facial hair, making him look like something that just walked out of a Bourbon commercial.

"Hunter, hey," I smile but I can already feel the strain as it doesn't quite meet my eyes.

"What brings you into town? Don't see you around much?"

I nod, "erm… just stuff, ya know!" *God this is awkward!*

He smiles, this time the strain is clear on *his* face.

"So when are you going to give in and let me take you out for that drink?"

I don't remember ever saying I'd *ever* let him take me out for a drink but he certainly earns a gold medal for trying.

One thing about Hunter Jackson is, yes he's good looking, but fuck does he know it.

Since high school he's been flying from one girl to the next and to be honest that could be due to the lack of hot men in this town but also because he clearly has the charm. Said charm will certainly not be working on me however.

He also works for the local sheriff's department, which he assumes automatically makes him the knight in shining armour, especially as I heard on the grape vine that he'd just been promoted to deputy.

"I'm far too busy at the minute Hunter, I'm sorry."

I push past him into the post office before he has time to

answer.

Please don't follow me in. He doesn't. *Thank god.*

I look back through the tiny side window to see him chatting to two blondes sitting at the little bus stop. A flirtatious smirk on his face. Definitely dodged a bullet there.

Turning to face the counter I'm greeted with the friendly presence of Mrs Potton.

"Bennett, what a nice surprise. It's been a while."

Jesus am I really that much of a recluse?!

"Mrs Potton, how are you?"

She glares at me with those gentle eyes, small wrinkles either side. "Good, thank you dear. How's your father?"

I hesitate for a second. "Yeah he's fine, as well as he can be I guess."

She looks at me with sympathy. I'm getting used to that look from the people in this town that know me and my dad. *Look there's poor Bennett, working at the strip club to support her lazy work-shy father.* I've even heard the words.

"That's good my lovely, now what can I do for you today?"

I glance over at the recruitment board.

"I was kinda hoping there might be something on that." I point to the large, cork board mounted on the wall, little pins dotted about holding small business cards and job descriptions scribbled onto pieces of notebook paper.

"Oh, not at the bar anymore?"

I roll my eyes, probably a little too obviously which I instantly regretted. Mrs Potton was nothing but nice to me and the last thing I wanted to appear to be was rude.

"They let me go, I need to find something else."

Her eyes followed me as I slowly walked towards the board.

It was filled with everything from waitressing to postal sorting to cleaning but nothing on there was paying even remotely similar to the money I was getting at Delilah's, especially with all the tips, being their best girl. Some nights I'd take home a whole months wage just in the extra cash that drunken, horny men were tucking into my g-string.

Defeated, I felt a soft, warm hand on my shoulder.

"You could always come here, help an old woman out."

I smile gently at the sweetest woman I think I've ever met. "Thank you, but I'm going to need a miracle to make enough money to keep things going at the house."

As I turn back to the board, something catches the corner of my eye.

A handwritten job advertisement jotted on a torn piece of lined paper but it's the black and gold business card that sits pinned upon it that really draws my attention. It's glossy sheen making it stand out apart from anything else on the board.

I unpin the card, glancing over the note.

"Knightchurch Manor?"

"Yes, came down yesterday," said Mrs Potton. "Printers have been playing up so I just scribbled down what it said on the email but, dunno, sounds kinda fancy. Found the business card posted through the letterbox this morning. Guess someone maybe wanted me to put it with the advertisement."

I nodded slowly, still staring at the paper.

The advertisement was for a general maid from what I could make out. A bit of cleaning and maintenance work I was guessing, but the salary was beyond impressive for what seemed to be required.

"This is insane." I didn't realise that I was speaking more to myself at this point than to Mrs Potton.

"Isn't it?!, some lucky person will certainly get the deal of a lifetime there." Mrs Potton hesitated, "it's perfect for you!"

I felt my eyes widen as I turned my head to meet her glare. Her cornflower blue eyes dazzling like two freshly cut jewels as she waited for my response.

I sighed, "It says a requirement of the job is that you have to take residence at the manor. I can't just leave my dad, even if the money is ridiculously good. Plus I don't know anything about Knightchurch."

Knightchurch Manor was a historic, gothic house about forty miles from Cedar Cross. I'd heard it, again in ghost stories when I was a kid, but I'd never actually seen it in real life. It had cropped up a few times in history books at school too and I'd never really thought too much about the place before. I certainly had no idea who lived there anymore. In fact I didn't even know anyone actually did. Whenever the house was mentioned in books it had always referred to the architecture, nothing had ever really been noted about the residents.

"Well petal, not many people do know much about the place," said Mrs Potton, pulling me from my thoughts. "But let me tell you one thing, that place is a god damn mansion and judging by what they're willing to pay for, what I can only assume is a housekeeper, I'd say you'd be a fool not to go for such an opportunity."

My brain struggled to process her words. I did need a job, desperately, but there was no way I could leave my dad.

Mrs Potton turned to walk back to her little kiosk.
"You know Bennett, I've always thought you were much too good for this town. A beautiful, bright girl like you never fitted in in this stuffy, old place."

I smiled, this woman really was the sweetest.

"That's why I think you should apply for this job, if you're lucky enough to get an interview then I'll take care of your father while you're gone."

"Oh Mrs Potton, I couldn't ask you to do that…that's…"

"It's my pleasure, and besides, it would give me the company now James and Verity are no longer home."

Mrs Pottons children were now grown and had flown the nest and her husband had passed away years ago. I didn't realise she even wanted any company. She always seemed so independent and fine on her own but then I guess everyone needs some sort of human connection eventually.

"I'd need to contact them first. I guess I could send an email, check it out."

Her gentle face brightened with a wide smile.

"Perfect, you deserve this Bennett. Let me know how it goes."

I giggled, "I will do, thank you." I gave Mrs Potton a quick hug before leaving the post office, the gold embossed business card clutched tightly in my palm.

Hunter was nowhere to be seen when I exited the shop *thank god*. I was finally feeling a bit of positivity and he was the last person I wanted ruining it right now.

Opening the emails on my phone, I jotted down a quick message with a bio and added a recent resume to the attachments. The note had said that no experience was necessary for the job but I had a couple of pretty good things on my resume which I hoped might work in my favour. I sent the email and headed home. One application down. I didn't have a clue how long I'd be unemployed for but at least this was a start.

Hurrying through the door, my dad was perched in his usual spot in the armchair. He smiled as I walked over, pressing a light kiss to his cheek.

"Working tonight?" He mumbled.

"Dad... I've actually applied for a new job today. It's a lot better money than Delilah's and... well it's at Knightchurch manor. It's a live-in position and I didn't know if I should apply, but then Mrs Potton said she'd help out here and well..."

"Sounds fancy. Glad you're considering getting out of that damn place."

My eyebrows raised with surprise. I knew my dad didn't like the bar, but I never thought he'd be okay with me leaving him.

"You don't mind that I'd have to leave for a while?"

He lifted his head from his newspaper, sliding his fine rimmed glasses down his nose.

"Bennett, you're an Angel, an absolute bloody godsend but I know you need your own life. You're a beautiful young woman and I'm holding you back."

My eyes began to prickle with emotion.

"Papa, you don't hold me back and anyway we don't know if I'll get the job yet." .

He smiled. "You'll get it." His gaze switched back to the tv as I walked quietly to my room.

I was stunned by the words coming from my dad's mouth.

I never knew he was feeling this way. I always felt like I needed to stay in Cedar Cross to be there for him, but the last thing I wanted him to feel was guilt that I was stuck here.

Dropping my bag on the floor, I let my body fall freely, backwards onto the bed, my arms splayed out either side of me, exhaling loudly. I'd sort this. It would be fine.

It had to be.

Chapter Three

Bennett

Usually when I've applied for a job position it's taken a few days. An interview is offered, you attend, and then there's that anxiety ridden stage where you're waiting for the employer to get back to you as to whether you've got the job, or just made yourself look like a complete inadequate tool. So imagine my surprise when upon opening my eyes, the following day from when I sent the email to Knightchurch manor, I received an email in response… offering me the position.

I stared at the wording on my phone, trying to make sense of how quickly it had all been processed. They obviously needed to fill the position rapidly.

The response was formal but basic.

Miss Bennett E Keane

Thank you for your interest in the position of general house assistant at Knightchurch manor.

I am pleased to inform you that after reading through your resume, we would like to offer you the role beginning September 8th 2022.

Please report to the main entrance on arrival at 11am where you will be escorted to your living quarters.

We look forward to meeting you and wish you the best in your

career at Knightchurch.

Kindest regards

Mr Andreas G Silvaro
Owner and Occupant of Knightchurch manor

September eighth was literally two days away. *Jeez* they really did need the position filled quickly.

Either they were desperate or I had a fucking amazing resume. *They were definitely desperate. My resume was complete and utter shit.*

I sent a quick thank you reply before throwing on some dark, ripped denim jeans and a black tank top. I grabbed my biker boots and headed down to see Mrs Potton to let her know about the email, and that my dad would need the care quicker than I anticipated.

I hadn't even reached the door to the old post office building before I spotted Hunter Jackson walking right towards me. His large strides filling the distance much too quickly as I did my best to speed up my walking. He'd trimmed his awkward facial hair and I had no idea why that just made me want to punch him in the face even more.

"BENNETT."

Oh fuck, here we go!

"Hunter, how are you?" My fake smile strains my face until I can feel my cheeks start to ache.

"Good, good," he replies, "but ya know I'd be even better if you let me take you out."

I try my best to contain the eye roll, exhaling my pent up sigh as quietly as possible.

"Hunter I really don't have the time, I'm so sorry but I've just accepted a job opportunity and I leave in two days so I really have to..."

"Job opportunity? Where?" His eyes widened and I felt an overwhelming urge to tell him to mind his own business, but getting into some petty argument with the town meathead wasn't something I really wanted to be doing right now.

"Knightchurch." I replied, giving him another awkward smile.

"Knightchurch?" His face twisted in disgust. "As in Knightchurch manor? What the fuck?!"

"Excuse me?" *What was this fuckers problem?*

"Knightchurch manor is something straight out of a fucking horror movie. The guys at the sheriff's office are always on about that place." He began to chuckle which only amplified my growing annoyance. "Bennett it's built on a fucking graveyard and people have gone missing there, like *missing* missing."

This time my eye roll was clear for him to see.

"Don't believe me then but that place is... it's weird! No one goes there. No one even knows who lives there anymore. It's fucking creepy and haunted to shit"

I'd had enough of his childish bullshit. *So much for the knight in shining armour.*

"Hunter, I know who lives there," *well I mean I kinda did.* "His name is Mr Andreas Silvaro and it's not weird. It's just a house. Plus I guess it doesn't matter if it's haunted as I don't believe in that shit. So now if you'll please excuse me, I have things I need to be doing that are more important than standing here talking about absolute rubbish with you...like packing."

With that, I smile and turn away, speeding up my steps before he has a chance to reply.

I feel him staring at me bewildered, as I head to the post office to see Mrs Potton.

One thing I'd become immune to, living in a town as old as Cedar Cross, was the amount of old wives tales that were always floating around. Whether it was the woods or Knightchurch manor, there was always some horror story being peddled.

Luckily I wasn't one to take notice of any of that drivel. People thought *I* was weird, so I was probably no different to the places these people spoke of in their stories.

Mrs Potton was only too glad to take over and help out with dad while I was away. She seemed ecstatic when I took the job and I suspected it was equally because she was finally getting the company, as it was that I'd found a ridiculously high paying job. I, for one, was happy to be helping her out as much as she was helping me.

Two days later, packing a small, moss green suitcase and chucking it into the back of my silver 1998 Subaru Outback, it felt surreal to be going off into the world without worrying about my dad for the first time.

I didn't know how long I'd be gone but I was definitely planning on coming back most weekends to visit, as a forty mile trip from Knightchurch wasn't that far in the grand scheme of things.

Dad hobbled out of the house with his stick as I threw on my leather jacket over the dark purple sweater and black pencil skirt I'd chosen for my first day. It was different to my usual style, but I felt like going to a place like Knightchurch would probably warrant some slightly more formal attire.

"I'm gonna miss you kid." My dad's eyes glistened with the tears he was trying to hold back.

"I'm gonna miss you too daddy, but I'll be back as much as possible. I love you." I pressed a soft kiss to his cheek, as he let a stray tear fall.

"Love you too princess." He whispered.

After many hugs and emotional goodbyes, I jumped into the car, turning on the ignition and typing the address into my sat nav. The map was pointing towards the dark wood. I'd never headed in that direction before and a small flutter erupted deep in my stomach, but I was ready for this next chapter.

Oh god knows I was so ready.

Chapter Four

Bennett

    The powder blue sky had already started to morph into swirls of smokey grey before I even reached the road trailing all the way through the dark wood. *Perfect, talk about the cliche horror story.*

    So many things were still a mystery about this new career venture, but I'd already accepted that beggars can't be choosers, and some creepy old wives tales were not going to keep me from an opportunity like this.

    I'd never even stepped foot into these woods before, to be honest I didn't actually know many who had, this direction headed straight to Knightchurch manor and no one ever had any business going there.

    As usual Darwin, my not so trusty Subaru, was already chugging as if she was going up, and the last thing I needed was to break down in these fucking freaky woods. I pleaded with the rundown, old motor not to give in, as the sky continues to whirl in a watercolour mix of blue and grey.

    Turning up the volume on the only ancient radio station that I could pick up, I decided to block out the sound of the collapsing engine, the only way I knew how.

    I finally cleared the forest and as I drove out into the open, I noticed for the first time, the sight of a grand building lying in the distance.

    The house may have a lot of mysterious horror stories but no one could deny the sheer beauty that stood before me.

Large wrought iron gates guarded, what looked to me, more like a palace than a Manor House. The pictures I'd seen in books did not do it justice at all.

The stone facades were a distressed grey with deep green moss growing throughout the cracks. They were crowned with ridiculously steep roof pitches and the house was dotted with row upon row of windows. Too many to count. Some square in shape while others were cut into more of a sophisticated arch shape. A couple even appeared to be stained glass with patterns of large, black roses adorning them.

The house itself was humongous, more like five manor houses joined into one. You'd need a goddamn map to get around this place.

The iron gates opened automatically as my car approached. I peered around to look for cameras but it didn't seem like there were any, or at least if there were then they were certainly well hidden.

A sliver of unease raced up my spine causing an unexpected shiver.

I rarely scared easily, so I had no idea what was causing this shred of anxiety that was just sitting in my chest. I was strictly putting it down to first day nerves.

Brushing off the shiver, I pulled up in the gravelled front parking area of the house.

A beautiful, gothic stone fountain consisting of two mischievous cherubs sprinkled lightly as I exited my car.

As I looked closer, I noticed long vines climbing and penetrating the stone of the building, making it appear like the house had veins, like it had taken on a life of its own.

I glanced around briefly but no one appeared to be in sight. *They must be inside.*

Lifting my eyes, I scanned the windows for any sign of life. Nothing. Until suddenly my eyes glazed over a window on the top floor and there, standing in the window, clear as day was a girl.

My eyes darted back to the window in which she was standing, as she stood still as a statue, just staring straight at me. Another chill zapped down my spine. The hairs on the back of my neck prickled lightly, my whole body turning cold.

I couldn't see clearly what she looked like, only that she was extremely pale with dark hair, but I could feel the intensity of her gaze. *Fuck this place was giving me the creeps already.*

I smiled and waved at the girl who continued to just stare at me but instead of smiling or waving back, she simply turned around and walked away from the window. *Okaaaaay then.*

I grabbed my cell to send a quick text to my dad to let him know I'd arrived safely, before realising there wasn't a single shred of a reception. *Perfect!*

Waving the phone around in the air like a crazy person proved absolutely fruitless, so I quickly tucked it back into my pocket. There must be a landline phone somewhere I could use. I made a mental note to look out for that later.

Turning towards the entrance, I jogged up the stairs and pressed my hand onto the large, golden knocker on the door, shaped into the head of a lion. The cold metal felt like it was penetrating the skin on my hand and after knocking twice, the door creaked open. *Full-on cliché horror. Perfect.*

"Oh hello there."

Relief flooded my bones at the sight of a petite and very attractive older lady, walking towards me down the huge stone staircase that sat straight ahead.

She was roughly my height with a slim frame and perfectly styled dark hair that hung in loose curls to her shoulders.

She smiled at me with a set of perfectly white, straight teeth that looked like they'd cost a fortune and were framed beautifully with a ruby red lipstick.

I wasn't sure which brand of designer had made the exquisitely tailored, cream dress suit she was wearing, but I could guarantee it probably cost more than my whole fucking wardrobe.

"Hi." I finally managed to snap from my thoughts and respond.

"My name is Estelle Silvaro, you must be one of our new girls?!"

New girls? The fact that it appeared she was saying that there were more than just one new starter actually made me feel a lot more at ease.

"Yep, I'm Bennett Keane, I was offered the general house assistant job, but I wasn't aware that there were any more employees starting." I glanced around the massive reception area realising how stupid my statement probably sounded. Of course there were bound to be lots of other people starting, the house was huge.

Estelle giggled. "Well my husband felt we needed a little more help at the house, so we've taken on a handful of girls about your age just to help out with some domestic duties. I'm sure you can agree that such a large house is quite the chore for someone like little old me." She giggled again and I could feel myself smiling.

I liked Estelle, she had a calming presence about her, and all of a sudden I felt myself filled with the positivity that I had, a hundred percent, made the right choice.

"Well now, I'll show you to your room. It's just upstairs, here in the north wing, where most of the other staff reside that don't sleep in the west wing. You can get settled and then you're welcome to take a walk around the place, get to know your surroundings a little better."

"Sounds perfect." I smiled. With that Estelle led me up the large staircase and down the corridor to a small door leading up to another staircase and yet another level of the house. As we walked through the long, red carpet covered corridors, I took in the sight of all the stunning artwork covering the walls. Portrait after portrait of men and women, all gorgeous in their own way.

"Are these portraits of family members?" I asked inquisitively, staring at the portrait of a handsome man with dark hair peppered with grey and a strong, sharp jawline.

"They are," replied Estelle. "Knightchurch has been in the Silvaro family for generations. It's a proud family home and one we hope you will be very happy in."

I nodded, still taking in all the breathtaking sights around me, from antique looking chairs to a tall, dark wooden grandfather clock stood by one of the windows.

Finally, after what seemed like a ten mile trek, we reached a large wooden door at the end of a long corridor.

"Here we are." Estelle took a large silver key from her pocket and unlocked the door, gently pushing it with one hand.

I gasped at the sight before me, my eyes widening to take it all in.

The room was all black wood with a red carpet and a striking black wooden four poster bed with red silk sheets folded perfectly on top of it. A black comforter spread neatly along the bottom.

"Do you like it?" Estelles voice hesitated and I could feel her holding her breath, hoping for a positive response.

"Oh Mrs Silvaro, I love it."

Estelle smiled. "Please call me Estelle, it isn't formal with me, I'd like to consider myself as your friend," her eyes appeared to glaze over for a second. "Unfortunately I don't have many."

I turned to look at her as she stood still, glancing at her glossy, black heeled shoes. A nervous expression gracing her slender face as if she was still worried I didn't like the room. I didn't understand how anyone couldn't like this extravagant room.

"It's perfect Estelle." I replied, doing my best to ease her anxiety.

She blew out a relieved sigh, a wide smile appearing on her lovely face before walking towards the door.

"Well I'll leave you to it. The grounds are large, due to that, we have staff who work in each section of the house. There's a lot of people around, you just might not see the same person regularly due to the size of this place and shifts etcetera, however you're free to go almost anywhere you please. My husband is incredibly busy at the minute so I'm sure you'll probably see more of me than him but he will be around. Tomorrow morning at seven AM sharp, we'll meet on the patio of the gardens, where you'll be informed of your duties. "

I nod in response.

"You may venture anywhere, however please avoid the east wing. That wing belongs to my son and he likes his privacy." With that she leaves, closing the door gently.

Son? Didn't know there was a son here.

I walked slowly around the room, trailing my fingertips over the dark wooden drawers and the stained glass lampshade that sat beside the bed. My curiosity for this strange, old house had definitely peaked and all I could think about now was getting out and exploring, really discovering what Knightchurch manor was all about.

Snapping open the clips on my suitcase, I carefully took out all of my belongings, slipping them into the old, heavy drawers. A light film of dust rose from the compartment I'd just opened. *Well I can definitely see why they need a few housekeepers around the place.*

After emptying the case of my clothing, I plucked out the last of the toiletries, heading to the en suite bathroom. As I stepped through the large wooden door, I was in awe of the sight before me.

Like the bedroom, the bathroom had dark furnishings with a rainforest shower and giant, free standing bath tub right in the centre.

It really did look just like something from a gothic fairytale.

My aching body already yearned for the bathtub but I was too eager to explore my new home, the relaxing would have to wait til later.

Changing into a pair of grey sweat shorts, a black tank top and my thin, battered chucks, I quickly scrunched my long dark hair into a messy bun on top of my head and headed out of the door.

One thing I should have asked Estelle for was definitely a map as this place was huge.

The interiors were definitely a bit dated and yeah all this black was certainly a bit weird, but nothing, except the freaky girl I'd seen in the window, looked out of place or sinister enough so far to warrant the ghost stories that were circulating in Cedar

Cross.

The only thing that seemed to unnerve me so far was the chill. It was like the place just didn't have any heating which seemed fucking absurd for a place this big.

It was only September so not exactly freezing yet which was good but still, the corridors were hardly warm and cosy.

After walking for what seemed like miles, I finally found the back doors to the house. The floor to ceiling glass panels allowed the dull shimmer of the upcoming autumn sun to dance through, illuminating the house.

I pushed on the large door knob carefully and it opened with a low groan. *Well I'm guessing this is the garden patio.*

Glancing around, it had never really occurred to me just how much this house was surrounded by the dark wood. It was literally in the back garden.

Even in daylight the forest looked gloomy and threatening, *now this was one place I understood where the ghost stories came from.*

The branches on the trees hung low like long, monstrous fingers and as the wind began to howl, I swear it sounded like whispers emerging from the darkness.

Looking to the sky, the grey clouds were still fighting with the sunlight and I could tell it was definitely going to rain soon, so if I was going to explore anywhere outside, then I better do it quickly.

I've always loved the rain, it made people keep their heads down, avoided awkward conversation. You never had to worry about bumping into someone you didn't want to see when it was raining. Rain blurred everything, turning the world into one big watercolor canvas.

I've also never been one for scary stories or even being that afraid of anything in general up until now, so taking a deep breath, I hopped off the patio and down the white stone staircase towards the beginning of the forest.

The wind began to pick up with a vengeance as I walked further into the wood. Twigs and branches cracked under my chucks and crows cawed from high above. The trees bent and swayed to the will of the wind, shedding their leaves like snow.

I followed an old looking makeshift pathway that looked like it had been here for quite some time. The greying pebbles, worn down with the amount of feet that had trodden over them.

The pathway spit into two lanes. I chose one at random as I couldn't even see where they led to anyway, they just continued winding into masses of dark bushes and greenery.

Continuing down the lane, suddenly something caught the corner of my eye, a sharp glint as if something had caught the light through the trees. I spun on my heel to face what I could see was another large iron gate.

Walking through the clearing, brushing the hanging branches and scattered leaves to one side, I finally reached it. The iron rusted, with vines of weed and thick foliage entwined around it, almost securing it in place. Placing both hands on the cold metal, peering through, a shiver raced up my spine and made everything in my body shudder for a split second as I stared at the entrance to a cemetery.

Chapter Five

Bennett

A chill skated along the back of my neck, making my skin pebble with goosebumps as I glared at the gates. They must have been at least twelve feet high. Emblazoned across the top was the word '*Silvaro.*'
Well at least we now know that Knightchurch isn't built on *a graveyard! Just has one practically in the fucking backyard.*

From the looks of things, it appeared that I was standing right in front of what I assumed was the family graveyard.

I shrugged away the shiver that quickly zapped through my body and pushed on the large iron gates. They parted easily, creaking as though it had been decades since they had been moved and the cemetery had been tended to.

I couldn't decipher whether it was the unpredictable September weather or the fact that I had stumbled upon a fucking old ass cemetery all by myself that was making my feel so damn cold all of a sudden.

Treading through the overgrown grass, I'm surrounded by large, grey, moulding headstones, some looking so ancient I can't make out a single letter that's inscribed onto them.

Weather battered and forgotten about, this graveyard screamed sadness as much as it did horror.

As I continue walking through the row upon row of graves, my fascination takes over and I find myself reading through each one that's clear enough to be seen.

They all appear to be past generations of the Silvaro family and although part of me wants to believe this is a sentimental thing, created by the family to keep their loved ones close even in death, I can't help but find the whole thing really fucking creepy.

Walking through the overgrown grass, I stop in my tracks when a large gravestone in the shape of an Angel catches my eye.

Thick, dark green and musty yellow vines twist around the statue making it difficult to read the name on the base.

I reach down and begin to tear away at the weeds, the sharp thorns from the plants covering the stone scratching my fingers and drawing tiny dots of blood.

Within seconds the old carving is clear enough to read.

Carlos Montgomery Silvaro
Born Dec 4th 1884
Deceased Dec 4th 1930
'Pasano le catene del diavolo finalmente comfinarte'

Pasano le catene del diavolo finalmente comfinarte? *May the devil's chains finally confine you.* My Italian was a little rusty, but I was pretty sure from the classes I took back in high school that that was what was written on the old, decaying headstone. Poor guy died on his birthday. *That sucks!*

My blood ran cold as I stared at the unkempt grave. Shrugging off the feeling of unease, I continued to walk slowly through the grounds.

Suddenly with a loud crack I stumbled backwards, the sole of my foot connecting with a large, broad, overturned branch that had fallen from an old oak tree. The sharp edge of the wood, piercing the thin bottom of my shoe and then into my foot.

I squealed as a burning pain radiates up my leg and I jump backwards.

Suddenly my legs gave way, forcing me backwards as I crashed to the ground onto my ass.

I grabbed my foot to inspect the damage and pulled off my shoe. Deep crimson blood began to soak into the material of my thin, torn sock as I tugged it off of me. *Fuck this was gonna need stitches.*

Looking around there was no one in sight. Large black crows hovered above the old cemetery in the dark trees, their squarks the only thing I could hear.

As they flew over my head, I was reminded of vultures circling their injured prey waiting for the opportunity to strike. *How the fuck was I supposed to hobble back to the house? It was too far.*

As I pushed from the ground, my leg continued to burn with hot rage and blood began leaking from the wound at a more rapid pace. I dropped back onto my bottom feeling my face pale at the thought of a painful struggle back to the house.

"What the fuck are you doing in here?"

I screamed in shock as the voice, deep and venomous bellowed from nowhere.

Whipping my head to the side is when I see him standing there. A tall figure cloaked all in black.

His dark, distressed jeans hidden at the bottom by the dying, overgrown grass and a hoodie covering the majority of his face. Only a light dusting of hair along a ridiculously chiselled jawline is visible.

The angle at which I was sat made the dimming sunlight create a gilded outline around his shadow-like form. Almost as if an Angel and a demon had clashed in battle and merged into one.

"Who... who are you?" I try to keep my breathing as calm as possible but my heart is beating so rapidly I can feel the pulsing in my mouth.

A large, tan hand grips the back of the hood of the black hoodie and peels it back slowly.

Instantly I feel my jaw slacken as I make a conscious effort to disguise my reaction, a shiver darts like ice up my spine.

There stood a vision of a man. The type of guy your mother would tell you to stay away from. Pure sin and danger in human form. Beautiful is the only word I could muster to describe him. Beautiful yet haunting.

His jet black hair, shaved shorter on the sides and longer on top with the most piercing blue eyes I'd ever seen in my life. They glittered like chips of ice, deep set under thick, dark brows. Even under the black hoodie and ripped jeans you could see the outline of a body resembling that of a Greek god that had my thighs clenching despite the searing pain I felt.

This man was the epitome of seduction and he was standing right here. In a graveyard. While I was on my ass. *Awesome.*

The scowl on his face however, told me he was not happy to see me.

"I said…What. Are. You. Doing. Here?"
Pain flared from my foot, just staring at this man for a second had made me forget where I was and what the fuck had just happened to me.

"I was just taking a walk, I just wanted to see the grounds, I'm… the new general assistant at Knightchurch." I pointed weakly in the direction of the house as his eyes narrowed, as if assessing if I was telling the truth.

"Always hang around graveyards do you?" His penetrating gaze glazed over my dark hair, piercings and outfit choice. *Sure, the goth likes hanging around the graveyard, very original.* A flutter of irritation emerged inside me.

I raised my eyebrows, a scoff escaping my throat.

"Same could be said about you, creeping up on people is not cool and anyway I wasn't hanging around, I was just passing through."

Even though every breath I take is laced with terror, I continue to look deep into his eyes. One thing I've learned in life is to never show fear. People pray on that shit.

He continues to rival my stare until his gaze flicks quickly to the blood seeping from my foot.

"You shouldn't be down here, it's private property for one thing, as well as the fact that it isn't safe… you're hurt." The tone at which he speaks makes me sound like an inconvenience he's stumbled upon. *I guess I probably am.* All that's missing was the eye roll and I'd know for sure I was fucking up his day.

I glance at my foot, pulling it towards myself.

"It's fine, I just need to get back to the house and I'll clean it."

Suddenly with two large strides, this striking yet terrifying man is standing right before me, looking down at me on the ground.

"You can't walk back." He growls. I'm not sure if his voice is intentionally threatening or if it's just the way it sounds but it sends another tremor racing through my body. I find myself automatically leaning away from him.

Before I even have a chance to reply to his words, two large arms sweep me up as I feel my body pressed against a solid, broad chest.

My breath catches embarrassingly in my throat and judging by the way, for just a second, I spot the corners of his mouth lift into an almost smirk, I can see that he caught my reaction too.

"I *can* walk, you know." My protesting probably sounds as weak as it feels, as my wound continues to throb and the thought of hobbling back to the house fills me with dread.

I hear a deep inhale fill his chest as if he's annoyed that I'm even speaking right now.

"It's quicker if I just carry you back."

Giving in, I wrap my slender arms around his neck and let him hold me. Heat radiates through his clothing and soothes the goosebumps on my body from the crisp chill in the air that's beginning to set in.

The heady scent of fire and brimstone mixed with citrus and washing detergent hits my scenes as I automatically lean back into his hold.

"As I'm letting a stranger carry me, the least you could do is tell me who you are and why you're on Knightchurch grounds."

"This is my home," he replies. "My name is Ezra Silvaro."

The Son! I remembered Estelle mentioning about avoiding the other wing of the manor as that was where her son lived. This guy was certainly not what I was expecting. *Wasn't the hidden son in a horror movie usually some kind of hideous beast? I'd clearly watched too much fucked up, make belive shit.*

"I'm Bennett, Bennett Keane. Mostly just Bennett but friends sometimes call me B." I was waffling now.

"Queen Bee," replied Ezra "The little creature with the nasty sting… figures!"

I frowned at his potential insult. This guy was full of cheer.

It doesn't take long before we reach the house.

A few workers are pottering around as we enter the large doors, but they don't even look up as Ezra carries me through the kitchen and out to a small seating area with a black, velvet chaise lounge in the corner.

He places me down onto the soft material before heading towards a tall, dark oak cabinet with several cupboards.

After several seconds of searching, Ezra returns with a small box which looks familiarly like a first aid kit.

Taking out a small needle and thread, he turns to me, his face still carrying the stoic expression.

"You need a few stitches, there's no need for a hospital but if I don't seal it, you run the risk of an infection. I need to clean it first, also we have no anaesthetic so I suggest you drink this," He reaches into the pocket of his jeans pulling out a small silver hip flask. I remove the lid, sniffing the liquid inside.

"Whiskey? Fantastic!" My sarcasm was clear as crystal as I received an irritated side eye from Ezra.

"Well don't drink it then, I don't give a fuck! Be in agony for all the fucks I give." He snarled.

I scoffed, shaking my head in disbelief. This guy was an ass.

I didn't care at all about not seeing a doctor or going to the hospital, *even though it was a bit fucking weird that he wouldn't just call one,* but being in such close proximity to this man, whoever he was, was making my stomach summersault and heat pool between my legs at just the sight of him. Even though he'd been nothing but a moody mother fucker since we'd met.

Sighing, I took a long, hard swig from the hip flask. The cool liquid burned a path down my throat and towards my stomach as I winced.

Now most girls, I assume would freak the fuck out if some

guy was preparing to stitch up their skin without pain relief, but for some reason I was in enough agony that I'd actually started to stop caring.

Ezras large hand laces around my ankle, gently raising my foot and placing it onto his lap. His thumb drawing soothing circles around my ankle making the flutter of butterflies within my stomach stir again.

Tearing open a small antiseptic wipe with his teeth, I couldn't stop my eyes travelling to his delicious lips. My teeth sank into the bottom of my own lip as I stared.

The cold, sharp sting of the wipe being pressed to my wound broke the trance I'd somehow fallen into as my eyebrows tightened with the pain. I let my breathing fall into a slow, deep rhythm as I took another swig off the whiskey.

After cleaning me up, Ezra settled to begin adding the few small stitches to my foot.

He glanced at me once before turning his attention back to the job in hand.

"Take a deep breath." He said quietly.

Inhaling quickly, I felt the force of the needle penetrate my flesh.

"Urrrrgghh!" I bit hard on my lower lip to stifle the moan of agony. Shit, this whiskey wasn't doing its fucking job. My leg began to tremble with the burn and tears formed in the corner of my eyes. I could taste the copper tang of my blood on my tongue from where I'd bitten down too hard on my lip.

"Take another drink."

I lifted the hip flask, chugging the honey coloured liquid. The burn in my throat almost matching the burn of my skin.

I squeezed the silver flask so tightly in my palms that my knuckles began to turn white as the pain traveled up my calf.

I kept my focus on the strand of black hair that dropped down over his right eye as he worked.

Cold beads of sweat ran down my forehead and I was doing my best not to puke. I was a second away from begging him to stop before he tied up the stitch upon completion.

As he finished up, he gently placed my ankle from his lap and onto the chaise lounge. His gaze never meeting mine, not even for a second.

I breathed slowly as the nausea began to pass and I began to feel a little more human instantly as he put the needle down. I quickly wiped the beads of sweat that had formed on my forehead with the back of my hand.

"So where'd you learn to do that?" My words attempting to come out playful but the expression on Ezra's face remained unreadable as he started to put away all of the equipment, out right ignoring my question.

"You should rest that foot, I'll let my mother know that you need a few days to heal so won't be starting work tomorrow." He stood, carrying the box and bloodied wipes that he'd just used on my foot towards the door.

"Erm... okay, well thank you."

He looked at me once before nodding in acknowledgment and exiting through the large glass door, closing it behind him.

I released a breath that I didn't even know that I'd been holding, dropping back until I was laid out flat on the chaise. *What the hell just happened?*

I needed to make a mental note to be more careful when out on my walks around the Knightchurch grounds.

My mind wandered between the creepy, tattered old graveyard I've just found hiding within the woodland of my new employer's backyard, and the man who essentially had been my rescuer. Knightchurch was a strange place, I'd give it that.

Who would want to have all their family, *dead family,* just chilling not even that far from where they slept at night?! I found the concept eerie and macabre, but whatever floats your boat as they say.

Pulling from the sofa, I carefully made my way back to my room. I needed rest. Curiosity had definitely killed this cat. At least it had until tomorrow.

Chapter Six

Ezra

What the fuck was she doing in there?

Slamming the door to my room, I took a few strides towards the bed, sitting on the edge of the black silken sheets. My head resting in my hands, the pounding agony in my head almost taking over my vision.

I don't know why I was bothered by another one of my fathers *assistants.* There had been many, but something about this girl sat differently with me and I couldn't put my finger on what it was.

Usually the girls that were employed here would just get in the way, fucking batting their eyelashes with that thirsty look in their gaze. I had no time for that. I entertained fucking them at first but now it bored me. None of them satisfied that urge that sat deeply in my soul.

The curse of my genetics was forever looming over me and I couldn't be trusted around anyone, especially not *her* or any other woman for that matter.

There was a sickness in me, one that had morphed me from the *normal* successful man I could have been, into a demonic creature that craved the darkness.

All I knew was that *she* shouldn't be here. In this house.

The sickness made me crave pain. I knew it wasn't normal, I knew I didn't deserve to breathe the same air as the girl, sitting helpless in the cemetery, but I didn't give a fuck. This was who I was and this was who I was going to be when I died. Nothing was going to change my fate.

Irritation flowed through my veins. I don't know why the fuck I helped her today, I should have let her hobble back to the house for being the snooping little wench that she was. *Dumb slut!* But I had to get her out of the fucking graveyard, hell knows enough blood had been spilled there already.

She was just sitting there helpless like a fragile little bird with a broken wing. Oh fuck, would I like to break her more.

She was fucking gorgeous I'd give her that. The thought of bruising her perfect creamy skin made my cock strain painfully against my jeans.

I found peace in the cemetery, fuck, I was the only one who ever visited that place anymore. Being amongst my family generations has always been soothing. Being amongst restless spirits like my own who knew what it was like to hear desperate screams and bask in the ecstasy. Like a prime steak to a starving lion. But today it has been far from that. All because of her.

If she knew the secrets, the demons this place holds, she'd run a mile, that I was certain of.

Pulling my hoodie and my thin, black t-shirt from my body, I stood before the full length mirror staring at my reflection. The image appeared to twist and contort. I knew it was all in my head but anger swelled within me all the same.

With all my force and a loud crash, I smashed my fist into the mirror, shattering it into thousands of tiny pieces. Staring at my knuckles, I felt soothed seeing the tiny shards glistening over my skin.

My blood mingled with what remained of hers, the blood that still stained my skin from where I repaired her wound.

I had things I needed to be doing, I couldn't be here right now. Kelvin Adams, a condemned man, was walking the street in fifteen minutes time and I was way behind schedule.

Throwing on an old sweater and pulling up my black hood on a thicker jacket, hiding the majority of my face, I headed out of Knightchurch, jumping into my black *Aston Martin* that was parked outside.

I'd have to put my foot down if I was going to make it on time into the city to see the corrupt, retired lawyer who'd been up to no good for a while now.

I spot him in the distance, leaving his apartment right on cue. I know where the disgusting cretin is headed but little does he know he won't be making that destination tonight.

The rage, revulsion and sheer adrenaline I feel, knowing this man is taking his last breaths in front of me is exhilarating. Blood rushes to my cock at the mere thought.

The wind begins to pick up, whipping against my face as I walk slowly, keeping to the shadows.

I feel the garrotte wire in my pocket. My fingers itching to touch it.

I see Kelvin slightly glance over his shoulder. I can't decide whether it's because he's afraid that someone is following him or he's afraid someone will know where he's heading. A sordid little peadophile meet-up.

As he turns his attention back to the path ahead, I see he's decided to take a back street alley.

Running my tongue over my teeth, I smirk. It's as if Hades is on my side today.

As the shadows of the alleyway engulf him, I speed up my steps. This will all be over with very soon.

The little bird enters my head. Her smooth, pale skin, her sweet scent, vanilla and something fruity as I held her tightly against my body.

This girl needed to leave Knightchurch, she wasn't safe within those walls, and she certainly wasn't safe around me.

Chapter Seven

<u>Bennett</u>

"Bennett, run. Run faster Bennett."

The wind whipped against my face, I couldn't see where I was going but I could feel the cold squelch of mud beneath my feet. I knew I was in the woods, my lungs aching through exertion. I could hear the terrifying sound of footsteps following me. It didn't even seem like he was running but he was right behind me all the same. My throat constricted as I fought to control the obliterating panic.

Suddenly my ankle gave out as my foot connected with a large branch sticking out of the cold ground.

Rolling onto my back, I stared up at the face before me. The face of the man chasing me, but it was his voice that I recognised first.

"You never should have come to Knightchurch little bird."

"Ezra?"

The bright flash of the knife blinded me as he raised his arm.

"Fuck"

My body jolted awake as I sat upright, sweat coating my forehead and behind my neck, making my hair stick to my skin. I rubbed a palm over my face.

A nightmare. It was just a nightmare.

I inhaled rapid, shallow bursts of air as I tried to calm my charging pulse.

Grabbing a tumbler from my nightstand, I switched on the bedside lamp and walked over to the bathroom, turning on the tap to get some water, gulping it down hard.

My silk pjs clung to my body.

The nightmare had seemed so vivid. So real. Ezras wolf-like eyes penetrated right into my soul as he lifted his knife to attack.

I decided to put it down to the creepy, old graveyard and the stress of my new surroundings. This shit was enough to give anyone nightmares.

Walking back to my bed, I lay down on the cool sheets closing my eyes. The tinge of pain in my foot reminding me that my encounter with Ezra Silvaro was most definitely real.

The wind battered against the window of my room. It almost sounded like fists hammering against the panes. I closed my eyes hoping it wouldn't take long for sleep to take hold.

BANG. BANG. BANG.

I bolted up right in an instant as the sound of someone hitting my bedroom door radiated throughout the room. My heart hammered in my chest as I again rose from the bed, tiptoeing in the dark toward the door.

Part of me wanted to hide under the sheets, I mean this was the part in the horror movie where the girl makes the wrong decision in the dark and gets murdered right?! Well I never was one for smart choices.

Slowly turning the golden door knob, I felt my whole body tremble as I fought to stay calm and steady myself.

I peered into the hallway. The freaky old paintings on the wall staring right at me. But no one was there. The corridor was completely empty. An eerie draft danced through the hall, gently blowing a lock of my hair across my face.

Releasing a relieved sigh, I quietly closed the door behind me as I walked back to my bed.

I wasn't one to believe in ghosts or scary stories so I wasn't sure why I was feeling so on edge right now. It was just this house. It had a weird aura that I just couldn't explain.

Walking to my window, I pulled back the oversized, black curtains revealing the darkness outside. The only lighting was the glow of a yellowing moon.

Cracking open the window slightly, I welcomed the light rush of air that hit my face. I closed my eyes, breathing deeply.

Suddenly, movement down below in the shadows caught the corner of my eye.

As I peered down below into the woodland area that crept towards the house, I saw the figure of a man. *Ezra?* No, this man appeared older in the way that he walked.

He wasn't taking the large strides I remember from Ezra carrying me back to the house, but he was trying to move quickly that was for sure.

He wore a thick, black coat with a large hood, but even covered, it was obvious that this man was more round than Ezra. Not quite built the same way.

I couldn't make out his face very clearly but one thing that struck me, one thing I could see even though most of him was shrouded in darkness was his hands. His old hands painted in, what looked like blood.

A gasp left my throat and I considered going down to see if he was hurt. It was only when his head snapped upwards that I saw those piercing eyes glaring right at me.

I quickly jumped backwards, releasing the curtain to cover me. My heart beating erratically, I walked back to the bed, climbing in and pulling the sheets up high, wrapping them tightly around my body.

Closing my eyes, I forced my mind to travel elsewhere, praying that sleep would take me soon but I couldn't erase the memory of my nightmare and I couldn't erase the vision of the hands, painted in blood.

The golden shimmer of the morning sunlight peered through the curtains, making the dancing dust particles glow like tiny stars.

Ezra had assured me yesterday that he'd let his mother know that I wouldn't be starting work today, so part of me felt like I should be resting but after my encounter with him yesterday, and my pulse-pounding nightmare on top of the man I saw from my window, I was feeling more agitated than ever.

Glancing in the mirror, I inspected the lighter roots appearing through my hair where it lacked the black dye I'd been using.

My golden nose and lip piercing glinted as it caught the light reflecting from the large, waterfall chandelier hanging from the ceiling. This was a new start and it called for a new look.

Entering the bathroom and turning the latch, I worked on washing out the semi permanent hair colour that disguised my naturally chocolate brown locks.

It came out pretty easily after a few washes, and as soon it was complete I started on removing my piercings.

It had been so long since I'd been my natural brunette, so when I next looked into the mirror, I felt like a completely different person was staring back at me.

Grabbing a black sweater and my black jeans, I combed through my hair and applied a slick of lip gloss and carefully applied my snuggly old, tattered Ugg boots, the only things I could find that would actually be comfortable right now.

Even if I couldn't get straight into working, I was still extremely curious about the house and wanted a bit more time to explore my surroundings.

Checking the small, silver watch that sat at my wrist, I noticed that it was eight thirty AM. Estelle would already have had her meeting with the new staff so I'd missed my chance to meet everyone all together.

As I stepped into the large foyer, the room of which I'd walked through when I first arrived yesterday, I spotted a young woman carrying a jug of what I assumed was water. She was very attractive, her tight curls of platinum blonde hair sitting neatly just below her shoulders.

Her face was immaculately painted in flawless makeup with a deep red lip. She reminded me of a fifties pin up. She stared at me, her judging eyes scanning my body from my face to my feet. She was dressed in a purple, tight fitted dress with a white apron sitting around her shapely hips. Her large, shapely breasts pushed high and sitting practically under her chin.

Our eyes met as she stopped in her tracks right in front of me.

"You must be the girl who couldn't make the meeting this morning." Her tone was cold, almost like she had no intention of making friends.

"Bennett, yes." I opened my hand and offered it to her. She glanced at the gesture moving her eyes from my hand back to my face without so much as a movement. Almost as if touching my hand would infect her with some life threatening plague. *Okaaaay then.*

"I hurt my foot yesterday, clumsy I know, I should be fine in a day or two." I felt like I was apologising to her for something. *Why the fuck did I feel like I was apologising?.*

The girl continued to glare at me, the fire and ice in her expression making me wonder if I'd suddenly grown an extra head.

"I'm Kara, I started working here a while ago now, I'll be covering the kitchen duties."

"Oh well it's nice to meet you, I'm sure…"

"I don't have time to be making friends." Kara's voice interrupted. "If we just stay out of each other's way, I think that would be for the best."

My brows furrowed in confusion.

"Erm… okay then, sure."

Without another word, Kara turned on her heel and headed towards the kitchen. I don't think I'd ever met anyone so hostile in my entire life. That girl was an odd one, that was for sure.

"I see you've met Kara."

The feminine almost musical voice sounded behind me as I turned to meet the sparkling eyes of Estelle.

Like yesterday, the lady of the house looked immaculate in a deep red dress suit with her silky hair in a high, twisted bun. Vibrant scarlet nails glistened as she moved her hands.

"She's… nice." I couldn't help the giggle that escaped my throat as I thought about my encounter with Kara.

Estelle laughed. "She's an interesting one that's for sure, but I'm sure you two will get on just fine in no time."

I doubted Kara and I were going to be best friends anytime soon judging by our first encounter but I just smiled at Estelles optimism. I'm sure she just wanted all her staff to get on for an easy life.

"How's the foot?" Estelles eyes lowered my feet.

"Sore," I replied. "But it should be fine in a few days ... thanks to your son."

Estelle visibly stilled. It was only for a second but I saw it there, the tension in her shoulders as her body seemed to freeze before relaxing again.

"Yes, Ezra informed me of everything that had happened. Take it easy today but I think maybe a day or two and you should be good to go?"

I nodded. "Of course."

Estelle smiled, giving my arm a reassuring rub as she passed by.

Heading to the kitchen, I picked up a slice of toast from the pile that had been left out on plates from breakfast.

The kitchen, like the rest of the house, was dark and dated. It still had an old stove and the tables which I assumed were used for chopping and preparing food, looked worn and in desperate need of an upgrade.

The walls were lined with built in, ageing shelves covered in crockery, pans and other bric a brac.

For people who were apparently as rich as royalty themselves, the Silvaros sure could do with updating their house. Had they not seen the bright white, vogue inspired kitchens you could get these days with the fancy islands?! Clearly not!

I wasn't sure what my plan of action was going to be today. I decided against going back outside to explore as yesterday hadn't turned out quite as I'd imagined, so maybe taking a slow walk around the house and resting in my room would be the best option for now.

The house was humongous. Every time I passed a door, it led to somewhere I hadn't yet explored.

Making my way back to my room, I suddenly heard the sound

of a piano being played in the distance. I hadn't met Mr Silvaro yet but I suspected it was probably him that was playing.

The melody was haunting, so distracting that I found myself gravitating in the direction from which it was coming from.

There were so many people around today. It seemed like Knightchurch had taken on a lot more staff than I first expected. Most of them were female and it could be my crazy imagination playing overtime but I swear they were all young and beautiful. Something told me Estelle was oblivious to the fact her husband may be a bit of a creep.

Stopping outside of the large wooden doors where the piano music was coming from, I gently placed both hands on the panels, pressing slowly. The door opened with a slight creak as I stared into the large open room. It's floor to ceiling windows letting in a blast of light. This had to be the most illuminated room I'd seen so far in the house.

In the middle of the room, positioned right beneath a glittering chandelier was a large, old piano and sat at its keys was who I suspected to be Mr Silvaro himself.

He stopped playing as soon as he spotted me hovering in the doorway.

"Who's there?" He asked. His voice thick and raspy as if he's spent his life filling his lungs with thick cigar smoke.

He looked towards me, his cold, steel eyes boring right into me pulling a quiet gasp from my chest. *It was him, the man I'd seen in the night.*

He was a handsome man despite the fact that he was obviously of the older generation. His inky black hair, thick with strands of silver littered throughout. My eyes instantly darted to his hands. No sign of any wounds so what was the blood all about?

"Sorry sir," I walked into the light so he could see me better. "My name's Bennett, I've just started working here. It's nice to finally meet you."

At first his gaze remained locked on mine as an eerie chill grazed the back of my neck, the hairs standing on end. His black suit looked moth-eaten and not what I expected from the man of the house.

"It's nice to meet you Bennett, I hope you're finding Knightchurch to your liking?"

The tone in his voice, unlike with Estelle, made me feel uneasy, almost unwelcome like he didn't really want me here but that he needed the staff. It was uncaring and lacked any emotion whatsoever.

"It's amazing," I replied, "such a beautiful, old building."

He nodded. "Yes, Knightchurch has been in our family for generations as I'm sure my wife has explained." *So this was Andreas Silvaro.*

I smiled, nodding in response.

"Do you play?" Andreas motioned towards the piano.

"Oh, only a little." I replied startled. "Nowhere near as good as you." I'd had a few lessons in school and at one point my dad tried to encourage me to take a few lessons with one of his friends - old Bill from the local pub - but I was nowhere near Beethoven standard just yet. I think I only attended two of old Bill's lessons and spent the rest of the time I should've been there chilling out with friends and a bottle of vodka at the local park.

His thin mouth curved at the side. "Come... show me."

Fuck!

"Oh I... I couldn't...I..."

"Please." He motioned to the instrument again.

Nervously I walked over to the grand piano as Andreas stood, holding out a hand to help me into his seat. I stepped forward accepting his palm and sat upon the heated stool which he'd just stood from.

Gliding my fingers over the ivory keys, I waited for some kind of inspiration to take over.

River flows in you by *Yiruma* was the only thing that sprang to mind and without thinking I began to play, my fingers effortlessly grazing over each note and my eyes closing as if this was the most natural thing in the world. *Clearly I remembered something from old Bill then.*

I didn't realise how relaxed and enveloped into my own world I'd become until I felt thick, calloused fingers sliding around the back of my neck. Goosebumps pebbled my flesh as I snapped from my trance, swinging round on the stool to see Andreas looking down at me, a heated expression on his face. My stomach churned with a sudden wave of nausea.

"Well I should go." I stood from the stool, quickly heading towards the door. The feel of his fingers across the back of my neck had sparked a feeling of unease and I wasn't planning on sticking around to see what kind of pervert Mr Silvaro was. I could still feel his fingers phantom trailing along my skin.

"I hope you'll join me again Bennett, that performance was... exquisite."

I nodded my head rapidly, anything to end this awkward conversation and get the fuck out of this room.

Tugging on the heavy door, I heard Andreas' voice behind me, smooth and spine chilling.

"Goodbye Bennett."

Maybe I was thinking too much into it, but that brief meeting had made me feel incredibly uncomfortable. There was just something about him that I didn't like, I just couldn't put my finger on what it was.

Heading back to my room, I silently counted the amount of portraits hanging on the wall. There seemed to be so many members of this family. Were they all buried in the cemetery out back?

Suddenly my eye caught the small silver plaque sitting below one of the paintings. Each portrait had a plaque at the bottom with the name and date of each member of the family, but this one seemed to stick out more than any other.

The painting was of a large, well built, (*it seemed*), man, somewhere in his late twenties, early thirties. He was ridiculously handsome with deep, icey blue eyes that seemed to be staring right back at me as I took him in.

The only eyes I'd ever seen as blue as his were... Ezras. The similarities were uncanny. He looked like Ezra but just in another time.

His clothes looked pre World War One and my guess was that he was slightly older than Ezra when this picture was painted. The date stated 1914. *Just what I expected.*

But it was his name that caught my attention more than anything. **Carlos Montgomery Silvaro.**

This was the guy in the cemetery. I suppressed a shudder threatening to escape as I continued peering into those sapphire blue eyes. He looked almost like he was smiling but the smile wasn't quite reaching his eyes, like he didn't want to be there. The whole vibe of this painting was just off and I couldn't explain what it was that was making me feel this way. This guy must be Ezras great grandfather, there was no denying the resemblance.

I made it my mission while I was here to find out more about Carlos Silvaro, but for now my foot had begun to ache again so I slowly walked back to my room with the intention of resting up for a while.

Pushing my door open, I screamed at the sight, my heart jumping straight from my chest as I saw her standing there in front of my bed. The dark-haired girl I'd seen in the window.

Chapter Eight

Bennett

I felt the blood drain from my face as she stared at me. Her skin, as pale as ice and her eyes dark like she hadn't slept in weeks. However despite the creepiness she emitted, I couldn't deny she was strikingly beautiful. I strained to regain my normal breathing. It was just a girl, seriously what the fuck was wrong with me.

I slowly closed my bedroom door, taking a few steps forward.

"Hey, sorry, you scared me... erm can I help you?"

Fuck! I shook my hands out in front of me to halt the stupid trembling.

The girl's eyebrows narrowed as her eyes crawled slowly up and down my body.

"No" finally she replied. "I'm sorry I scared you."

I smiled, a relieved sigh evaporating from my lungs.

"No really it's fine, I saw you yesterday... when I arrived. In the window. Sorry I haven't had a chance to meet any more of the staff yet, I erm... hurt my foot." I wiggled my hand at the wrist towards my injured limb.

She took a quick glance to where I was pointing before her eyes snapped back to my face. Silence.

"Ok well anyway, can I help you?"

Running her hand over the silk bed sheets, she sat down carefully.

"I don't really have any friends and I suppose after I saw you yesterday, you just looked like someone I could get to know."

My brows furrowed. "Oh ok," I replied. I guess judging by the reception I received from Kara and Andreas Silvaro, it didn't surprise me that this girl was lonely. People were hardly the most welcoming here I'd discovered so far.

"Well…" I walked over, sitting down beside her on my bed. "What's your name?"

"Millie." She smiled and her beautiful face seemed to light up for the first time.

"Okay Millie, well I'm Bennett, it's nice to meet you."

We both giggled.

"I'm sorry." She smiled. "You must think I'm so weird. Some creep, hanging around in your room."

I laughed, "not at all, although I haven't met the friendliest people here that's for sure."

"Yeah they're not the nicest, I have to admit," replied Millie. "The girls here can be a bit bitchy."

My eyes widened in agreement as I nodded slowly.

"Yep, I've only met one but she wasn't the best."

Millie smiled. "Kara?"

We both laughed again. "Yesss, do you know her?"

Millie silenced for a second. "No, but I've seen what she's like since she's been here and she has an attitude with everyone. Don't take it personally. Wait til you meet her minions Elaine, Riley and Summer."

"Elaine, Riley and Summer?"

Millie laughs. Guess I'll have to wait to find out what that is about.

"So have you been here long?" I ask.

Millie rolled her eyes and it was the first time I'd seen any kind of sass from her. "Too long… so how's the foot?"

I looked down to my feet. "Sore… but I guess that'll teach me to look where I'm going."

Millie's eyes stay fixed to the floor. "How did it happen?"

"I decided to go for a little walk, explore the grounds of Knightchurch, came across an old graveyard…"

"Graveyard?" Millie's gaze shot up to mine again, catching me in surprise.

"Erm... yeah there's some creepy old graveyard out back just through the woodland area. Think it's the past generations of the Silvaros or something."

Millie stilled. I couldn't read the expression on her face. Something between concern and... maybe a tinge of fear was all I could make out.

"Anyway," I continued, "I didn't get far, tripped on some branch and then got the pleasure of meeting Ezra Silvaro. Mr and Mrs Silvaros son."

Millie's features seemed to soften for just a nanosecond. "Yeah I know him." Her voice was soft and quiet, almost a whisper.

A small thread of jealousy weaves its way through my core. *Why the fuck did I feel jealous?* Of course Millie and Ezra knew each other. She worked here and he lived here. He was sex in human form and she was a petite, little stunner. *Yeah now I was jealous.*

I inhaled deeply, pushing the feeling of the green eyed monster back to the pit of my stomach.

"So what's he like?" I asked. Part of me didn't even know why I was asking, he made it no secret that I was an inconvenience yesterday and I hadn't seen him since but something just kept me wanting to bring him up in conversation.

Millie smiled. "He's complicated, but I guess when you see past that..." she waved her hands instead of finishing the end of her sentence and I decided hearing about my new friend's potential crush probably wasn't something I wanted to continue talking about.

She had a look of something in her face when she spoke about him and I couldn't quite place what it was.
I was tempted to push on but I refrained.

"Well I should go." Millie stood from the bed, brushing down the pretty, navy blue summer dress she was wearing and brushing out her thick, chocolate brown hair with her fingers.

"Well let's hang out soon." I said, mirroring her movements.

"Sure." She smiled, walking towards my bedroom door. Grabbing the door handle she twisted it, opening the door slightly before turning back to me. "I'd probably avoid that creepy cemetery if I were you, but if you're looking for somewhere to explore, take the path on the right side through the woods. Knightchurch lake is just through the clearing." With that she gently nodded her head and left, closing my door behind her.

Knightchurch lake? I wasn't aware of any lake here. I hadn't gotten round to taking the right side path on my walk yesterday before disaster struck but I was keen to keep exploring the grounds. *And avoiding fucking graveyards.* I decided maybe a little more *careful* adventure would be my plan for tomorrow.

"Bennett, Bennett"
The voice grew louder and more threatening. I searched my surroundings. The woods. Cold, dark, the feel of blood thumping through my veins.

I look left. Right. Forwards. Backwards. How did I end up in the woods? In a thin nightdress? No one is here. I search frantically for the source of the voice.

Staring forward a silhouette catches my eye as my breathing accelerates. A woman. Her hair, the brightest shade of silver. She looks young, she can't possibly be any older than I am.

"WAIT." I scream but she doesn't hear me, she's running. I need to catch her. I catch a sliver of her face, only briefly before she turns and continues running towards the house.

"PLEASE." I continue to yell desperately.
"SOMEONE IS AFTER ME. PLEASE WAIT. I NEED HELP!"
She continues on, ignoring my plea.

I chase her into the house. Wait! Where am I? I frantically searched around the room. My room? My bedroom in Knightchurch?
"Bennett."
The voice is barely a whisper as I turn round, the silver haired woman on my floor before me. Blood coats her white nightdress. A terrified expression on her pretty face, a face also streaked with

bright red blood. The nightdress looks dated, not the kind of nightie that I'm wearing right now. Her pale skin, covered in dark, stain-like bruises.

She claws desperately at the floorboards of my room. Her nails, breaking against the thick wood. Snapping and bleeding, I can hardly bear to look.

"What? What is it?" I call to her but she stares at me with blank, dead eyes, continuing to claw at the floor, no sound leaving her lips.

The floorboard comes away leaving a dark hole. I walk slowly to where the woman sits, waiting for me to look inside the hole. The sound of my breathing, the only thing audible in the room.

"Bennett." My name leaves her lips one last time.

Suddenly a blood curdling scream radiates from her body as I dive back in pure horror.

"Shit"

For the second night in a row, I jolted awake in my bed. These fucking nightmares need to get the fuck out of my head now. After only two days, I'm starting to feel like this house is making me go crazy. I'm starting to lose my mind.

I lean over, grabbing the small, jewelled clock on my bedside table. Three AM. The witching hour. *Of course.*

Letting my head fall back onto the soft, cloud-like pillow, I let my eyes adjust to the dark. Why was I having these nightmares? And who was the girl? The image of her silver hair and blood soaked nightdress burned into my brain. In my dream she was clawing at the wooden panels of my floor. *What the fuck?!*

Standing from my bed, I stared at the panel on the floor where the girl was sitting in my dream.

Dropping to my knees, I carefully pried away the chunk of wood. However, unlike in my dream, the section of the floor came away easily. Leaving a deep hole in the floor.

Hesitating, I dipped my hand into the hole. Dust and cobwebs met my fingers, making me wince.

I felt around, finding nothing but debris until suddenly my fingers grazed upon what felt like a box.

Grabbing it, I carefully pulled it from the hole and placed it on the floor before me.

It was an old looking, bronze coloured box. Pretty, intricate lattice detailing swirled around it, as I twisted it in my fingers trying to figure out what the hell I'd just found. Pulling the lid, the box opened with a sharp click.

Inside, I found a small book. It looked like it had just been rolled up and shoved inside the box, which I realised was some kind of keepsake box.

The paper of the book looked brown and tarnished, covered in a lacing of creases.

Opening the first page I noticed a date, *January 1911,* and a name *Theodora Alcott.*

A journal, I'd just uncovered someone's journal, and by the looks of things, no one had read this for a *very* long time.

Chapter Nine

Bennett

My fingers glided over the cool exterior of the pretty bronze box as I slid the folded journal back into the tiny compartment. Who was Theodora Alcott? And 1911? The book was well over a hundred years old.

Pushing up from my crouched position on the floor, I slowly walked back to the bed, when I heard the sound of music floating through the air.

The haunting melody filled the room and as much as I wanted to uncover the mystery surrounding the journal I'd just found, I couldn't help but feel compelled to see who was playing. It was three AM, who would be awake at this time? *Andreas Silvaro*

The thought of bumping into Andreas again sent shivers over my skin. I should ignore the music and go back to bed but I never was one for making the smartest of choices.

Grabbing my silk nightgown, I slowly opened my bedroom door, carefully making sure the low groan from the hinges wasn't enough to wake anyone, *or worse, alert the person who was playing the piano that I was there.*

My bare feet touched the cold, stone floor of the hallway as I tiptoed down, past the creepy portraits and huge, ugly grandfather clock at the end of the hall.

Stalling outside the room where the piano was located, I inhaled a deep breath, pressing against the large mahogany door and peering inside.

Darkness met my gaze, the only light was the soft golden glow of the candles sitting neatly on the sideboards.

There he sat, his tall form slightly hunched forward over the keys as his slender fingers worked in a hypnotic rhythm... Ezra Silvaro.

The light from the candles reflected off his flawless skin, almost creating a ghost-like image.

A strand of jet black hair fell over his eye as he played, completely oblivious to me watching him.

For a second I stood paralysed, completely mesmerised until my focus was met with a pair of eyes, blue, yet dark as the shadows and deep as the ocean.

He let out an audible sigh. The kind you release when feeling frustrated or just plain annoyed with someone's presence.

"To what do I owe this honor little bird?" His voice was smooth as silk. *Little bird.*

I flinched at the memory of him calling me little bird in my nightmare. *Has he ever called me that before? How would I know that was what he would call me?*

"Well?" His tone changed from annoyed to annoyed with a fizzle of anger.

"I couldn't sleep" I lie, "I heard the music and..." my voice trailed off as I stood scrutinised under his gaze.

No man had ever made me feel so much unease and I hated it. A flutter of something glided through my stomach. Ezra was attractive but something felt off about him. *Way off.* His whole aura was mysterious, dangerous even, and I found myself wondering if being alone with him in this creepy house was the best idea. But the danger was fucking addictive, I couldn't deny that. Like a foolish moth to a flame, I just kept feeling drawn even closer, even though the ultimate destination was getting burned to death.

Instead of replying to my words, Ezra went back to pressing the keys on the piano. A soft tune filled the air as I entered the room and walked over to where he was sitting.

"You play well," I smiled. "Who taught you?"

He slammed his eyes closed. "Why are you here?"

I arched my brow in surprise. "Excuse me?"

"Why are you here?" He repeated. "In this house?"

I wasn't sure what he was expecting to hear at first, before I replied. "I applied for the job, the one in the local post office."

He looked at me with pure intensity. "I don't know what you're talking about but you should leave. You're not right for the job"

He looked back down to the piano keys, breaking my gaze. *Unbelievable.*

"HA!" I scoffed in disbelief, walking closer to where he was sitting. "You think I'm not good enough for this job? This house? To make a few beds and mop a few floors."

In a second, he lunged to his feet, his hand shooting out and grabbing my throat, pressing me backwards as my back slammed against the piano.

"What the fuck…"

His face was so close to mine, I could feel his warm breath on my face, his masculine smell was intoxicating as a mixture of fear and adrenaline surged through my body. Outrage filled my mind but my core pulsed, a wave of heat travelling directly between my legs.

"You have no idea what you're getting yourself into, little bird. No idea at all."

Trying hard to mask the tremble in my voice, I swallowed hard. Ezras gaze dropped from my eyes to where his hand was still connected to my throat. *God he was beautiful. That tanned skin and eyes that had somehow transformed from blue to ebony. If death was a person, this man was him.*

I forced myself to stand up as straight as I could.

"I'm not afraid of you." I hissed, pushing into his hold in defiance. The truth couldn't be any further away but I'd be damned if I was going to show any weakness to this mother fucker.

His mouth twisted up into a snarl. "You should be."

His free hand glided down the side of my body, skirting over every curve and valley of my hips and the top of my thighs before travelling up the dip of my stomach and between my breasts.

My lips parted, releasing a slow breath before my teeth dug into the bottom one, pressing firmly.

His eyes flicked from my eyes to my lips. The moment felt like it had frozen in time and that no one else existed, only us.

Just as I thought he was going to press his lips to mine, his eyes jolted back up.

"Get the fuck out." He released me with a sharp shove against the piano. I inhaled in surprise. *What the fuck?!* My hand gripped my throat where I could still feel the phantom touch of his fingers.

Without any further explanation, Ezra turned and headed straight for the door in powerful strides, leaving me alone in the darkened room wondering what the fuck just happened.

Chapter Ten

Ezra

My footsteps echoed through the halls as I stormed through the house, back to the east wing.

Why was this girl testing my patience? Her eyes, the colour of emeralds, pierced right through me. I feel like I can't fucking breathe when she's there. Like she can see me for who I am, and it terrifies me.

She looks fucking hot. Gone are the piercings and the dyed black hair. Her naturally dark locks cascade down her back like a waterfall, swaying just above her ass. *Fuck!* My cock springs to life at just the mere thought of her perfect, round backside. It's been way too long since I got laid, I need to go back to fucking my fathers waste of space staff.

Holding onto her throat, I was one second away from squeezing, one second away from ending it all and she had no fucking idea how close to death she just came.

I've never met someone who looks at me with such defiance. It's like she can see right through me, see the depths of my soul where the darkness hides. But that's ridiculous, if she could really see that far into my being, she would see the monster that lurks there. The monster, just waiting to be released.

I run my hands through my hair. Frustration fills my every bone and I struggle to contain my ragged breathing. Struggle to contain the urge to destroy something. Because that's who I am, that's what I do. This girl needs to go now!

Arriving back at my room, I push open the heavy, wooden door, slamming it behind me before taking a deep breath to calm myself.

Suddenly as I turn towards my bed, I'm met with an even more infuriating sight.

Kara sits in my bed. *In my fucking bed.* She's covered in one of the light sheets, but I can tell that behind that, she's naked.

Her blonde hair falls loosely around her shoulders. I should be happy, *hell I should be fucking ecstatic* that this bitch is in my bed. She's hot and my dick is throbbing, liquid heat from my encounter with Bennett is still racing through my veins but all I feel is anger. Pure, agonising rage.

"Get the fuck out!"

Kara looks at me with confusion.

"I thought you'd be pleased" she replies, her voice low and laced with a faint tremble.

"How dare you let yourself into my private quarters. You're a fucking maid and you fucking don't belong here."

Her eyes flicker with hurt and then I notice they gradually glass over as if she's fighting back the tears.

"I can give you whatever you want." She slowly peels back the bed sheet and yep, just as I fucking knew... naked! Not a fucking stitch of clothing.

However instead of the reaction she was hoping for, it only served to make my anger spike even more.

Without another word I stride over to the bed, snatching her wrist in my hand and dragging her from where she's laid.

She squeals in surprise and drags the sheet with her as she flies from the bed.

"Get the fuck out." I demand. "I don't EVER want to see you in here again."

I open the door, pushing her roughly through it and without warning, I grab my bedsheet and tear it from her grasp leaving her naked and exposed.

Her hands fly to conceal herself but I slam the door in her face without remorse.

She can fucking walk back to her room in the buff. I have no time for that. That's the kind of shit Caleb deals with, not me.

Kara's had a thing for me for long enough now and I've never returned the affection. This little obsession is getting fucking annoying.

As soon as she's gone, I walk slowly back to the bed, my whole body aching with exhaustion. I've suffered with insomnia for as long as I can remember and tonight my demons feel like they're playing overtime.

It's been three weeks since the last time I let my demons play. Three weeks since I drew the blade of my knife over skin, watching it part like butter. Three weeks since the screams of evil fed my soul and eased the cravings that consumed me.

I let my body slump back into the bed as I run my palms over my face. My cock still painfully hard from the encounter in the piano hall.

I could have fucked Kara, probably should have fucked Kara, but the only person in my head right now is the pretty little brunette, too curious for her own good.

I've managed to control the urges ingrained into my DNA, only letting them take over when I've had to, but seeing *her* is making things more difficult by the day.

I loosen the buttons on my jeans, pulling them down far enough to release my cock. It springs free, bringing a small sense of relief. I'm rock hard already, a bead of pre cum glistening on the tip.

Wrapping my hand around the base, I begin to slowly pump my hand up and down the shaft, gently to begin with and then picking up rhythm as I picture the little bird's lips wrapped around my length instead of my fingers.

A low groan rumbles in my throat. Her full, luscious pink lips. Her firm round tits, just the right size to fit perfectly in my palm. Her sweet, tight cunt.

With a few more strokes I shatter. Thick ropes of cum spurt over my lower stomach as I come down from the temporary high.

I lay there spent for a few more minutes, thinking of ways I could get Bennett to leave this fucking house, and soon. Nothing good is going to come of her being here. She has no idea the secrets that Knightchurch holds or the monsters lurking underneath her bed.

Chapter Eleven

Bennett

As always, the strobe of light peeked through the crimson curtains as I opened my eyes. I thought I'd pulled them tighter last night. My head felt swollen and heavy due to lack of sleep.

I tossed and turned after getting back to my room following my run in with Ezra. Thoughts racing through my head.

He was an enigma that I just couldn't get my head around. He had this cold, almost frightening demeanour but yet he didn't leave an injured girl to struggle, walking back to the house from a derelict, old cemetery. I just didn't get what his issue was.

The small bronze box sat neatly on the bedside table where I'd placed it before leaving to seek out the source of the music a few hours before.

I lifted it, opening it up again to see the folded up journal inside.

The writing was so pretty, it almost seemed a shame that it was in a screwed up book, hiding under a decaying floorboard, home to cockroaches and god knows what else.

I knew I didn't have long to sit and read the book as today was supposed to be the day that I actually did what the Silvaros were paying me for, but curiosity was seriously getting the better of me as I opened the first page, desperate to at least read a little of what was in here.

Laying back against my fluffed up pillow, I relaxed and began to read.

Theodora Alcott January 1911

Life begins today. I've arrived. Knightchurch is more beautiful than I ever could have imagined. I never thought a girl like me, coming from nothing at all, could finally end up in such luxury, yet here I am. Even the sound of the drizzling rain can not pull me from my happiness. I spend my days surrounded by such opulence that I have only ever seen in my dreams. This place is like a palace from the fairytales that my mother would read to me when I was a small child. Its endless rooms and vast, open outdoor spaces are simply divine. I feel like God has truly blessed me.
The Silvaros are kind. They welcomed me with open arms. Genevieve is beautiful and Carlos... Well Carlos is something else entirely. Is it sinful to say he makes my heart flutter by just one glance? I know it is, so I shall not think such things as working in this heaven is more than I could have ever asked for and right now life. Is. Perfect.

    I pull my eyes from the page. Theodora Alcott, she was a worker who came to Knightchurch, pretty much the same way I did. I wanted to tell someone what I'd found but my intrigue was forcing me to keep this a secret, at least until I'd had a chance to finish reading it.

    I wanted to stay and continue reading more than anything but I had work to do and could already hear the sounds of people scurrying around, so I knew I was probably going to be late if I didn't get a move on.

I hurried into the shower, the warm water easing my aching bones. I washed quickly, drying myself in record time and picking up a black swing dress, pulling it on as I grabbed my *Doc Martens* and headed out of my room.

    Jogging down the marble staircase, and into the sitting room, I was met with the stone cold stare of Andreas. His suit looked more polished today, his demeanour more that of someone who came from wealth. Estelle sat close by on a moss green chaise.

    I smiled over at her, expecting her to be her usual, warm,

friendly self but she seemed distant, distracted, her eyes glazed with a kind of sadness. It also wasn't hard to notice how her eyes were circled with the darkest shadow-like circles. Almost as if she hadn't slept in days. Before I had the chance to speak, Andreas' voice rose above everything else.

"Ahh Bennett, nice to see you again."

I force a smile as best I can, my eyes still locked on Estelle who doesn't move a muscle. It's almost as if she's frozen in place.

"Today there are beds to change and rooms to clean. We expect nothing but perfection here at Knightchurch. I'm sure you understand. I will call Kara and she'll help you get sorted for the day." *Great!*

I nodded. Spending time with Kara was definitely not going to be my idea of fun, but I hoped there would be so much work to do that it would keep me busy and keep my mind off a certain tall, dark and handsome Silvaro who was playing with my sanity and invading my nightmares.

Almost as if the devil himself had heard my thoughts, the door opened and Ezra walked in. Dressed in his usual black, ripped jeans and a black hoodie, he looked every bit as sinful as he always does.

Frustration mounted inside me at how my body responded to this man every time he was within twenty feet of me. I'd never reacted to a guy like this and god knows I'd met plenty of them working at Delilah's.

His blue eyes met mine before turning to his father.

"I'll be away today, hopefully back before sunset." His words were basic but very to the point. The tone abrupt as if he didn't really give a shit what his father was thinking.

Andreas let out a sigh. "Of course." He smiled but the smile again didn't meet his eyes.

This man was as fake as anything and the way my eyes caught Estelle flinching every time he spoke was throwing red flags in every direction.

Andreas placed his hand on Estelles shoulder and squeezed. It appeared to be a sign of affection but she looked uncomfortable, almost frightened. Before I had a chance to say anything, she rose from her seat, not even looking in my direction and heading towards the door. Andreas followed slowly.

"If you need anything, Kara will help you." He said as he joined his wife outside the room, leaving Ezra and I alone.

The silence was palpable, my heart thundered in my ears as we stared at each other.

The door swiftly opened again, behind where Ezra was standing.

"Did I miss anything bitches?"

A handsome, dark blonde stranger entered the room. He must have been around the same age as Ezra and looked to be about the same height.

His broad chest heaved under a fitted white tee and my eyes directly flew the bulge in his fitted, light blue distressed jeans. *Fuck.*

I forced my eyes back to his face where he was throwing me a cheeky look with emerald green eyes that rivaled my own, looking like he knew exactly what I'd just been checking out.

Where Ezra looked dark and dangerous, this guy looks like mischief and light. His delicious smile framed with light stubble made my cheeks flush pink with heat.

Ezra looked between us shaking his head.

"Caleb, get the fuck out of here." Said Ezra.

The new guy fake pouted at him, drawing the tiniest smile from my lips.

"Out!" He shouted, "we've got shit to do."

The guy, Caleb, rolled his eyes, holding his hands up in mock surrender and heading back to the door.

Just as he was about to exit, he turned towards me, giving me a cheeky wink and a smile that I'm sure has had more panties dropping than I've had hot dinners.

I covered my smile with my hand, waiting for Ezra to turn his attention away from his friend and back to me.

"Fuck sake." Ezra cursed under his breath before looking back at me.

I inhaled deeply, plucking up the courage to speak.

"Erm... I'm worried for your mom." The words sounded strangled but at least I managed to get them out. I felt like I was going to melt into some slushy puddle just being in the same vicinity as him. *Fucking ridiculous.*

Ezras expression remained unreadable as he fiddled with a zippo in his hand.

"My mother is currently on medication, she's struggling."

My eyebrows raised. I had no idea Estelle was struggling with anything. She seemed so bright and cheerful. *Well from what I'd seen so far.*

"May I ask..."

"My sister died." His voice cut off my sentence as my stomach churned in surprise. *His sister died.*

"Oh I'm so sorry I..." Now I was struggling with something to say. No wonder Estelle looked the way she did. She'd lost a child.

Ezra shook his head. "It happened two years ago, she vanished, into thin air, no signs that she was leaving, no signs of anything. One minute she was there and the next she was gone."

The look of shock must have blatantly been painted on my face at this point.

"But you said she was dead, have they never..."

"Found her? No but my sister was a happy girl, she would never just up and leave the way the police tried to make it out. We've had a lot of... trouble with the police over the years. Ghost stories about our family, rumours, the police didn't want to help, so they put it down to a runaway. But I know something happened to her. Elenor was no runaway."

"Her name was Elenor?" I ask softly. Something about the way Ezra talks about his sister brings out a vulnerability in him. One I would never have imagined was there.

"Yes," he replied, "she would have been twenty five now."

His sister would have been the same age as me. I wanted to reassure him, tell him that if she hadn't been found, the likelihood was that she was probably still out there somewhere, but for some reason he seemed like his mind was made up. Like he just knew she was... dead.

"My mother is struggling, she takes medication but at times it's not enough. My father is trying to pull her through it."

It was only there for a split second but I saw it. A coldness that flashed over his eyes when he mentioned Andreas, almost like he knew something was wrong there, just as I thought I did.

I walked slowly to where he was standing, leaning on his arms over the table, his hands curled into fists. I placed my hand onto his to offer reassurance but he jolted upright, almost as if my touch had scolded him. The pain in his eyes from talking about his sister had vanished and was replaced by the familiar hardness.

"I have to go, I have a lot to do today."

With that he stormed through the door and out into the large foyer before striding out through the front door of Knightchurch.

I ran my fingers through my long, tousled hair. Shaking off thoughts of Ezra and these strange feelings he ignited in me. He never mentioned a single word about anything that had happened last night. It was obvious me being here stirred some kind of rage within him but I still have no idea why. In a way I felt relieved that he was acting like last night never happened but part of me wanted to know if he was feeling anything, even the smallest amount, like the way I was feeling.

Kara stood by the entrance to the kitchen, chatting to three other girls who I assumed were Elaine, Riley and Summer.

Millie had mentioned about these girls, they looked like the mean girls you always got in high school and I knew instantly today was probably going to be a struggle.

Speaking of Millie, I hadn't seen her for a while. I missed her smile already and I didn't even really know her.

I made a mental note to go looking for her after I'd finished up today. Knightchurch was huge so it wasn't really surprising I hadn't bumped into Millie yet. I wasn't even sure what jobs she'd be scheduled with today.

"Beds throughout the south wing need changing," said Kara, walking towards me without so much as hello. "There's an old cart over there, it's a bit dodgy on the wheels but I'm sure you'll manage."

The urge to flip her off was overwhelming but if we're both gonna be working here, the least we can do is try to get on.

The three girls Kara was talking to giggled like petty school kids as I walked towards the old cart, a basic sack on wheels and started pushing it towards a small lift I'd come across to take me up to the bedrooms.

"So how are things with Ezra?" I heard one of the girls ask, directing the question to Kara. My footsteps slowed as I pretended to be having trouble with the cart's wheels as I listened in to the conversation. Kara flipped her hair, a smug grin on her stupid face.

"Perfect!" She replied. "In fact I was with him just last night, he couldn't keep his hands off me."

They all giggled, carrying on their juvenile conversation. My chest tightened at Kara's words. *Was I jealous? What the fuck?!*

It didn't make sense that Kara and Ezra would be together last night unless it was before or even after our little encounter in the piano room. But regardless I was feeling pretty shitty. *Was she his type? Why did I even care?*

Speeding up, I headed to the bedrooms to start stripping the beds. This place had a lot of rooms so this was going take me a fucking long ass time.

Several bedrooms later and I was starting to lose the will to live. I'd lost count of the amount of beds I'd stripped. God knows why this place needed so many bedrooms when the family consisted of only three people. What a waste.

Just as I pulled the last sheet from the bed, a little redhead entered the room, I recognised her straight away as one of the girls who stood with Kara earlier in the day.

"Hey, Bennett isn't it?" She began. "I'm Summer, thought I'd come and give you a hand."

Okay, this chick knew exactly what she was doing, helping out on the last fucking bedroom. I forced a smile while she beamed, what I could tell, was an equally forced grin.

Summer grabbed the new, white Egyptian cotton sheet and began folding it onto the bed.

"So what brings you to Knightchurch?"

I wasn't feeling particularly in the mood for chit chat but went with it anyway.

"Well, I lost my previous job and this one came up and so… yeah I'm here."

"Oh," Summer nodded. "What was your last job?"

"A stripper." The words came out without hesitation and I had to bite back my smile as I saw the surprised, judging look on Summers face.

"Oh okay." She replied. The atmosphere between us in that second could have been sliced with a knife and I was loving it. I had to do everything in my power to keep from laughing. I was fucking proud of my previous career. Why shouldn't I be?!

"So why are you here?" I guessed it was probably best to repay the curiosity.

"Duh! It's Knightchurch." Summer looked at me as if I'd just grown three heads. "I wanted to see if all the rumours were true. You know about all the missing people, ghosts and all those fucking freaky things." She wiggled her fingers as if she was casting some kind of mock spell.

"I don't believe in all that shit." My reply was probably a little blunt but I was getting a bit tired of all these old wives tales.

"Well you should. The police have raked over this place loads of times over the years. People have been reported missing so many times and the creepiest thing is that they just vanish into thin air. No trace. But everyone knows the Silvaros had something to do with it."

My eyebrows pinch together in confusion.

"So nothing was ever found?"

"Nope. Nothing at all. The police looked everywhere, even dug up that creepy graveyard they've got hidden in the woods." *She knew about the cemetery.* "Obviously people thought they were stashing bodies where all their manky, old ancestors are buried."

Summer shuddered, before regaining composure.

As much as I fucking hated gossip, I had to admit these weird stories were drawing a curious side out of me.

"I'm a psychic." The statement was so random. "Like I can sense things, and I read Tarot cards. My aunt taught me. That's another reason I came here, I'm into all that spooky stuff."

All that spooky stuff? Was this girl for real?

"Maybe if people have gone missing and there's no evidence of any foul play here then maybe... oh I dunno... they just left?" I wasn't even trying to hide the sarcasm in my voice at this stage.

Summer just looked at me like she was trying to figure out if I was being serious or not.

"Nope, the Silvaros did something to them. I know it. I can sense it. Plus it was all women. I reckon it's something to do with Andreas. He's creepy as fuck. Kind of exciting though isn't it? All the mysterious shit?"

My lips tightened as I nodded in response. There was no point giving my opinion, this girl was deluded clearly. But even I had to admit Andreas was... strange, and that was putting it lightly. However, exciting it was not!

"So, you good friends with Kara?" I wasn't sure why I was changing the subject to Kara. She'd already made it clear that we weren't going to be friends and to be honest I wasn't that interested in her, but something was nagging me inside about her relationship with Ezra. I had no idea why but I wanted to know just what his feelings were.

"I guess." Summers' response wasn't the enthusiastic one I thought I'd be getting. "She's ok, I mean she came from money so she doesn't need this job. Her dad sent her here because she was getting a bit too spoiled. He wanted her to see how the real world works, get an actual job. But when she saw Ezra there wasn't much more convincing needed to get her to stay. She says she and him are a thing but I'm not so sure. I never see them together, in fact he never even seems to acknowledge her."

I nodded. Something told me Summer wasn't quite as friendly with Kara as I thought.

We finished the rest of the stripping and Summer offered to take the cart down to the laundry room so I could finish a bit earlier. It was a nice offer and to be honest it did make me like her a little bit more, even if she was a bit of a strange one.

Walking down the steps outside the house to the garden, I was pleased to see Millie sitting by a little patch of dirt, a small trowel in her hands.

"Hey." It looked like I had pulled her out of a deep thought.

"Hey you." She smiled. Her pretty face lighting up. "Come help me."

I bent down into the mud where Millie was now crouching.

"What are we doing?" I asked, grabbing another trowel from the floor.

"I'm trying to turn this little patch into a flower bed. I've planted some red roses here but they just don't seem to grow. No matter how much I look after them or water them, just nothing. It's like the ground is dead... almost... poisoned."

I glanced at the small patch of earth that Millie was trying to garden. The ground looked dry and cold. The only thing growing there were dirty looking weeds. All yellow and broken.

Picking up the small watering can that Millie had brought out with her, I sprinkled some water onto the flowerbed. The dirt sucked up the water but within seconds it's cracked appearance had returned. No signs of life or anything other dry and rot. *Weird.*

It wasn't the right time of year for gardening anyway, but this patch looked worse than anything I'd ever seen in autumn.

"I guess I should stop trying huh?!" Said Millie. She wiped her hands on her sunshine yellow apron.

"Maybe.. I mean it could be the time of year but what do I know?! I'm no expert." I replied with a sigh. "You been on gardening duties today?"

"Yep." She replied, grabbing her little tools and dropping them back into the bucket by her side. "It's not the time of year though,

I've been battling with this for months. You had a chance to see the lake yet?"

With everything that had been going through my mind, I'd completely forgotten about the lake that Millie had mentioned."

"Oh no, I forgot all about it. I'm not even sure where it is."

Millie smiled. "It's about a ten minute walk, not too far, maybe we could go there tomorrow. If you'd like?"

A day at a pretty lake sounded good and I reckon I could probably finish the house duties early if I got a move on with it. *And Kara wasn't being a bitch adding extra stuff on.*

"That sounds like a fantastic idea." I said.

"Bennett."

The silvery voice came out of nowhere as I turned to see Estelle standing on the steps, looking down at Millie and I, hunched over the rotten flower patch.

She stared at us with a gentle smile on her face. She looked far from the scared, shell of a woman I'd seen with Andreas which was a little more reassuring.

"Would you mind helping out with a few jobs in the laundry room? We're snowed under today."

I forced a strained smile. The last thing I wanted to do was more housework but as they say, needs must.

"Of course I'll be right there."

Estelle nodded, spinning on her heel and going back up the stairs.

"Great. No rest for the wicked!" I rolled my eyes.

Millie laughed, going back to her digging.

"So lake tomorrow?" I stood, brushing the dirt from my knees.

"Sure thing." Said Millie, not looking up from the task in hand. "Bring your swimsuit. I'll meet you there."

I had to admit I was loving getting to know Knightchurch. I intended to discover as much about it as I could. I had no idea why people would make up rumours about a place as beautiful as this. I suppose jealousy probably played a part.

The villages nearby probably hated the fact an attractive, and seriously loaded family lived in this gothic masterpiece of a house. It seemed like a reasonable argument for all the childish gossip. After all there were no such things as ghosts anyway.

Chapter Twelve

Ezra

Everyone has skeletons in their fucking closet. Granted, my family has more than anyone I've ever come across, but still, I'm yet to meet a human who isn't harbouring something dark and desperate deep down. We all have secrets. Some are just worse than others.

I live by that fucking fact like it's a mantra. One that I recite to myself every time I walk to the soundproof room hidden deep beneath the walls of Knightchurch. The room that I know at this precise minute holds a killer more depraved than any I've known in my lifetime. One of the worst kind. Too bad he's also a cowardly sack of shit.

The trap door under the oversized, black Egyptian rug in my room leads to the corridors underground, laced with cobwebs and dust so thick, I have to cover my mouth and nose with my hoodie.

I use my flashlight to see where I'm going even though I've made this journey many times in my twenty eight years. I could probably reach the room with my eyes closed.

It's cold and grim down here, not somewhere a normal human being would want to venture, but I've never pretended to be a fucking normal human being. *If only.*

I'm the only one of three who walks this path. Myself and my father, we're the only ones with this burden, this curse, and Caleb when he's working with me. Unfortunately due to some other issue, he isn't with me right now, so today I walked alone.

My mother had been told strictly to make sure staff never entered the east wing. Despite the soundproof walls, you could never be too careful that someone might hear.

I reach the large, iron door at the end of the corridor leading to the room that holds child killer Donavan De Luca.

He's been hiding out for months since he was finally charged for the murder of his twin stepdaughters and their friend. All the girls were only six years old.

My blood simmers as I unsecure the padlock and thick, metal chains on the door. It creaks as it opens and seeing him sat there, half naked, tied to a battered, wooden chair in the middle of the cold, damp room, it feels like someone has doused the flames inside me with a bucket of gasoline.

Releasing my fury would be the only way I could get any potential sleep, but even that wasn't a guarantee.

Donavan whimpers as he rolls his head attempting to regain consciousness. The drugs I stabbed him with earlier today should just about be leaving his system and I can tell by the glazed expression on his face that he's beginning to realise he has no clue where he is. I wait for the panic to set in.

"Fuck… fuck…" *there is it.* "Who are you? Where am I?"

Donavans head snapped back and forth between me and the room as he took in his surroundings. His pale almost transparent, veiny skin pricked with goosebumps as he trembled like a terrified dog.

I narrow my eyes as I grab the only other battered, wooden chair in the room, spinning it around and straddling it, draping my forearms over the back. I clutch my pen knife loosely between my thumb and forefinger, twisting the point of the blade over the pad of my other thumb. I struggle to hide the bored expression on my face.

"Donovan." My voice makes him tremble more. Fuck I haven't even touched him yet.

"W… what do you want?" He stutters. His eyes widen, glinting with fear and I begin to worry he's going to pass out before we've even gotten to the good part.

"You're probably wondering why you're here?!"

Donavan nods furiously, still looking around the room.

"My name is Ezra Silvaro and you are the VIP guest at my home. You may know it formally as Knightchurch manor but for today you will know it as... your own private hell."

Donavan begins to sob, tugging at his restraints. Horror is etched on his face as he snivels, snot and tears combined, his face turning an unhealthy shade of red.

"Please, please let me go, I won't tell anyone." He cries.

I run my fingers over the stubble on my jaw.

"See I can't do that Donavan because, see I've been hearing all about you and how the police are searching for you regarding the death of three little girls. Ring any bells?"

He shakes his head slowly, his face contorted with how heavy he's now crying. *Fuck he's ugly.* I rise to my feet, my patience is wearing thin with this motherfucker now.

This man had overpowered and harmed these children. The monster your mother tells you is hiding under your bed, yet here he was, weak and begging in his underwear about to meet the monster underneath his own.

I walk over to where he's sitting, still waiting for some kind of response to my question, but still he sits sobbing to himself. Spit dribbling from the corners of his disgusting mouth.

Suddenly without warning and without any more words from Donavan, I plunge my penknife as hard as I can into his thigh. He screams in agony and no doubt shock as his eyes bulge and he stares in horror at the knife sticking out of his leg.

"AHHH FUCK, FUCK"

The screams are like music to my soul as I inhale deeply, almost as if his suffering has transformed into oxygen and my starving lungs can breathe again.

I rip the knife from his thigh, wiping the dark red liquid on my jeans. His blood paints the denim like beautiful paint on blank paper.

"Now are you ready to talk, Donny boy?" I ask. His wailing

continues, *god it's fucking annoying.*

Snot and tears continue to pour from his face.

"I'll tell you anything." He sobs as I smile, running my tongue over my canines.

"Oh I know you will, Donny. Now let's start with why you killed your stepdaughters and their friend. Three innocent children. Someone's daughters, granddaughters. Tell me Donny. What made you do it?"

He looks at me with fear and desperation in his beady little eyes.

"I didn't mean to kill them, I was just… just…"

STAB.

I ram the knife into his other thigh, this time ripping it back out instantly. He screams like a bitch, thrashing violently against the restraints. But he's going nowhere. He's my toy and I'm far from done playing with him today.

"You need to speak quicker Donny boy, I'm a busy man. I don't have all day."

"They were pictures, I just wanted to take some pictures. A guy, a guy said he would buy some pictures of the girls, offered me ten grand… they started crying, saying they were going to tell their mum. I panicked."

My stomach rolled in disgust.

"So you strangled them. At least I think that's what the police report said. You silenced three children for good so they couldn't expose you for the pervert you are?!" My blood boiled. My hands shaking, struggling to hold back.

"Please I didn't mean to…"

I drive my fist into face, connecting hard with his cheekbone. His head whips to the side, a spray of blood decorating the floor from his mouth.

He whimpers in desperation.

Walking to the far side of the large room, I grab the large black rucksack that I keep down here for when I play my games. It contains knives, tasers, saws, pretty much everything someone like me could want. My own bag of treasures.

I remove the cable wire laying at the bottom of the bag.

"Now you ended those innocent girls' lives in one of the most horrific ways so Donavan before you die, I'd like to give you a little taste of what hell is going to be like."

With that I wrap the cable around his throat, pulling as tightly as my arms will allow.

His eyes bulge and his face reddens to the same colour as the blood on the concrete floor as I continue to tighten, locking off his air supply and crushing his windpipe.

He thrashes before convulsing, the colour in his face changing rapidly from red to purple. I can see unconsciousness starting to set in. Just as he's about to pass out I release the rope. *It's a grizzly job but hey, someone's gotta do it.*

Donavan desperately inhales, coughing and choking as he tries to regain his composure. However, just as his breathing begins to regulate, I grab the cable again, pulling it taut against his throat and cutting off the air supply yet again, waiting for him to teeter on the edge before I'll let up and subject him to it all over again.

A sense of calm washes over me as I absorb his cries and his terror. It's like a drug, except nothing I've ever taken could ever hit this kind of euphoria. It's otherworldly.

The pain inside my own head is torturous and wild but it's all I've ever known and it's all I'll ever continue to know. All I want to do is inflict this pain onto others. Make them suffer.

I don't know how many times I'll repeat the torture on Donovan. Until I get bored or my arms begin to ache I suppose but either way, he'll be dead by the end of the day and the world will be free of one more perverted monster. It's just a shame that the world still won't be free of one more monster like me.

Chapter Thirteen

Bennett

Theodora Alcott   March 1911

It's only been two months and yet I can not remember what my life was like before Knightchurch. This place is like a dream. If only mama and papa could see me now. I've written to them several times over the last couple of months but sadly I've heard no reply. I'm sure papa is just busy with the farm and mama has my sisters to care for so I can not expect too much from them right now. Carlos has started paying me attention. He is the most beautiful man I've ever seen. His eyes sparkle like sapphires. I know it's a sin to have these feelings for him but I swear sometimes when I bathe in the lake, he's watching me from the woodland. Hidden. I like the thought of him watching me. I've never been with a man before, yet when I'm in his presence all I can think about is what his touch would feel like. I imagine his lips, softly caressing the delicate spot below my ear and his fingers gliding lower between my legs. I must stop. Just writing this is making me giggle like a small child. Genevieve has been so good to me, I shouldn't be having these impure thoughts about her husband but I just can not stop. The weather has just begun to get considerably warmer and it's more tempting than ever just to spend time out in the open. There is just endless space here. I've always been someone who loves the outdoors and now I can indulge in this as much as I like. I must go now as I have work to do. I know I will see Carlos today and my stomach is already in knots. Nothing can erase this smile. How did I get so lucky?!

Wow! This bitch had it bad.

I giggle to myself as I roll the battered journal back up and secure it was an elastic band I found in the kitchen.

I was tempted to read more but I had work to do and I'd already promised Millie I'd head down to the lake.

I thought about showing Millie what I'd found but something felt good about having this little secret that no one else knew about. I doubted even the Silvaros knew about the small box and journal.

To save time, I grab my blue bikini and put it on underneath my black smock dress and pull on my *Doc Martens*.

I hadn't questioned Millie yesterday when she mentioned about bringing the swimsuit, as to whether swimming in a lake this time of year was a good idea but the sun was shining, casting a warm glow into the room so at least it wasn't torrential rain. Plus I wanted to explore the grounds as much as I could and Millie sounded like she really loved this lake. *Fuck it!*

After finishing up getting ready, I headed to the kitchen. I hadn't even made it to the bottom of the stairs before I heard the shrill voice like nails on a chalkboard.

"BENNETT!" *Dear god!* Summer bounced out of the kitchen, her mop of reddy auburn curls bouncing on her slender shoulders. I tugged my lips into a strained smile.

"Hey." My wrist managed a limp wave.

"We're together today." Her enthusiasm was nauseating. What the fuck! "Karas in the kitchen, Riley and Elaine are taking the laundry and we get to clean the bedrooms."

I had no idea why the fuck she seemed so happy about cleaning the bedrooms but hey who was I to comment. Whatever rocks your world right?!

As if reading my mind, Summer winks. "Sorting the bedrooms is fun, you find all sorts of things."

Ahh now it made sense. Our Summer here was a grade A fucking snoop. Perfect! *Nosy bitch!*

I considered making excuses and trying to land a job where I could work alone or at least with Millie but Summer, for some strange reason, actually seemed like she *liked* my company, so pushing down my irritation I forced a smile and headed to the cleaning cupboard.

The stench of bleach and something like citrus invaded my nostrils as I opened the door. Pulling out the box of supplies stuffed with dusters, cleaning polish and other bits and pieces, I headed back upstairs to the first floor.

"We're starting in mister and missus Silvaros' room," said Summer, following me up the staircase. "The bedroom is on the top floor, hope you're up for a workout." She began taking the steps two at a time. I dragged my feet up the stairs, continuing to walk at a snail's pace. I was in no hurry to start cleaning although the thought of clocking off was already on my mind.

When we arrived outside the Silvaros bedroom, we were met with a large, mahogany wooden door. Intricate detail was carved into the large panels depicting what looked like roses with thick vines and thorns.

Summer pulled out a small, gold key and placed it into the lock, clicking it open. Grabbing the large brass doorknob, I pushed the heavy door, both of us peering around it like we were about to look into Aladdin's cave of treasures.

The room was magnificent. A gigantic, gothic looking four poster bed sat in the middle of the room, covered in peach and blush pink silk covers and luxurious white fur throws. The bed itself was surrounded by mirrors. They were everywhere, even on the ceiling.

"Filthy bitch!" Summer snickered. "Mirrors on the ceiling." She pointed to where I was already looking. "I bet Andreas and Estelle get up to some kinky shit in this room."

The thought made bile rise in my oesophagus like battery acid. I shuddered the feeling away.

"Let's just get cleaned up in here. I assume the beds will be left to Riley and Elaine so we'll just do a bit of dusting."

Summer smiled. "Of course."

She picked up a shocking pink feather duster and started waving it around towards the large, silver chandelier in the room. Grabbing a cloth, a tatty black apron and a bottle of some random spray, I started dusting the bedside tables. A picture of a young Estelle sat on the small unit. She was wearing a floor length, midnight blue gown, her hair in tight ringlets and a huge, enthusiastic smile showing off her row of perfectly straight white teeth.

"Wow, Estelle was a hottie." I pick up the gold frame, examining the picture closer. Summer turns her head to face me, body still contorted towards the job in hand.

"Hhmm, doesn't surprise me, the woman is stunning. Hell knows what she sees in Andreas?! She could have been a model."

I nod, placing the picture back in its original place.
A small rose gold jewellery box sat at the back of the bedside table. I wiped around it quickly until the duster slipped from my fingers and landed on the floor. Bending down to pick it up, my hip suddenly clashed with the table forcing the contents including the jewellery box to shudder.

The lid dropped from the top revealing no jewellery, just pack after pack of Xanax. *Fuck someone was having trouble sleeping.* Estelle was clearly struggling.

My mind cast back to the conversation with Ezra about how his sister had gone missing and was presumed dead. I couldn't imagine the amount of pain it was causing that poor woman. My heart ached for her. I quickly placed the lid back on the box before Summer started her snooping.

Taking in the sights of the bedroom, I don't think I'd ever come across a room so big. I was pretty sure you could fit a small apartment in this room.

The grand en suite bathroom was just off to the left. It housed a gorgeous, white marble bathtub, big enough for two.

Entering the bathroom, I quickly got to work wiping away traces of dust and soap scum inside the bathtub before starting on the sink.

A large, antique, oval mirror overlooked the sink. I stared at my reflection in the glass. My pale face, my long chocolate brown hair, the faint trace of darkness marking the delicate skin around my eyes where I'd woken so many times with nightmares.

Even before coming to Knightchurch, I wasn't the best sleeper in the world. Maybe swiping a few of Estelles pills wouldn't be such a bad idea.

Scrubbing the sink, I spotted a small chip that looked like a spillage stain in the marble.

Bending down I began to rub at it. A rustling sound came from the bedroom, it seemed like Summer was doing her digging around already.

Realising the chip on the sink wasn't a stain of dirt after all, I rose back to my feet, my eyes meeting my reflection in the mirror.

Although instead of my reflection, there stood a woman staring right back at me. Her face, deathly pale and her eyes both covered in bruises as if she'd been horrendously beaten.

The cut on her forehead looked angry and deep as a trickle of thick, crimson blood leaked across her eyebrow and ran into her left eye.

Her tattered, silver hair was matted with mud and congealed blood which also tarred her battered, white nightdress. *The girl from my dream.*

I dove back in shock as she stared at me, her eyes, deep, black pools of nothing. Piercing and haunting at the same time. The blood vessels in the whites, all burst and inflamed, creating the illusion of some demonic possession.

My heart thrashed against my rib cage and I feared at any minute it would break out of my chest. The feeling, verging on painful as my voice lodged in my throat, making it impossible to speak or even breathe.

I watched in slow motion as her dry, chapped lips parted and her mouth opened wide. But instead of speaking, she screamed, the noise so loud, just like in my dream. She screamed so viciously, I was sure I could feel it in my soul and that any minute the glass in the mirror would shatter.

Without thought, I screamed back in terror. My hands instinctively fly to my ears to stop the noise coming from the glass. My eyes squeezing closed so I no longer had to witness that tortured face.

I don't know how long I was screaming before I felt small, warm hands shaking my shoulders.

"Hey, hey Bennett, what's wrong, what is it?"

I opened my eyes to see Summers' concerned face in front of me. Her hands on either side of my shoulders.

"The woman... she was screaming at me... it...it was there, the woman, she was screaming...I..."

Summers eyebrows furrowed in confusion. "Bennett, the only person who was screaming was you, what happened, you scared me half to death."

My trembling hand shot out, pointing towards the bathroom mirror.

"There..." I shouted. "She was..."

"Bennett, there's no one there. See." Summer moved out of the way, giving me a clear view of *my* reflection. My terrified, gaunt face stared back at me but that was all I could see, just Summer and myself. No one else was there.

I pressed a hand to my chest to calm my breathing.

"I'm so sorry, I..."

Summer smiled gently. "It's fine, come on, we're done in here now but before we go, I want to show you something that might cheer you up."

I sighed at the mischievous look on Summers face.

Walking out of the en suite, back to the bedroom, Summer pointed to the peachy coloured silk sheets on Andreas and Estelles bed.

There, spread out, was rope, handcuffs and a number of sex toys I don't think I'd ever come across before. These looked more like some kind of kinky torture devices rather than something used for pleasure.

"Where'd you find those?" I asked Summer.

"Oh just in the draw," she gave me another cheeky smirk, "told you the Silvaros were filth."

I giggled, brushing aside the incident in the bathroom. My breath, still staggering to reach its normal pace. I must be exhausted if I'm seeing fucking ghosts from my dreams. I need a holiday or some shit, clearly.

"At least we know what Estelle sees in Andreas," laughs Summer.

I smile awkwardly. A feeling of spiders creeping slowly up my body makes me shiver.

Summer scoops up the rope and toys, pushing them back into the drawer where she'd just found them.

I was still wary of Andreas, and seeing his little 'collection' was doing nothing to expel my worries.

I guess you never know what people are like, or what they're into behind closed doors but I never would have imagined Estelle using half of this fucked up looking stuff. Just proves you can't judge a book by its cover.

Leaving the bedroom, I began speeding up the cleaning of the rest of the rooms. The sooner I was done for the day and chilling out with Millie by the lake, the better.

Throwing my apron onto the laundry cart, I dusted down my dress, grabbed my bag and headed outside.
The sun was still shining and I hoped Millie had finished her work for the day so we could relax. I had no idea where she'd been allocated, this house was a fucking maze, but I'd planned to see her down at the water anyway.

I followed the directions Millie had given me, making sure I avoided the old cemetery this time and followed a path in the opposite direction.

Despite the dusting of browning leaves in autumn, the sun was blazing today. The woods were looking a little less intimidating in the gentle sunlight but some sixth sense still kept telling me something felt off around here.

I hadn't been walking long before I heard the gentle lap of water hitting the banking up ahead.

Pushing the low lying branches aside, I stepped into the clearing to reveal the most idyllic lake I'd ever set eyes on.

Sunlight bounced from the dark crystal waves as they softly rippled in the gentle wind. Millie was laying on the still plush, green embankment. Her silky hair spread out above her head. She was wearing just a crop top and tiny shorts that she must have been wearing beneath her usual dress.

It was almost October but this day could have easily been compared to any August summer's day.

Pulling off my dress, I adjusted the strings on my bikini bottoms before laying down next to Millie.

"Hey." Millie's smile was infectious. "So glad you could join me. How was your day?"

I sighed, dropping my head to the cool ground.

"Yeah it was... fine." I held back on mentioning what I saw in the Silvaros bathroom mirror, I'd only just met Millie and the last thing I wanted to do was make my new friend think that I was a complete nut job. I was starting to believe it myself.

Millie giggled, her eyes still closed, lapping up the last of the sun.

"You sound enthusiastic."

My eyes rolled involuntarily. "I had the pleasure of working with Summer today."

Millie opened her eyes, sitting up and looking down on me.

"Oh and how was that?"

I shrugged. "It was actually fine. I don't think she's as close to Kara and her little minions as we thought. She seems to want to avoid them more than anything."

Millie nods. "I guess maybe I had her wrong then."

I sat up to face her.

"She's actually not that bad, maybe I could invite her down here with us one afternoon?"

Millie's smile looks forced and slightly uncomfortable.

"Well I mean, I guess you could."

Millie seems like such a sweet girl but something tells me she isn't that big on socialising. She never speaks about any friends and she's always on her own. I really do feel for her. *I think that's why I so desperately want to be her friend. Maybe I feel sorry for her more than anything.* I'm quite an introvert myself so I'm hardly one to judge but I just don't know how to take this girl sometimes.

"Seen anything of Ezra?"

The mention of his name pulls me from my thoughts

"Erm... not today."

Why would she mention him? Would it be weird if I started probing her on whether she was interested in him? Yeah it definitely would and anyway was I interested in him? I don't even know anymore.

"He likes you, you know."

My eyebrows raise and I'm pretty sure they're about to get stuck in my hairline.

"What makes you think that?" I ask.

"I've just seen him around," Millie's smile turns mischievous. "I'm good at picking these things up."

I try to stifle the laughter that's about to come out of my mouth.

"Well I don't know about that, maybe he's more into Kara?!"

This time Millie laughs. "Believe me, Ezra has no interest in Kara. She's just..." Millie waves her hands in the air, a look of distaste on her beautiful face. "Trashy!"

I smile, hearing someone who looks as sweet and innocent as Millie make a bitchy comment seems surreal.

"Anyway change of subject, I can see why you love the lake so much."

Millie's eyes slowly scan the horizon of the lake, lingering in the middle where a small bird has swooped down looking for its lunch, the soft ripples slowly melting into nothing.

"Yeah, I spend all my free time here. Only at the house when there's stuff to be done but otherwise, rain or shine, I love to sit down here. I love the peace, the sound of the water and the wildlife. There's nothing more soothing."

I nod in agreement. "Fancy a swim?"

Millie's eyes sparkle at my words.

"Sure."

Walking the edge of the embankment, we both pause.

"It's a little cold in there," smiles Millie.

My teeth begin to chatter already at the thought of my body even touching the water.

"Maybe we should just jump. Get the shock over with."

Millie grabs my hand. "I'm game if you are."

With that we bend our knees, holding tight to each other's hand as we plunge into the murky depths.

In an instant, icey pain encases my body, the feeling of hundreds of knives piercing me from head to toe.

My mind goes blank as all I can concentrate on is the agony of the cold.

My eyes open instinctively, the water is much darker and dirtier than it appeared on the surface. Millie's blurred face comes into view, and for a second it's almost like she's smiling at me.

Fear rips through me as I also realise it's a hell of a lot deeper than I had first anticipated. *Jesus I'm an actual fucking moron!*

I kick my legs as I struggle to make it back to the surface. *What the fuck?! I'm a good swimmer.* I might as well have been thrown into the fucking ocean, why can't I make it to the surface?

My body jolts involuntarily, arms flailing and I feel as though I'm falling through space, no control over what's happening to me or how I can stop it.

My lungs begin to ache, starving for air as I fight with what little energy I have left.

All of a sudden Millie's slender arm grabs me by the hand, pulling me upwards, as I break the surface, coughing and spluttering.

"Bennett, are you okay? I didn't know you weren't a strong

swimmer or I wouldn't have…"

"I couldn't get back up." Those were the only words I could get out as my body continued to gasp for air.

"Maybe we should've just got in a little slower," Millie giggles.

I brush my long wet hair out of my face, pushing it back. Wiping the remaining water from my stinging eyes.

Something was wrong, I could feel it. I might have been having some weird ass hallucinations in the house but this felt real. I couldn't get the surface, something was keeping me under, stopping my arms and legs from working properly.

I was pretty confident how fucking ludicrous that sounded, but I know how I felt. My legs had turned to lead. I was trapped under there.

Millie had started swimming around the lake happily, not a care in the world, seemingly oblivious to the fact I almost fucking drowned. *Shit, this place was making me question my sanity.*

I began to swim slowly in circles, keeping an eye on Millie and making sure I only swam where she did.

One thing I knew for sure was that next time we hung down here at the lake, I'd be staying on the fucking grass.

I spent another couple of hours with Millie before the cold had finally started to set in and I was beginning to see just why swimming in a lake in a tiny bikini is a bad idea in September. I decided to head back to warm up but Millie insisted on staying on her own.

Grabbing my dress, I slung it over my soaking two piece. Ringing out my long hair, I left it falling in messy, damp waves down my back as I picked up my belongings and got ready to head back to the house.

"Same time tomorrow?" Millie called, her tiny arms still parting the water in a graceful breaststroke.

"Maybe." I smiled, giving Millie a quick wave and heading back into the woods. I wasn't so sure I was up for another day down here just yet.

Even in the daytime these woods were definitely not the most pleasant place to be.

Large black crow's squawked above my head, gathering in the trees.

I wrapped my exposed arms around my body, my dripping hair creating prickling goosebumps over my skin.

This forest was ancient, it made me think just what these trees had seen. If only they could speak. Share their haunting secrets.

A twig cracked behind me. Spinning around I was met with fiery blue eyes, glinting with venom. I knew those eyes only too well by now.

"Ezra?"

His tall, dark form came further into view. Those chiselled cheekbones, that raven hair, that ink. *Fuck Bennett get it together.*

His dark grey sweater and black jeans were covered in mud as were his hands as if he'd been digging. My eyes flicked from them, back to his eyes.

"Are you following me?"

He scoffed, "don't flatter yourself little bird, I was walking from the cemetery."

I felt my face turn a deep shade of pink. Of course, the cemetery was just the other way.

"Well you shouldn't creep up on people." I said. My stomach somersaults like I've done three rounds at a theme park.

The ice chips in his eyes bore into me as heat pools in my stomach and travels between my legs.

"You shouldn't be playing in the woods, little bird. It's dangerous," His face is void of any emotion except the glitter of lust in his eyes as he slowly begins to prowl closer to where I'm standing. I begin to reverse, my back hitting the ragged trunk of a tree, stalling me in my tracks.
"There could be monsters or anything in here."

I swallow hard, it feels like a golf ball has become lodged in my throat.

His hard, strong body presses against me, pushing me further into the rough bark. The unforgiving wood clawing against my bare skin, making me wince.

"Well it's a good job I don't believe in monsters then isn't it?" I say, my voice is barely a whisper as I fight against the feeling that having Ezra Silvaro so close to me evokes.

His face is now within inches of mine, I can feel the brush of his breath on my lips. His heady smell of wood, smoke and something masculine invades my senses. I don't move. Don't blink. Don't even breathe. It's like a toxic aphrodisiac clouding my mind.

Suddenly his lips brush against my ear in a feather-like touch, his tongue meeting my lobe, the warmth prying a low groan from my throat.

My eyelids flutter with need as I feel him grin against the sensitive area of skin between my ear and my neck.

As his lips reach the side of my throat, he begins to suckle roughly, I can already feel the bruise emerging as my legs tremble with desire.

Without warning, Ezra sinks his fang like teeth into my neck. The shock of it forces me to cry out, unable to conceal it any longer.

He runs his warm tongue over the bite, soothing the sting in an instant.

"Are you sure you don't believe in monsters, little bird?" His husky voice is oozing sex and there's nothing more I can do besides rub my thighs together in hope of creating some friction.

Ezra notices my sudden movements, looking me straight in the eye as his eyebrows raise in surprise.

"Well, well, well, the little whore gets off on the pain?! Interesting."

I nod, the degrading name he just used, turning my brain to putty as I struggle to string together a coherent sentence.

His hand travels round the back of my head, grabbing a fist full of my damp hair. He yanks my head back sharply, pain lancing through my skull. I release a heavy exhale.

"If it's pain you want, pretty girl, then believe me it's pain you will get."

His delicious mouth lingers so close to my own that I'm sure he's going to kiss me at any minute. But instead he releases my hair and pushes off the tree with both hands, standing straight in front of me. My heart hammers as he looks at me with hooded eyes. A smirk rising on his handsome face.

Without another word and mimicking the scenario in the piano room, he turns and begins walking back to the house in long strides, leaving me alone, confused and horny as fuck!

Chapter Fourteen

Bennett

More sleepless nights followed. If I wasn't haunted in my dreams by the girl with the silver hair that had appeared in the Silvaros mirror, I was plagued by those terrifyingly beautiful, pale blue eyes. Ezra Silvaro was a mystery I couldn't quite manage to wrap my head around.

Since our encounter in the woods, all I could focus on was trying to avoid the man who made my chest tighten and my blood heat with lust.

Nothing about him had been particularly that pleasant but yet I felt like that was drawing me further towards him. Like I was begging for his punishment. *Fuck what was wrong with me?!*

I'd spent a few more days, after my shift, by the lake with Millie. She loved that place, and to be honest I was starting to see how calming it could be as long as you weren't fucking swimming in it. I settled for sitting on the edge of the banking, dipping my toes in.

I hadn't bumped into Ezra on the way back which I was extremely grateful for. I wasn't even sure what I'd say to him if I did see him.

Finishing up polishing the cutlery until they were sparkling like the fucking sun, I dumped the marigolds under the kitchen sink and decided to skip the lake for today.

I was feeling exhausted from lack of sleep and I hadn't had a chance to read the journal, tucked in my drawer for a few days.

My fingers were itching to take it out and open it up again.

Before I left, I filled the old, copper kettle up with water to make some strong coffee to take to my room.

I placed the coffee into a mug, scouring the cupboards for some crackers. My stomach was growling and even though the Silvaros had made it clear that we were welcome to help ourselves to food, my appetite had dwindled and I'd hardly eaten a thing.

Tonight I would try to find a landline phone as my mobile still had zero reception and I desperately wanted to check in on my dad and Mrs Potton. I was sure she was taking good care of him but I was desperately missing the old fool, even if he was a pain in the ass.

As I shuffled through the cupboards, I heard a loud smash behind me.

Turning I was met with the gloating face of Kara. My mug of coffee lay spilled across the stone kitchen floor, the ceramic, shattered into tiny pieces. Rage flared in my veins as Kara tapped her red heels in the mess.

"Ooops, I am so sorry, I must have knocked it." Kara mocked a fake expression of surprise, raising her perfectly manicured hand to her mouth.

"You did that on purpose." I snarled. This bitch was grating on my last nerve.

"Look Bennett, like I said I must have knocked your mug, I really am so sorry."

Deciding to let the drama drop, I walked over to the broken mug to start picking up the pieces.

I crouched down as Kara walked past me slowly, bending slightly until her lips were almost at my ear.

"That's what you get for messing with my man." With that she kicked a piece of the broken ceramic, sending it flying to the other side of the kitchen.

Oh fuck this shit!

"You bitch!"

I shot up in anger, grabbing Kara's perfectly curled blonde

hair, ripping her head back like she was a rag doll.

She squealed, her hands thrashing out to claw at my face. She was like putty in my hands as I wrestled her to the ground, straddling her and landing a perfect right hook on her sharp cheekbone. She screamed in agony and oh god did it feel good?!

Kara fought like a little bitch, so much clawing and scratching. My hair was the first thing she attempted to grab as we wrestled like rabid dogs on the kitchen floor.

"What the hell?!" I heard the voice before I saw who it was. Riley and Elaine, Kara's little lap dogs ran in, both of them needed to tear me away from the bitch on the floor. Cowering. Her hands up to her face in a pathetic attempt at protection.

I fell back, landing on my ass in the spillage of coffee. My hand landing on a shard, leaving a small cut on my palm.

Kara got to her feet with the help of her minions. I sat where I was, breathing heavily. Adrenaline rushing through every part of my body.

"You fucking psycho!" She shouted. "You're going to be in so much trouble when the Silvaros find out."

I laughed. I didn't give a fuck what anyone thought. This bitch deserved everything she got.

Dusting off her dress, now stained with coffee, Kara stormed out of the kitchen, followed by the other two girls, leaving me in the mess.

I released a sigh, pushing up from the ground.

"Here let me help you." The gruff voice was like sandpaper as I raised my head to the smiling face of Andreas. Holding out his hand, reluctantly I placed mine in his as he helped me up.

"I'm so sorry about that." I didn't know what else to say, I just hoped he hadn't witnessed everything and was here to sack me on the spot.

Instead, he smiled, no sign of stress or irritation on his face at all.

"Don't apologise for her, she's nothing."

I frowned. "Right...erm ok."

"I'll get the mess taken care of, there's plenty of staff."

I smiled in appreciation. "That's really not necessary, I am the staff... I..."

"I insist," he replied, cutting me off mid sentence.

I looked down at my hand, realising he was still holding my palm in his. He turned my hand over to see the dripping cut in the middle. It wasn't deep but my skin was painted with the blood. I'd forgotten about it in my frustration at the situation.

"Oh I'm sorry, I'll just run it under the tap, I must have..."

Before another word was spoken, Andreas took my hand to his lips, licking the blood still pooling from the small wound. *What the fuck?!*

I'm pretty sure in that moment my heart beat fucking stopped. My blood ran cold as his hot tongue lapped at the skin on my palm. I yanked my hand away quickly, pulling it into my chest like I'd been scolded.

"It's fine." I barked.

I didn't mean for the harsh tone in my voice but goosebumps broke out over my flesh as I caught a flash of something dark and sinister in his lingering gaze. A smidge of my blood smeared across his bottom lip. The sight, sickening me to my core.

I turned to walk away, all my instincts screaming at me to run for the hills.

"Did you enjoy driving your fist into her face?"

The question catches me off guard, stopping me in my tracks.

I turned to see Andreas, staring at me like every ounce of his being is put into my answer to this question.

"No," I replied. "I didn't *enjoy* it. It was just a misunderstanding."

I was willing to say anything right now just to wrap up this weird conversation. I was feeling more and more uncomfortable by the second and all I could think about was getting back to my room and locking that mother fucking door.

"Oh come on Bennett, I saw the rage in your eyes, felt good didn't it? Hurting her, making her suffer for what she did to you? Seeing that bitch get exactly what she deserves?" His voice dripped with malice.

My eyebrows dipped into a deep frown as I let his words sink in. Horror shaking me from the inside out.

"Mister Silvaro, with all due respect I have no idea where you're going with this, but like I said it was a stupid misunderstanding and I don't take pleasure in the suffering of others, no matter the situation. Now if you'll excuse me, I'm not feeling well and I need to lay down." My eyes skirted to the broken mug on the floor. "I'll take up your offer of that cleaner."

I spun on my heel towards the kitchen door, not looking back. Still I felt his sharp, dangerous eyes burning into my back like lasers.

I brushed off the shudder that wracked my body and headed up to my room, this time I was the one taking two steps at a time.

Creepy old men were always pacing the floors of Delilah's, I'd had plenty of experience with them so this should be no different. I just need to see it as exactly the same situation as I would have encountered at the strip club. So why the fuck did this feel a million times worse?

I continue running up the stairs and down the corridor to my room. The further I got away from Andreas Silvaro right now, the better.

A wave of relief hit me like a ten ton bus as I rushed into my room, slamming the heavy wooden door closed, dropping the latch. Leaning against it and closing my eyes, I let out a pent up sigh. *What the hell was that?*

The room was silent except for the frantic sound of my breathing. Pushing the eerie feeling aside, I walked over to the bedside table, yanking open the drawer. The little red journal sat in its usual place at the back.

Jumping on my bed, I shuffled to get comfortable on my stomach, opening the dusty old pages to find out what happened next.

Theodora Alcott   May 1911

Today I am about to make the biggest confession of my life. I've taken Carlos Silvaro as my lover. I feel weak and giddy and oh so many things that I can not explain. Genevieve is my friend and I know she can never know about us, but I genuinely, in my heart, believe that I am in love with him and that he too feels the same way.

I wasn't sure where his feelings lay at first but he has made no secret of how much he lusts for me. It makes me feel like a real woman.

I gave him my innocence, the greatest gift a woman can give and I can not explain the feelings that stir within me when his tongue brushes my skin or I feel him inside of me. Oh I know what I speak of is a sin.

My mother and father would be ashamed but he says Genevieve just doesn't understand him and I know I can give him the love and happiness that he so craves.

We often meet by the lake. It's such a beautiful, idyllic place. When we are together there, it's like no one else in the world exists. We steal any moments we can with each other and I find myself hanging on to his every word, waiting for the next time we will be alone together.

I also feel like Carlos needs me right now with everything going on with the residents of Cedar Cross. The accusations thrown his way regarding the mayor's missing daughter, those demons in that village will point the finger at anyone. Ridiculous if you ask me . I can't explain how happy I am right now. Nothing and no one can destroy how I feel.

I scoff, famous last words.

So Ezras great - grandfather was nothing more than a horny womaniser.

I bite my lip to hold in the smile. I wonder if he knows how grandad was having a fling with the staff behind granny's back. Wow, this journal would make for a great novel.

My eyes scan the page again. '*The accusations thrown his way regarding the mayors missing daughter'* what the fuck was all that about?

Staring down at the small cut on my hand, my mind traveled back to the encounter with Andreas. It was becoming painfully obvious as the days went on why this place was the centre of so many horror stories.

Before arriving at Knightchurch, I'd refused Hunter's irritating jibes and pleas to look up the house's history on Google. I didn't trust or believe anything I saw on the internet, so looking up some stupid stories didn't appeal to me very much, especially as I was living in the place.

Now, however, I was starting to regret that decision with a passion. I knew nothing about this house or this family and it was the first time since I'd arrived that I was starting to get a little anxious.

If I wasn't having nightmares, I was hearing strange noises in the walls as if the pipes needed a good clearing out. This house was old as fuck, what did I expect. I'd lost count of the amount of times I told myself to get it, the hell, together.

Shoving the rolled up journal back into the drawer, I pulled out my phone, switching it on and trying desperately to get some kind of signal.

Nothing. Not a single bar. *Perfect.*

I needed to speak to my dad, I needed to hear his voice. It felt like years since I'd spoken to him.

Flopping onto my back, I rolled over onto my side, slipping both my hands under the pillow below my head. Sleep was calling me and I wasn't about to turn it down.

My eyelids grew heavy, and I sank into the soft, silken sheets ready to let my dreams take over.

"GET OUT!!!!!!"

The silver haired woman's face flashed behind my eyes.

I jolted upright with a scream. Breathing erratically as my eyes flew around the room. A dream. I'd fallen asleep.

Checking the clock on the table, I realised I'd literally nodded off for no longer than ten minutes.

Sweat beaded on my forehead. I was going insane. I don't know what it was. This house? The Silvaros? God knows but one thing was for sure. It was time to start doing some serious digging.

Chapter Fifteen

Ezra

Thick, black dust settled over the windowsill of my room. Sliding my thumb through the small, delicate fragments, I let out a loud sigh. My chest feeling heavy and tight.

I sometimes wondered why the fuck my family hadn't just sold this monstrosity of a house, but then who really would want to buy a Manor House that held more ghost stories than the fucking Tower of London?!

Today my demons were stirring loudly, causing me to feel unsettled and agitated.

I needed to get away from the claustrophobia of my room and into a place where my mind felt more settled... and there was only one place that would provide the calm I needed right now.

Leaving my room, I hesitated as I spotted her from a distance. That long, dark hair, creamy skin and outrageous body walked across the landing at the top of the large, grand staircase. My mind was transported back to our encounter in the forest.

I loved playing games with the little bird. I wanted to see the fear in those jade green eyes but she never showed me what I was looking for and it infuriated me.

However, the way her body responds to me is fucking addictive. I can see through all that defiance, the need and wanting in her eyes.

I'm willing to bet my life on the fact that her pussy was fucking soaked when I caught her off gaurd in the forest. Just the thought causes a rapid surge of blood to flow straight to my cock.

She hides her weakness well but I'm stronger, I'll break through that solid exterior that she portrays so well.

She continues walking, unaware that she's simply prey walking in the eyeline of a predator. Unaware that my eyes are trained on her, watching her every move.

As soon as she's gone down the stairs and out of sight, I begin to descend from the shadows, making my way over to the South Wing where I know I'll finally find some peace for the day.

Not many people are around. The halls are derelict which is what I prefer. No one speaks to me when they do see me walking the halls anyway. They know better. I know I'm unapproachable. Intimidating. That's the way I like it. I don't have any interest in talking to anyone. I'd prefer it if this house was as empty as the pitch black hole in my heart.

Passing the horrific, narcissistic portraits that covered almost every fucking corridor wall in this house, I finally arrived at my destination.

Pushing the heavy mahogany doors to the library, I was met with the familiar face of our library manager Winston.

"Sir, what a nice surprise, I didn't expect to see you today. I would have been a little more organised had I known you were coming for a visit, tidied up a little."

I placed my hand on Winstons shoulder. "No need."
I replied. "I'm not staying long, just go about your business, old man."

Winston nods. The white haired pensioner is probably one of the only people in this whole goddamn house that I actually would give the time of day for.

He's been at Knightchurch for many years now. I think it was my grandfather who hired him.

One thing about Winston is he was good with minding his own business. I think that's why he's always done so well here and been in the house for so long.

He has no other family that I'm aware of so Knightchurch is his entire life. He loves this dusty old library, probably even more than me.

He cares for it well and he's probably the most respected person around here.

I look around at the row upon row of books. All collected over the generations by the Silvaros.

There must be more books here than in the whole of Cedar Cross combined. I love this place. It's the only section of the house that I actually do love.

This room is the one thing I would say my family got right, even if it's the fucking *only* thing they got right.

When my urges and the sickness in me stirs, this is one place where I know I can come to try and calm myself.

Each book in this magnificent library is therapy. Rows upon rows of deep, tranquil therapy and luckily it's big enough to hide away amongst the stacks when I don't want to face the world, which lets face it is most of the fucking time lately. I love it when my mind gets lost in this never ending ocean of words.

They say a man who reads lives a thousand lives yet he who doesn't read lives but one *or something like that* and fuck is that true.

I walk to the furthest point of the room, and begin looking through a row of books at the end of one of the bookcases.

Growing up I'd had a *probably unhealthy* obsession with monsters and villains. I had a kind of empathy for Frankenstein's monster and I could genuinely get into the headspace of Bram Stoker's *Dracula.* Both of which sat amongst the dusty, moth eaten, special editions that lined the shelves.

Most of these books I had highlighted and annotated. I'd written so many notes within the browning pages. Jotted down poems and quotes when they appeared in my head, scrambled and without a purpose.

I'd always loved poetry and old ramblings even though I knew when people looked at me, that was the last thing they would have expected.

This place held my heart and soul. Knightchurch was damned but the library was its shining beacon of hope.

Slumping down at a small, beat up, old table and chairs that were hidden behind some of the bookshelves, I pulled out a few copies of some of my usual reads and opened up the dusty pages.

An hour later I was still in the library, tucked away and in my own world when I heard the hard footsteps behind me. I already knew who it was before he spoke a single word.

"Alright mother fuck!"

I looked up into the fucking, over enthusiastic face of Caleb. A wide smile on his face showing all his bright white, perfectly straight teeth.

"Don't you have something more important to do than piss me off right now?"

Caleb laughs, his voice is deep and thunderous as it echoes through the silent library.

When Caleb and I met, years ago, I don't think either of us had any idea how important we would become in each other's lives.

Caleb, a vigilante, hell bent on destroying the evil who torture and maim the innocent for fun, and me, a monster feeding the sickness that resides inside myself with the bitter screams of the cruel and depraved.

It was a match made in hell but that didn't mean I didn't want to knock him the fuck out ninety percent of the time.

I was night and he was day. I was the silence and he was the noise. We shouldn't work but we did.

I guess they do say opposites attract but this was next level opposite shit.

"Put the books down, we're going to The Falcon."

He drops down on the battered, three legged chair opposite me. The seat, straining to accommodate his weight, I'm unsure as to how it's still remaining upright.

"I thought you didn't go to The Falcon any more. The last time you were there, that chick was hoping for a marriage proposal from what I remember."

Caleb smirked, giving me a sly wink. "Naaa Ruby knows where she stands. We're cool."

This asshole was unbelievable.

The Falcon was a strip club almost two hours away from Knightchurch. Caleb visited the place regularly, and I'd joined him a few times, but the owner Ruby was obsessed with him and this was beginning to cause problems as I knew he saw her as nothing more than a quick fuck every now and then.

I knew she had a thing for me too as she'd made it clear on more than one occasion that she wanted my cock and would take both of us at the same time if we were up for it.

Caleb would do it in a heartbeat, he was pure filth but I couldn't be less interested in the girl. She just didn't do it for me at all.

There was a strip club in Cedar Cross, Delilah's, that I knew of. We could have gone there instead but the place was too close to home and the last thing I wanted to do was mix with the Cedar Cross scum.

"Let's go, the books can wait."

I considered throwing back some shitty remark but I couldn't be arsed.

Grabbing my jacket from the table, I gestured for Caleb to lead the way. His sly smile, indicating he felt like he'd got one over on me. *Bastard.*

Heading out of the house and jumping in my black Aston Martin, I drove us all the way over to the town where The Falcon was located.

It's slick, black bricks and vibrant yellow neon lights screamed 'trying too hard but still tacky as fuck' yet Caleb didn't seem to give a shit. He loved it here.

The atmosphere stank of money and there was always some lowlife snorting coke from a strippers tits or doing shots from a slick belly button. Yeah not my thing.

Nodding once to the doormen, we bypassed a line of people waiting to enter and headed through the large, glass doors.

Heavy thumping penetrated my ears as I walked through the corridor of The Falcon. *I did something bad* by *Saphs Story* charging through the air.

Sweaty bodies greeted us as we entered the main room,

swarms of people struggling to move out of the way as we walked towards the bar.

This had got to be the busiest I'd ever seen this club. I hated it. I hated people in general so to be amongst this many was fucking torture.

Caleb whistled over the bar to a cute girl in bright pink booty shorts. She threw him a wink before handing a bright blue coloured drink to the guy she was serving and then coming straight over.

A chorus of groans called out as the barmaid came straight to us next allowing us to que jump. Caleb threw them a look which silenced them in an instant. People knew not to disrespect Caleb or myself here, it didn't end well for you if you did.

We ordered two straight whiskeys, no rocks and leaned against the bar, ignoring the disgusted looks of the men around us, too pussy to say a word. These pieces of shit were nothing to us so they could stare all they liked.

Caleb knew what he was doing when he jumped in my car instead of bringing his own as he ordered three tequilas. Slamming the small shot glasses back one after the other.

"Hey handsome." A tall, gorgeous blonde with legs for days slid her red, manicured hand over Caleb's shoulder.

"Ruby." Caleb smiled. His eyes glowing with sin. "How are you tonight?"

She ran her hungry eyes over Caleb's body before turning her head and doing the same to me.

"Even better now I've seen the two of you."

Ruby could probably get any guy she wanted. She owned a strip club that had belonged to her husband before he was killed in a car crash, racing some morons for a high. Now she had endless amounts of cash and guys drooling over her on a nightly basis. However the only guy she was interested in was the one who didn't and never would feel a thing for her.

Caleb would never settle down. He didn't have it in him. I'd never seen him give a shit about any woman for longer than the few hours he was fucking her.

"Come on, let's go somewhere a bit more private."

Picking up Caleb's drink, Ruby downed the whiskey and gestured for us to follow her into one of the back rooms.

The private booth was lined with black wood and gold velvet sofas. Small round tables stood in rows in front of the seating. Each table contains an ice bucket built into the centre.

A square table was perched to one side of the room, and an old, vintage record player on the other side.

The room seemed to block out the sound of the music from the club, which I was actually glad about because they were now playing some shit I hated anyway.

Ruby ran her long, slender fingers over the old record player before lifting the needle and beginning one of the albums that was already loaded up. I had no idea what or who was playing but some kind of slow, sensual music began to leave the speakers.

Caleb and I dropped onto the sofas, his eyes remained glued to Ruby as she began to sway her hips. Her black mini dress, barely skimming her ass and her tiny black g-string almost on show.

She licked her enhanced lips as she closed her eyes and dropped her head back. The waves of golden hair brushing the bottom of her slender back.

Caleb sat, legs spread, slouched back. His eyes heated with every move she made.

I sat forward, my elbows resting on my knees as I continued to finish my drink. A look of boredom on my face because that's what I felt... utter boredom.

Sure Ruby was hot, that was a given, probably even an understatement, but she wasn't the little bird living under my roof and that was what was driving me crazy.

I didn't want to crave this girl so badly and I hated myself because I didn't know why I craved her the way I did. She was stubborn and strong willed yet it seemed like danger called to her, like she was just a magnet for bad things to happen to.

That's why I knew she was made for me. I needed to break things, and she was begging to be broken. An unlucky charm, a piece of meat thrown to a wolf.

My head was filled with thoughts of Bennett while Ruby continued to gyrate around us. With one swift movement, she gripped the bottom of the little black tube dress and pulled it over her head, leaving her standing there in nothing but her back g-string. Her firm tits and small pink nipples erect and begging for a mouth to take them.

She walked over to Caleb, pulling his shirt until he stood and then walked over to me. As she reached down, I knocked her hand away, I wasn't going to even let her think I was having any of this, or that I was even the slightest bit interested. Caleb could ride this pussy all he wanted but I was not getting involved. The only pussy for me was hiding back at Knightchurch surrounded by monsters she didn't even have the slightest idea about.

The knock back earned me a scowl from Ruby but she soon regained her composure and leaned into Caleb, bringing her lips towards his. He grinned cruelly before pushing her face to the side and gliding his tongue down her throat.

Caleb never kisses, it's like his trademark. He uses women... and men for his own accord and tosses them aside when he's finished like last nights fucking takeaway.

I lean back in my seat and watch the shit show unfolding right in front of me.

Ruby and her fake tits lead Caleb over to the table at the side of the room. She hops on spreading her legs wide. Her tiny g-string and tacky red heels, the only items on her body.

Caleb continues licking and nipping down her throat to her collar bone, his eyes meeting mine, flaring with lust for a second until he carries on trailing his tongue down Ruby's chest and taking one of her pink buds into his mouth.

She moans like the whore that she is and he continues to suck, grinding his jean covered erection against her pussy.

He grips the nape of her neck as he devours her. Her hips bucking forward.

As tempting as it is to join in, Ruby just does nothing for my cock whatsoever. She's no Bennett, that's for fucking certain.

Caleb's hands slide down Ruby's side before he laces the side of her g-string around his fingers.

In one quick swoop, he tears the small piece of material clean off her body and pulls back, staring at her, sat there completely naked.

"Ez, come on baby, there's plenty of me to go round and I'm a demon with my tongue."

She swipes her tongue over her bottom lip, a glint of a stud catches the light as I try hard not to roll my eyes. *This bitch is relentless.* I stare hard at her, making sure she knows her advances are not welcome and she needs to stay the fuck away.

Caleb grabs the bottom of his shirt, tugging it off as Ruby drops her mouth to his chest, licking his abs and flicking the piercing in his nipple.

She tries to kiss him again but everytime she gets close, he grabs her jaw, squeezing hard. She lets out a squeal each time he squeezes before going back to his chest, licking and biting like a wildcat.

Bringing his hand to her cunt, Caleb works two fingers inside her. She thrusts against his hand before grabbing it in hers and pushing his fingers deeper.

Caleb looks over at me, a chuckle leaving his throat as Ruby continues to ride his fingers. She looks like she's teetering on the edge as a loud gasp passes her lips and her eyes begin to roll back.

Caleb looks like he's getting bored as he spins her around on the table, dragging her over the edge so her ass is up in the air. I can't help the laugh that escapes me as he unbuckles his jeans and pulls out his throbbing erection.

Ruby looks over her shoulder, her bottom lip pulled in between her teeth, her eyes begging.

"Last chance." Caleb says to me as he runs his hand over Ruby's smooth bare ass, raising it up and landing a firm slap on her ass cheek. Her scream turns into an irritating giggle.

"Be my guest." I'm bored out of my skull and the quicker he gets this over with, the fucking better.

Giving me a wink, he looks down, parting Rubys butt cheeks

and spitting on to her ass crack.

Massaging his saliva over her puckered hole with his thumb, I can see the hesitation in her face as she realises just where this is heading.

Just when I think she's going to stop him, she spreads her legs wider, throwing her hands across the table and gripping the sides to secure herself.

Caleb spits on his rock hard cock before lining it up at her back entrance.

He doesn't even ease it in slowing, instead slamming home inside her ass forcing a feral scream from Ruby's mouth. Her face contorts in pain but as soon as Caleb reaches round, pressing two fingers back inside her pussy, she relaxes down on to the table, pushing into his vigorous thrusts.

Their combined moaning fills the room as I check my watch wondering what my little bird is up to back at the house.

She infuriates me because she forces me to think of nothing but her, but fuck she's addictive. There isn't a drug on this planet that could compare.

I plan to check on Bennett later while she sleeps but for now I'm stuck here with this asshole and his flavour of the night.

I considered leaving but judging by Ruby's wailing, I'd say they were pretty close to wrapping this bullshit up. Caleb and I had been busy recently with our work so I had to grant him some way of getting his frustration out, even if I did want to get the hell out of here.

The sound of skin slapping on skin is disrupted by Ruby's cries of ecstasy as she comes and soon Caleb is roaring as he empties himself inside her ass.

Pulling out, he tugs his jeans back around his waist and buttons them up before pulling his shirt back over his head.

Ruby spins around, a look of pure bliss on her face, cum dripping from her ass as she reaches for Caleb. He steps away joining me at my side, before picking up the tumbler containing the last of the whiskey I'd just poured and downing it in one.

"So." Ruby smirks at both of us. "How about a few more

drinks?"

Before I can answer, Caleb picks up Ruby's dress and throws it at her naked body.

"Some other time." He replies as he taps me on the shoulder and we head to the door.

Rubys smile instantly changes to rage as she begins screaming in our direction.

"You assholes. You're barred, never come here again Caleb Fox."

I slam the door, cutting off her cursing as Caleb smiles.

"Mother fucker."

He chuckles at my remark as we head to the door and back to my car. I've had enough excitement for one day. Now I need to see my little bird.

Walking up the steps back at Knightchurch, I walk quietly to Bennett's room. It's late and the room is in darkness. Shadows dancing around the room and the little bird, the only thing illuminated by the light of the moon peering through the heavy curtains.

I watch her as she sleeps peacefully, laying on her back, the smooth covers around her waist. One hand on her stomach and the other up by her face on the pillow.

She snores softly, her lips parted slightly as I watch the way her chest moves up and down in delicate breaths. I lean down gently, brushing a strand of her silky, dark hair away from her face.

She stirs slightly but continues her light snoring. I press my lips together tightly, a feeling resembling a heavy weight settling in my chest. I force myself to swallow the lump in my throat.

Bennett looked at peace in her bed as I left her room, praying that even if only for tonight, her nightmares would stay away.

Chapter Sixteen

Bennett

Weekends were strange at Knightchurch. I longed for the time to do whatever the hell I wanted, but asking Estelle if I could head back to Cedar Cross to see my dad was shut down quicker than I could even get the question out.

Apparently some bullshit excuse about staff being required to stay on site in case they were needed.

Clearly these guys had never heard of cell phones. Speaking of phones however, Estelle did agree to let me use a battered old landline phone, so at least I finally got the chance to speak to my dad.

He sounded amazing, so chirpy and healthy. Having Mrs Potton there seemed to be doing him the world of good. At least my mind was put to rest if nothing else.

If I didn't know any better I'd have suspected this connection between the two of them wasn't quite as platonic as they were having me believe.

I swore I heard my dad call Mrs Potton 'my darling' from a distance, while I was checking with her that she was giving him his correct medication. Something in that made me feel a bit warm and fuzzy inside. If anyone deserved a bit of happiness it was them.

So it was looking like it was another weekend spent in my room or touring the grounds.

Millie had spent a little time hanging out in my room so that

I wasn't completely alone all the time, but I hadn't seen her at all this weekend.

The rooms of the house were sectioned off more like college dorms so I wasn't surprised I hadn't seen her about. Plus she was often off doing her own thing it seemed, and there were only so many times I wanted to hang out, freezing by the lake. That girl seemed to have no concept of 'I'm freezing my ass off here.'

Walking past the lounge, I heard the faint echo of voices. It sounded like Andreas and Estelle. As I crept closer I heard Andreas, his voice raised as he spoke.

"NO!" The only word I heard thundering from his mouth. I turned the corner to the lounge seeing him standing over Estelle, her small frame looking fragile next to his broad physique. He towered over her at that moment and if I wasn't mistaken she actually looked… afraid.

"Everything alright?" I kept my voice stern and strong. If Andreas was threatening her, there was no way I was going to stand by and let it happen. He wasn't going to bully me, but I'd love to see him try.

"Everything's fine darling." Estelle gave me a pained smile. She wasn't alright, that much was obvious.

"It's just I heard…"

"Like my wife says, Bennett, everything is fine!" Andreas' voice was thrown at me like a dagger.

I pressed my lips together to stop myself from saying something that was probably going to get my ass fired.

"Okay, well, I'm just going to go for a walk, let me know if you need anything." My response was aimed purposely at Estelle. I wanted to silently somehow tell her that I was here if she needed anyone or was in trouble. It wouldn't suprise me if Andreas was some fucked up abuser. He definitely came across that way. I'd be keeping a close eye on him from now on.

"Why don't you visit the horses?" Estelles face seemed to lighten as she spoke.

"Horses?" My eyebrows dipped in confusion.

"Yes dear, we have the stables, they're just a ten minute walk north of the front of the house. We have three horses. If you'd like to see them?"

My eyes gleamed with excitement.

"Absolutely, I love horses."

Estelle smiled. "Well what are you waiting for, get out of here."

I smiled back, barely able to contain the butterflies erupting in my stomach. I'd always loved animals and the fact that there had been three horses here, the whole time, I can't believe I had no idea.

Luckily I was wearing a black sweater and black leggings so I was pretty much in suitable attire for a stable.

I headed off in the direction that Estelle had told me, and ten minutes later, I arrived at a pristine building. The beautiful stables, surrounded by neat piles of hay and equestrian equipment.

I could hear the rustle of the horses already as I walked slowly towards the entrance.

Walking into the warm stable, I was met with the striking sight of three, magnificent black horses. Their beauty was mesmerising. Thick, glossy coats, shimmering manes and eyes that shone like diamonds.

The horse nearest to where I was positioned made a nervous snort. Edging slightly backwards, away from where I was standing.

Desperate to prove I was no threat, I slowly walked towards her, gently placing my hand on the side of her mane. Her rigid body relaxed under my touch.

"Hey girl, it's alright. I'm Bennett, what's your name ey?"

"Aaliyah."

The rough, deep voice startled me as I jumped back, turning to see Ezra.

Gone was his usual hoodie get up, replaced by dark blue, distressed jeans and a laid back, grey shirt. The buttons at the top left open, creating a relaxed look and revealing a smidgen of ink.

If sin and pure carnal lust was personified, it was standing right here in front of me.

I wrestle my gaze back to his face.

"Oh I... didn't realise anyone was here."

Ezra began to walk slowly towards me, his hands balled into fists by his sides and a wicked glint in his eyes. I couldn't explain the feeling he was evoking inside me. I knew I should be terrified. Being here. Alone. With him. But it wasn't fear that I was feeling. It was... something else.

Delicious heat flooded between my legs, a tight clench of need, as my mind flashed back to his lips just below my ear, his teeth grazing my skin and his tongue erasing the sharp sting. *Jesus.*

He stopped right in front of me, placing a hand on Aaliyah's mane, right where mine had been seconds before.

She shuffled slightly into his touch like she felt comfortable being near him, like she felt... safe.

He stroked her carefully and it was the first time I'd ever seen this side of him. His expression softened as he looked into the horse's eyes.

I turned towards the other two horses.

"Are they all yours?"

"Yep," he answered, still looking into Aaliyah's eyes, before turning to face me. "This one's Wolfe," he pointed at the next horse along. "And the one at the back is Matteo."

The horse at the back began to buck slightly, he looked like the feisty one. Both horses were truly magnificent just as Aaliyah was.

"Do you ride?"

Ezras question emerged from nowhere.

"Well I have before, a little." I answered, my voice sounding like I was desperately trying to remain cool and collected.

"The stables have been in my family for generations. We've always been a family of horse lovers."

I nod as we both stand in silence. The tension crackles between us like electricity that's almost palpable.

"You don't like me very much do you?" The words slip from the box they've been tightly compressed in inside my chest as Ezra turns back to look at me.

A low chuckle leaves his lips, it's almost a scoff. He briefly looks to the floor, shaking his head almost like it's in disbelief.

A strand of his raven hair falls forward giving him the most beautiful, relaxed look. *God he's gorgeous.*

His eyes meet mine again, this time they're tainted with something unrecognisable. Something that sends shivers racking up my spine.

"You know nothing about me, about this place, if you did you'd get the fuck out of here and never look back." *Not this bullshit again.*

I frowned, shrugging my shoulders.

"Why do you keep saying things like that? What does that even mean? Is it because of your father? Has he done something?" The questions rolled from my tongue one after the other. But all he does is shake his head in frustration.

"Well?" I could feel the anger beginning to rise inside me. I was done with his stupid cryptic games. I wanted answers.

"I'm trying to protect you, you stubborn bitch!" His words hit me like a bulldozer as he spat them with rage.

"Excuse me?" My eyebrows raised so high I was sure they were going to get stuck in my fucking hairline. "Protect me from what?"

Closing the gap between us, Ezra took two strides, standing before me.

Invading my personal space, he stood almost nose to nose with me.

I swallowed hard, the heady scent of smoke and citrus invading my nostrils. Every thought in my mind dissolved in that moment, my legs turning to jelly.

"They're beautiful creatures...the horses," I mumbled. "I can see why you would love them so much."

Ezra's eyes narrowed. His expression turning dark and I notice a flash of heat in his eyes for the smallest of seconds as his gaze travels down towards my covered breasts and back to my face.

"Beautiful creatures." He replies, his voice barely a whisper.

With that he lunges forward, his lips crashing onto mine and his fist tangling into my hair, gripping hard. The sharp sting from my scalp, only pushing me to want even more.

My mouth instinctively opens, teeth clashing as his tongue invades my mouth, the feeling like velvet, eliciting a soft moan of pleasure from deep within me.

I claw my nails down his chest, forcing deep growls to vibrate against my lips.

My mind is no longer functioning. No longer wondering whether or not this is a terrible idea. Instead my body has taken over, doing whatever the fuck it wants, and right now it's never before wanted anything as much as it wants this man right here.

Before I can even comprehend what's going on, we're tearing at each other's clothes. Battling for dominance as we rip the fabric from each other's bodies.

Ezra skims his hands under my ass before lifting me, my legs wrapping around his toned, trim waist. My tight, wet heat pressing against him, I roll my hips desperate for more friction.

I'm left only in my red bra and panties as he stands only in his jeans. His shirt, completely torn away and discarded somewhere on the ground.

He carries me to the back of the stables where soft piles of hay are stacked. Laying me down on the warm, straw covered floor, as he hovers above me.

I take in the sheer perfection that is Ezra Silvaro.

His chest laced with deep cut definition. A light dusting of dark hair trails below his belly button, between that perfect V that leads to the bulging in his pants.

I can already see his cock straining against his jeans, confirming he's just as desperate for me as I am for him.

His chest is decorated with the most intricate ink. All black, no colour at all. So much unique artwork makes up the canvas on his body but it's the large cross, right in the centre of his chest that catches my attention most of all. The urge to trace my tongue over the beautiful lines is overwhelming.

Ezra stares down at me as I lay beneath him. Vulnerable and at his mercy. With one swift tug, my bra is torn from my body exposing my full, round breasts.

"You are fucking perfect." He hisses, cupping my tit. The perfect handful.

The pad of his thumb teases my small, rose pink nipple until he leans over, replacing his fingers with the warmth of his mouth. My eyes roll to the back of my head in ecstasy as his tongue flicks over my sensitive bud. He roughly paws at my other breast as he continues to suck until suddenly without warning he clamps his teeth down, biting into my flesh.

I scream out in surprise as, just like with the bite on my neck, he begins to soothe the sting with his tongue.

He lifts his head. His heated eyes catch my gaze as I notice a drop of blood from my nipple, the deep red smear on my tit and also on his lush bottom lip.

I expect to feel fear. I expect to feel regret but the only thing I feel is so ridiculously turned on.

My panties are soaking and all I can think about is how I want him to punish my other nipple in the same way he just has with this one.

As if reading my mind, he focuses his attention on my other breast. Repeating what he had just done until I'm writhing below him in an intoxicating mix of pain and pleasure. My spine bowing in bliss.

His hand glides down, over my flat stomach and the deep curves of my hips until they reach my panties. With one rapid swipe, he tears the material from my body, leaving me completely exposed. Every piece of restraint leaves my body as I watch him sit back on his knees observing the view.

"Fuck, Bennett look at you. Laid out in a fucking stable for me to do whatever the fuck I want to you."

My body arches, begging for his touch.

Gently he brushes two fingers up the inside of my thigh and

between my folds, circling my clit.

"Such a good girl. So fucking wet for me."

My pussy throbs with desire as Ezra continues to work the little bundle of nerves before sliding his middle finger inside me, quickly followed by a second.

I cry out from the feel of him stretching me with his digits and as he adds a third finger, I feel the pressure begin to build inside my stomach.

I bite my lip to muffle my cries as he thrusts his fingers in and out of my pussy. His thumb applying just the right amount of pressure to my clit.

As heat courses through my veins like electricity, Ezra pulls his hand away. I groan as my body aches from the feeling of emptiness left behind.

"Please." I beg. *I actually beg,* as a dark shadow crosses Ezra's face.

He slides down to settle between my thighs, licking and nipping the sensitive flesh between them. Drawing lapse circles on my skin until he's worked his way up and is face to face with my glistening pussy.

"Ezra." My voice is breathless as I rock my hips, pleading with him to give me the release that I was so close to getting before he so cruelly extracted his fingers.

He raises his head, a smirk on his luscious lips.

"That's a good girl, little bird, beg for my cock like the dirty little whore that you are."

Fuck me, those words are enough to push me over the edge before he's even touched me.

"Yess." I cry.

"Yes what? What do you want, Bennett? Say it! Tell me what you are." He's taunting me now and as frustrating as it is, the agony of the wait ripples through me in exquisite bliss.

"I want your cock, please, I'm a filthy whore and I want your cock inside me." I can't even believe the words that are coming out of my mouth. I've never spoken to anyone like this before but this man, this beautiful, mysterious, terrifying man just forces them out of me and although my head is telling me this is insane, my body has never wanted anything more.

Ezra smiles like he knows exactly the effect he's having on me. "All in good time, little bird."

He dips his head and drags his tongue up my centre in one agonisingly erotic motion. A gasp leaves my throat as ecstasy engulfs me. A million different sensations invade my body, from hot, to cold, to dizzy. The feelings overwhelming.

His large, calloused hands splayed out on my sternum, holding me in place on the soft, warm hay. My own hands slam to my sides as I frantically try to grip onto something, the only thing being handfuls of straw. As my body rocks, Ezra chuckles, the vibrations from his mouth driving me even more crazy.

As his tongue begins circling my clit, he digs his fingers deep into the flesh of my thighs almost painfully, the feeling contrasting with the gentle way he flicks his tongue over my sensitive bundle of nerves.

Without warning he releases a thigh and plunges two fingers back inside me, swiftly adding a third stretching and taunting me.

My moans fill the whole stable as he sucks and fucks me with his fingers.

My orgasm begins to build deep within my core and just as I think I'm about to go over the edge, he gives my clit one final swipe of his tongue before sitting back again on his heels. This time his eyes connect with mine. Those dangerous blades of ice never leaving mine as he unfastens his belt and unbuttons his jeans.

My jaw almost hits the straw covered ground as he pulls down his boxers letting his cock spring free.

Sweet Jesus this man is huge.

Ezra keeps his gaze trained on mine as he wraps his hand around his long, hard length. Pumping a couple of times.

The sight of it sends shivers down my spine and I feel the pricking of goosebumps erupt down my chest and over my breasts. My nipples hardened to painful points.

"Is this what you want?" His voice is gravelly and masculine, tainted with arousal as heat flashes in his gaze.

I nod. The words lodged in my throat. As soon as he has my consent, Ezra grabs my hips, pulling me down towards him until his cock is pressed against my entrance. Then his mouth is back on mine, his tongue tangling with my own in a punishing kiss.

His hips buck forward as he sinks his throbbing cock into me an inch at a time. My eyes widen as my body struggles to accommodate his size. I begin to pant, small deep breaths until he's finally fully seated all the way inside me.

A loud moan leaves my lips as Ezra releases a hiss between his clenched teeth.

"So fucking tight." He groans, his body shuddering on top of me.

He moves slowly for a couple of thrusts to allow me to adjust before speeding up his movements, gaining a rhythm as he drives into me over and over again.

The stable fills with the combined sounds of our panting and moans as pleasure fills me from my head to my toes.

Ezra thrusts as deep as he can go, holding roughly to my hips before placing a hand under my knee and lifting my right leg, allowing him to go even deeper. The new position, achieving just the right angle to hit something euphoric inside me.

My nails dig into his sweat-licked back as my core goes tight and all of a sudden a powerful, all consuming orgasm wracks through my body. The feeling so intense that stars burst in the back of my eyes.

"OH GOD!" I scream. Ezra continues bucking into me, hard and fast.

"He can't save you now, little bird."

His smile is almost chilling as I ride out my orgasm, until my body is left trembling. With a few more grunting thrusts, Ezra follows, spilling his hot cum deep inside me.

He shudders as he drops down on top of me. Satisfied and spent. Both of us, a tangle of sweaty, naked limbs.

After a few seconds, Ezra rolls off of me onto the hay, pulling me into his chest and wrapping his strong, inked arms around me. His warmth encases me like a cosy blanket.

Within minutes our heaving, combined breathing calms, leaving us both laying in silence.

The sounds of the horses grazing and our gentle breaths were the only thing I could hear.

My fingertips trail across the inked lines of his chest.

"What are your dreams?" I don't know why I ask the question. Whether it's to fill the silence or to find out more about this enigma of a man who surprises me at every turn.

Ezra releases an exhale that sounds slightly tinged with frustration. "I don't think I dream the same way as other people."

I could sense he wasn't feeling in the mood to open up right now…but I wasn't gonna shut up anyway.

"My dream, deep down, has always been to get out of Cedar Cross and live by the sea. Sit on the shore with the sand between my toes and the salt in my hair. Sometimes I can picture it so vividly it's like I can almost touch it." I've had this dream in my head since I was a little girl. I still lived in the hope I would get my wish one day.

Ezra remains silent beneath me.

After a few minutes, He gently slides his arm from underneath me, sitting up straight. I can't help but smile as I prop my head up on my elbow. Strands of hay twisted into my hair looking like a murder of crows had been nesting in it.

Ezra turns towards me. His hand, reaching out and pulling a stray strand of hay from the front of my locks.

"I have to go." His voice, almost a sigh, sounds pained, almost like he's carrying the weight of the world on his shoulders.

I nod. I guess I shouldn't really have expected anything more than what this really was. Sex.

"What are your plans for today?" His question startles me. Such a mundane, normal thing to ask someone and yet Ezra Silvaro is the last person I expected to hear it from.

"I don't have many plans," I admit. "I guess I could hang out with the girls from the house. Summer or Millie maybe."

I looked to Ezra, who at the moment, was just staring at me. His lips slightly parted.

"Are...you okay?" I asked. *Did I say something wrong?*

"Of course." Ezra scowled, his usual dark expression gracing his face once again. I could tell in that second that the Ezra from ten minutes ago was long gone.

"Do you know Summer or Millie?" I asked. Something seemed off about the way he's just reacted to what I'd said and I desperately wanted to know what the fuck had just happened.

"No," snapped Ezra. "The house is full of staff, it's impossible to know all of them." He jumped to his feet, slipping on his jeans and buckling them back up hastily.

Annoyance flared in my veins.

"Just the ones you're fucking hey?!" I instantly regretted the words as they left my mouth and I had no idea why the fuck I'd just said them, but the anger in his face said it all.

Without another word, he grabbed his shirt and just like he always does, he stormed off out of the stable, leaving me naked on the floor, surrounded by my torn clothing. *Great.*

I let out a loud sigh, dropping back down onto my back.

What the hell was this guy's problem? He said he didn't know Summer or Millie but he definitely knew at least one of them because I saw it in his eyes.

That look that flew across his face when I mentioned them. Something was going on. Something he obviously didn't want me to find out. But I wasn't giving up that easily. I would find out what kind of secrets Ezra Silvaro was keeping.

Chapter Seventeen

Bennett

Sneaking back to a large Manor House when you're half naked with torn clothing and cum running down the inside of your thighs is not the easiest thing in the world that's for sure. Yet here I was, tiptoeing back to my room before anyone saw the absolute state I was in following a perfectly innocent morning visiting the horses.

Entering my room and slamming the door behind me, a wave of relief came over me.

Tossing my ruined clothes aside, I jumped straight into the shower. The hot, waterfall spray battering against my worn out body as I stood against the cool tiles.

My nipples ached where Ezras teeth had abused them and I could still feel his hands on me, his mouth drawing pleasure from my very core.

As I closed my eyes to imagine myself right back there in the stables, a rough bang on the bedroom door pulled me from my fantasy.

Jumping from the shower, I pull a large, fluffy towel from the rack and wrap it tightly around myself. The rapping at the door continues.

"I'm coming." I yell as it carries on. *Jesus.*

I open the door to see a wide eyed, smiling Millie standing on the other side.

"Jesus girl, for someone so small you don't half make a lot of racket." My voice turns into a giggle as Millie continues to smile at me.

"Sorry babe but I thought maybe we could have a girly night tonight. Just me and you? Fancy it?"

I shake my head in disbelief. This was what was so important?!

"Sure, yeah, of course."

Millie jumps up and down, squealing like an excited child.

"Perfect, see you tonight at eight."

With that she skipped off down the corridor. I continued giggling as I closed the door behind me, heading back to the en suite to finish cleaning up. It seemed like I wasn't the only one not wanting to spend the weekend alone.

After freshening up, my growling stomach was alerting me that it was dinner time, although the last thing I wanted to do was go downstairs and strike up any conversation with Andreas or Ezra, so a quick trip to the kitchen with snacks for my room would have to do.

Jogging down the stairs, I passed the entrance to the lounge. Estelle was sitting alone at the elegant, white tea table, silently staring into space, holding her little floral teacup between her thumb and forefinger.

Continuing to walk, a jog of guilt tugged at my insides forcing me to walk back and check that she was alright.

Estelle was probably the strangest woman I'd ever met. When she was her usual bubbly self, she was the loveliest human you could ever meet, but other times she was just so spaced out and looked so painfully lonely. It was as if the pills she kept on her nightstand were her only friend.

Gently I tapped on the door, pulling her from her daydream.

"Estelle, are you okay?"

She blinked at me before the smallest smile curved up on her full, red lips.

"Of course. Bennett, do come in." She gestured her hand towards the empty seat at the tea table, opposite to where she was sitting. "Please join me."

Despite the fact that this felt weird as hell, I wasn't going to be the one to turn down a clearly lonely and vulnerable woman who needed a friend.

Entering the room and closing the door behind me, I took the chair opposite, as Estelle picked up the little china teapot and poured the beige coloured liquid into the matching teacup.

"Have some tea. This one's my favourite." She pushed the little teacup towards me.

"Erm...thank you."

Feeling obliged to take the offering, I raised the teacup to my lips. A sweet blend of honey and herbs exploded on my tongue, enveloping my senses. *She wasn't wrong, this was pretty good shit.*

I smiled at Estelle as I started to relax a little. Her face was deathly pale. I wanted to poke around, find out how she was feeling.

Ezras tone when he had told me about his sister Eleanor, who'd gone missing, was playing on repeat in my head. I couldn't imagine losing a child. This woman must be crushed on the inside. Sometimes it was as if you could see that she really was only half alive, a former shell of a woman she once was.

After a few minutes, the silence between us was starting to get a little on the uncomfortable side and I desperately wanted to address the elephant in the room.

"Estelle, are you sure you're alright? I don't mean to pry but Ezra told me about Eleanor."

Estelle turned towards me, the look of pain etched on her face.

"She was never found, my Eleanor."

I bit into my bottom lip so hard I could taste the coppery tang of blood. The grief radiating from Estelle was tangible.

"She was your age. A bright, beautiful girl, everyone said so. She always got all of the attention. We were all just second fiddle to the perfection that was Eleanor."

I smiled letting her tell her story.

"You must miss her terribly." My hand instinctively reached

out covering Estelles cold, pale closed fist. A single tear dropped from her crystal eyes.

"I do, of course I do." She smiled softly. I wanted to comfort her, tell her that Eleanor was alright and that she hadn't been found, therefore she was probably still alive. Yet after Ezra had been so sure that his sister was not one to just go off on her own without letting her family know, it did seem strange that she had just vanished for two years. I hoped there would be some closure for this family eventually, but two years was such a long time.

Estelle took a sip of her tea. The long, emerald green sleeve of her silk shirt sliding up slightly to reveal hideous, dark blue and purple bruising. Bruising like she'd been restrained.

Noticing where my eyes had landed, Estelle quickly put down her cup, tugging the sleeves back into place.

"Estelle?"

She looked at me with a fear in her glittering eyes.

"Estelle, is Andreas hurting you?" The words tumbled out before I could stop them, but I needed to know, needed to find out why she was so terrified of her husband the way I could see in her face that she was.

"Andreas is my husband and he loves me." She replied quietly. "He wants what's best for me, I know this."

I narrowed my eyes. *What the fuck.* It felt like she was justifying his abuse, and that's what this was. Abuse. It was painfully obvious.

"Does Ezra know you're covered in bruises, all over your wrists?"

Her gaze snaps to mine. "I don't want Ezra involved." Her tone is much more harsh now. Like she's demanding I drop this.

I take the hint. "I just don't want to see you hurt, that's all." I replied.

Her expression slowly softens.

"I'm fine." she smiles. "The villagers of Cedar Cross have been starting up rumours again. We're always the talk of the town for one thing or another. This time it isn't just the kids making up nursery rhymes about us. How we're secretly demons hiding out here or vampires who sneak out into the night to drink the blood of virgins. It's the vicar's daughter, she's missing and of course all fingers point to us."

"River Oakwell? She's missing?" My mouth widens in surprise. I'd known River from school, although not personally as she was a couple of years younger than me. Stunning girl, with long, curly dark hair. *She's missing?!*

"I don't know her name, but we had nothing to do with it. Yet, of course we're the targets all over again."

I sigh at Estelles' defeated tone.

"Have you thought about showing the villagers what it's like here? Making them see it's just a beautiful home, filled with beautiful people?"

Estelle looks at me like I've grown another head.

"How would I do that?" She asks, scratching her chin with her slender finger.

"Well... I dunno." I stare at the ceiling hoping for an idea to hit me. "That's it!" I feel like I'm having some sort of epiphany. "It's almost October. Halloween. Why not open Knightchurch for a Halloween party? Fancy dress is popular."

"Well... I" I feel the hesitation radiating from Estelles body. She glances around the room. "I suppose we could. As long as Andreas is fine with it." A large smile draws on her face and I can't help the cheesy smile I can feel on my own.

"Perfect. I'll get together some helpers and we can start the decorating soon."

The idea of a project that didn't involve mopping or making beds sounded pretty damn good to me. Plus I always knew how to organise the best fucking parties at Delilah's so this was going to be wild. Also Knightchurch had its own ballroom and if I had to hazard a guess from just passing by its high, glass doors, I'd say it hasn't been used in decades.

Estelle smiled as she continued drinking her tea. She reminded me of a fragile doll. One that would break if she was hugged too tightly.

I wanted to get to the bottom of what she was going through with Andreas, but she wouldn't say a word.

She was afraid, clearly and I couldn't help but wonder if Ezra had any idea about any of this. I found it difficult to believe that he didn't have a clue at all.

The door to the lounge swings open as Andreas enters. The more I see him, the more I realise just how large and intimidating he actually is.

The night in the kitchen after my altercation with Kara pops into my head. *Did you enjoy driving your fist into her face?* I release a small shudder at the memory.

"Ladies," Andreas nods towards the table. "To what do we owe the pleasure Bennett?"

I stand from my chair, dropping my napkin to the table. I won't be hanging around here.

"I was just saying to Estelle, as it's nearly Halloween, maybe we could hold a party here at Knightchurch. Let everyone see how amazing you all are and their ghost stories are nothing more than juvenile gossip."

Andreas looks at me. A stern expression on his face. There was no way he was going to buy into my idea, not a chance in he...

"I think it's a wonderful idea." His mouth turned up into the most unnatural, horrifying smile, it actually made me wince. "I assume you'll be the one to organise this?"

I coughed, clearing my throat, still startled by his reaction.

"Erm... yes, yes, of course." I stuttered.

"Perfect, well that's settled then. October thirty first, we open up Knightchurch manor."

The rest of the day was split between planning for the Halloween event and picking over every little word Andreas Silvaro had ever said to me in the hope that I could work out just why in god's name he'd agreed to open up his house.

However, I was far from going to complain about it. This was the perfect chance to show the busy bodies of Cedar Cross,

Hunter Jackson included, that there were no ghosts and goblins hiding in the walls of this old house. Just a misunderstood family *with a father who scared the shit out of me and a son who gave me the most mind blowing orgasm of my entire life.* Yeah I'll probably leave those details out.

By eight PM, when Millie arrived at my door, I was more than happy to relax and go over plans with her about how we could make this party extra amazing.

"How about paper lanterns, like silver and gold, hanging from the rafters in the ballroom." Millie chirped excitedly. She crouched on her knees, before sitting on her feet on my bed as she munched popcorn and threw ideas my way.

"And how do you suppose we get up to the rafters Mills? Fly?"

We both laughed.

"There must be some way, come on Bennett, you're in charge of this, you gotta get creative."

I rolled my eyes. "I am being creative, I already said we can make some cob webs and shit... I dunno."

Millie smiled at me. Her delicate features lighting up.

"It's going to be amazing," she said, her voice low.

"Yeah." I agreed. "It is."

Sitting on the bed, Millie began to stroke her slender fingers through my hair.

"Do you ever wear your hair in braids?" She asked.

"Erm... sometimes, I guess."

She began lifting the shiny, dark strands of my hair and entwining them into little plaits.

"My mom used to braid my hair all the time." I felt the sadness in Millie's voice as she spoke the words.

"What happened? To your mother?" I didn't want to pry but I did want to ease some of the pain I could hear in Millie's voice. The heartbreak was evident and the need for me to just reach into her heart and tear out that pain was overbearing.

"She was sick... she..." I could hear the break in her voice, like she was fighting back the tears.

"Is that why you're here?" I asked. "At Knightchurch."

I hear a quiet sigh leave her lips.

"Yes." She continues braiding my hair. "It is."

I inhale deeply. "You know, you can talk to me at any time. About your mother, your father maybe? Whatever you want."

Silence sits heavy between us for a few moments.

"Can we talk about something less depressing." She forces out a small giggle as I turn my head, returning the strained smile.

"Sure." I'm not going to poke the fire where it isn't needed. Just like with Estelle. I hate prying into things that are none of my business. I'll never be one of those people.

"So... Ezra."

His name feels like I've just taken a bullet. A sensual, beautifully agonising bullet... but a bullet none the less.

"What about him?" Since when was my voice so fucking squeaky?

I can almost feel Millie smirking behind me. "You like him right?"

I consider denying it, telling her it must all be in her head but that would make me the worlds fattest, fucking liar.

"Urgh!" My palm hits my face, which I'm pretty sure is turning a rather unattractive shade of pink. "Yes, I do like him, but he's... he's so frustrating. So hard to figure out."

"Does he like you?" She asks, finishing one braid and pulling fine strands of my hair to start the next one.

"I think he does. I mean... I hope he does. It's just one minute he's pushing me away and the next... he's all over me."

I wait for Millie's reaction. I feel like I've already revealed too much, but I'm desperate for someone to talk to about this whole messed up situation I've found myself in.

Millie doesn't respond. I'm beginning to wonder if I've offended her or something. I turn to face her before she's had a chance to finish the plaiting.

"Are you interested in Ezra?" I need to ask. The question has been burning away inside my chest for the longest time now.

I expect to see a blush, an embarrassed reaction, anything but what I'm faced with as Millie bursts out laughing. I purse my lips in confusion.

"God no." She continues howling with laughter.

"Okay, okay, Jesus he's not that bad looking." I giggle.

I think the jealousy in me has suddenly melted into defensiveness.

Millie's laughter dies down. "No, of course he's not," she smiles. "It's just, I kinda have a bit of a thing for someone else."

My eyes widen at her admission. I swivel my body fully around until I'm sitting crossed legged in front of her.

"Oh my god who? Spill?"

Millie laughs. "Caleb... Caleb Fox."

I pause, trying to think back to who she's referring to.

"Caleb? Ezra's friend?" My memory jogs and the penny finally drops as I'm reminded of the handsome guy with the mischievous grin. The shaved, dark blonde hair and eyes of jade.

Millie grins, nodding her head. *Now there's the tinge of red in her cheeks that I was looking for.*

"Oh my goodness, I would never have guessed. I mean I've only met the guy once... briefly, but wow, he's good looking. You should go for it girl."

Millie's smile depletes slightly as she looks down, twiddling her fingers.

"It's too late for that now, plus I don't think he even knows I'm there."

"Millie you're gorgeous, the man would be insane to miss a chance like this with someone like you. You should definitely tell him how you feel. It's never too late."

Millie's whole demeanour seemed to brighten and I was hopeful that she'd take my advice and act on it. Caleb was cute, granted I didn't know a single thing about him but things couldn't possibly be as messed up as they were with Ezra, so what was the harm in going for it?!

Spending the evening with Millie was exactly what I needed. We laughed, we chatted, we seriously took the piss out of each other.

I joked about Millie's fascination with the lake, asking her if she'd spent time there today, already knowing what her answer would be. She was an outdoor girl through and through. Give me my home comforts anyday.

She laughed, giving me the usual "If you ever can't find me, I'll be at the lake." I rolled my eyes and we continued to laugh and joke into the early hours of the morning.

We might be polar opposites but one thing was for sure, Millie certainly made Knightchurch a better place.

Chapter Eighteen

Ezra

A god damn Halloween party? Was my father fucking insane?

Attracting that kind of attention into Knightchurch was the last thing I needed and could end very, very fucking badly.

Opening the door to my room, I was met with the shit eating smirk of Caleb, laying on my bed, legs crossed in his fucking muddy boots, cleaning his teeth with his knife.

"Get the fuck off my bed, you animal." I scowl.

A thunderous laugh rumbles from his chest as he jumps up from the antique, black wooden bed.

"What's got you in a strop?" He asks. That silly, smug look still painted on his face. *I'm gonna punch that fucking look straight off at any minute.*

"You, putting those shit covered things on my bed."

Caleb clamps his lips down, stifling a smile and looks down as his filthy boots.

"You sure that's all it is and not something to do with the pretty brunette I saw you talking to the other day?"

Flashbacks of my tongue in Bennett's pussy and her groaning beneath me in the stable invade my mind. My cock strains against the zipper of my jeans, begging for release.

Caleb smirks as if he's got it all figured out.

Bennett Keane is too good for me. I don't deserve someone as pure as her. All I'll do is taint and tarnish her. Destroy her with my shadows. It's a constant battle inside of me.

"Cedar Cross has it in for us again, The vicar's daughter is missing and guess who suspect number one is?"

"River Oakwell is missing?" Caleb's eyebrows narrow as if he's thinking about something.

"Yep, and it has fuck all to do with us but you know what those old mother fuckers down in the village are like."

Caleb nods.

"So apparently we're having a fucking party to make friends with the same ones who would gladly burn us at the stake."

Caleb chuckles. "Andreas Silvaro has agreed to an open house party?" Caleb stares in disbelief.

"So it seems." I can hardly believe it myself. "Come on," I gesture over my shoulder, "we've got work to do."

Lifting up the rug and opening the dusty trapped door, we both descend into the darkness, covering our mouths against the attacking debris.

Slowly we make our way through the tunnels until we arrive at our destination. My favourite sound proofed room.

Being this close to my prey is like a silver bullet to a werewolf. It was toxic but oh fuck was it my weakness.

Caleb had been busy collecting our little friend who was strapped to a bed on the other side of the iron door we were about to enter.

Caleb is one of the only people who knows what lies within me. He sees my darkness and he adds to my demons with his own. That's why he's my brother to the end and there's no one I'd rather have by my side right now.

As the iron door opens. I'm met with a terrified gaze. The man, tall and lean, lays out on a bed that wouldn't look out of place in a centuries old, psychiatric hospital. He's naked except for his stained boxers, *are those shit marks? I fucking hope not!*

Straps confine his arms and legs with two thick ones across his neck and his forehead. A ball gag is secured into his mouth, I assume to silence him. I look to Caleb for confirmation.

He shrugs his shoulders. "The fucker bites."

I smirk, walking over to the man, ripping the gag from his

mouth. He shouts in horror.

"HELP! HELP ME!"

I scoff. "No one can hear you."

The man's eyes widen in terror. "What do you want? Why am I here?"

It's the same drawn out story with every kill. The pieces of shit are knocked out, drugged up to their eyeballs and dragged back here where they scream, ask what it is they're suppose to have done, and cry like fucking babies when they realise their dirty little secrets are out in the open, ready to gut them from the inside out.

I release a tired sigh. My little bird is playing heavily on my mind today, which in turn is stirring an even deadlier darkness inside me.

The man in front of me, Zachery Kane, had been on my radar for sometime. He'd been beating his wife, his six year old son and his elderly mother who lives with them for a while now and I'd been biding my time, waiting for the moment to strike.

It didn't seem to me like things could possibly get any worse with old Zachery here, until three weeks ago when his sons babysitters mother called to say her sixteen year old daughter had taken an overdose, and left a letter claiming Zachery had raped her and she couldn't live with the pain anymore. Of course the piece of shit denied it, and having money when the young girl's family had none, meant that nothing was able to touch him… well almost nothing.

I smile at the thought. Oh sweet justice.

"WHY AM I HERE? TELL ME!"

Wow, Zachery was getting edgy. I couldn't blame him. I mean if I was strapped to a bed, minutes away from being hacked to death, I'd probably not be feeling too great either.

"You know very well why you're here," I reply with a bored expression. "Tell me how long have you been beating your wife Minnie? Hhmm? Your mother Marie? Or what about your child? Lucas isn't it?"

The look on Zachary's face confirms he knows the reasons

why he's here today. I circle around the bed. His eyes trained on mine.

"I didn't do anything to anyone, I don't know what you're talking about!" He spits, his lips curl in defiance.

I look to Caleb, who's smirking in the corner.

He's checking out the table where I've placed all the equipment I'll be using today. I made sure to bring some of Caleb's favourites.

"See I think you're telling porkies now Zachery." I pull out my favourite pen knife from my jeans. The little blue handle engraved with an 'E.' Soon that engraving will be on the flawless skin of my little bird. Nothing turns me on more than the thought of that.

Zachary's eyes widen at the flash of the small, sharp, silver blade. I can't wait to play.

"Care to tell me about Christy Lomax, your sixteen year old babysitter?"

I always liked to hear them say what they've done. I guess it's almost like I'm a priest and I'm getting some kind of fucked up confession.

I know they did it. I always know. Caleb is careful when sourcing out these people to make sure they really are the scum we suspect they are. The rotten, bad to the core cretins of society. We stalk them for a while to see what we can find and then bam... we take them down.

Zacherys breathing begins to speed up. His eyes refusing to leave the knife in my hand.

"There's nothing to tell, she was some messed up kid who looked after Lucas a few times. She was having problems at home, did herself in and tried to pin the blame on me."

This guy still refuses to own his shit, getting a confession out of him was going to be tough. Luckily I was a patient man.

Lowering the blade of my pen knife to the corner of his eyeball, I slid the blade over his eyelid, careful to only make a surface scratch.

Zachery begins to thrash against the straps that hold him in place, unable to move his head due to the thick double bands holding his forehead down on the bed. They've already started to cut into the skin with his constant attempts at escaping.

Red liquid drips from the small gash I've just made.

He starts crying, fucking sobbing. His tears mixing with his blood.

"Care to share anything?" I ask again. I don't know why I'm giving him the option to confess. Guess I'm just nice like that.

"No please, I haven't done anything." This guy is officially the ugliest cryer I've ever seen. *God what did his wife see in him.*

Zachery is far from an attractive man. He's skinny, pale, has patchy hair where it's thinning in places, and don't get me started on the body odour. I guess fear will do that to you.

Tired of waiting for an ounce of truth to leave Zachary's mouth, I walk back over to where he's laying. His whole lanky body is trembling so violently it actually looks like he's convulsing.

Angling my pen knife at just the right height, I slowly dig the blade straight into his eye socket. Blood spurts from the wound, decorating my shirt as Zachery screeches in horror. The sound is fucking unholy.

Not stopping there, I begin to cut. My hands slicing through thick skin as I serate a perfect circle around Zacherys eyeball, slicing the muscles underneath, before plucking the slimy, blood soaked object straight out of his head.

Adrenaline surges through my veins as he howls in agony. I feel like the pain is so tangible, I can practically taste it.

I breathe in through my nose as if I'm inhaling some kind of prestigious cocaine. The high from this torture creating a euphoria no drug could even imitate.

Caleb smirks at me from the corner. A heated gleam in his eye. He's reaching down, his hand rubbing over his rock hard erection in his jeans.

Caleb and I have fucked plenty of women and I know ultimately that's what we both prefer, however we've always had an unspoken connection between us. One that we've explored a few times. A connection that's only cemented our unbreakable bond.

I see him more as a brother than a lover but there's no denying the attraction is there. Even though lust is all it'll ever be.

The eyeball makes a sickening pop as it lands on the cold, stone floor.

Blood pools in the abandoned eye socket. I'm no doctor but my guess is I should probably do something before the fucker bleeds out.

As if reading my mind, Caleb picks up a small, gas blow torch, *one of his favourites,* and brings it to the bed.

Vomit begins to erupt from Zacherys mouth like lava from a fucking volcano. It's a good job I have a strong stomach because that shit smells rancid.

Holding the blow torch to the wound, Caleb begins cauterising the eye socket.

Zachery howls more, unable to move an inch.

"So my friend, anything you'd like to say?" I ask again, looking straight at the now deformed monster on my table.

"Pleeeasse!" He begs, saliva dripping from his thin, dry lips.

"Not the right words, Zachery boy."

With that, I grab the rusty hack saw I found round the back of the house and begin sawing into Zacherys shackled wrist. The rust has severely blunted the blade, making the sawing long and slow.

When I hit the bone, it's a challenge to break through. At this point, Zachery is sweating and verging on unconsciousness.

With a thud, his skinny hand hits the floor. I walk to the other side to get started on the second one.

"Please no!" He cries. "Ok I admit it, I raped her, I did it. I did it and I told her that if she told anyone I'd do the same to her mother." Saliva sprays from his mouth as he sobs, the shame of his actions dripping from his body like acid. "There, are you happy now?" His voice is so high pitched, he's practically screaming the words at me.

"Did you just ask if I'm happy now?" A laugh rumbles from

my chest as Zachery continues trembling in fear. "And what about your family?" I continued.

Zachery continues sobbing, his whole chest heaving with the force.

"I hurt my family, I did, I need anger management." *A bit late for that now.* "Please I'm sorry, I've told you everything, now please let me go."

This was the best we were gonna get out of him, I knew that for certain. I was done with talking.

Without even acknowledging a single thing Zachery had just said, I began to hack at the other wrist with my blunt, rust covered saw. More screaming came and with every slice of the blade, my arousal was climbing higher and higher. My cock now painfully hard. I needed my little bird.

I know what I'm doing right now is the right thing to do, it's the only way to control my urges and make sure I keep my sickness locked inside its cage.

I'm using my curse for good, to make the world a better place than it was when my heartless ancestors lived.

After removing both of Zacherys hands, the things he used to deliver so much pain to so many people, I nodded to Caleb, I was done. He was free to finish things.

Taking a large carving knife, Caleb stood directly over Zacherys body before plunging the weapon deep into his chest cavity and dragging it downwards towards his navel, spilling the contents of his stomach onto the already tainted floor.

A bitter gurgling sound filled the room as Zachery began to choke on his own blood. The thick, red liquid trickled from the sides of his mouth.

He convulsed a couple of times before the light in his beady eyes went out for the final time. The whole area underneath the bed, swimming in a crimson pool.

Caleb looks to me, his toned chest heaving. I fucking love the way we can communicate with only our eyes. No words need to be spoken.

In an instant he's on me, his mouth crashing into mine. A

battle of teeth and tongues and ravenous gasps, as he grips my hair and I latch my palm around his throat. Squeezing firmly.

He brushes his hand over my bulge.

"Fuck Ez, you're hard as a god damn rock."

He unbuttoned my jeans before pulling my cock free from my boxers. A low groan of appreciation leaves his plush lips as he stares at my dick. Throbbing and begging for his mouth.

"You know what to do." I let out the words in a gasp, and that's all it takes before Caleb is down on his knees in the pool of sticky blood coating the floor, taking the whole of my length into his mouth.

Gripping the back of his shaved head, I press harder, forcing myself to the back of his throat. He gags but it only makes me force myself in even more.

I begin to buck my hips, my head dropping backwards as I brutally fuck Caleb's face.

Within a few more thrusts, I come apart, the orgasm charging through me as I spill my seed down his hot, tight throat. He swallows every drop before standing to face me, kissing me once, letting me taste myself on his tongue.

"Suck your cock better than Kara?" Caleb jokes. *He's a fucking prick!*

My lip curls in disgust at the mention of her name.

"That bitch won't get within ten feet of my cock."
I sneer.

Caleb laughs out loud, the sound rumbling through the dirty old room. "What about the brunette?"

I freeze at the mention of my little bird.

"What about her?"

"Well she's clearly on your radar, just the mention of her seems to have an effect on you."

He was certainly right about that.

"She's out of my league." I don't have anything else to say, even to my best friend.

Buttoning up my jeans, we both turn back to the butchered corpse behind us.

"What's the plan for him?" Caleb asks, nodding towards Zachary's body.

"The usual," I reply. "We cut him up to make him easier to hide, clean this place up and wait till nightfall. Then I'll take him as far away from Knightchurch as I can and dispose of him. Just like always."

Caleb nods, swiping his tongue over his bottom lip. *I swear he knows exactly what he's doing sometimes.* "Sounds good to me."

"We need to be careful, more than usual. With the rumours about the fucking vicars daughter, I don't want anyone sniffing around."

Caleb gives me a mock salute.

I scoff at him, turning to sort out Zacherys body. As long as I'm hurting the demons in this world, I know I'm not hurting Bennett Keane.

Chapter Nineteen

Bennett

Not much scares me, I've come to realise that now. However for some reason the harsh wind, battering against the old window panes of my bedroom is freaking me the fuck out tonight.

The bedroom I was given when I arrived here is certainly not situated in the best of places within this house.

Tall, gangly trees lean towards the glass, beating and drumming every time there's even the slightest bit of a breeze and look like spirits hovering outside when it's dark.

I pull the large curtains closed to help muffle some of the noise but I can still hear it. The trees by the window tapping like fingernails. For the first time I'm actually starting to miss Cedar Cross.

Today has been a fairly boring day. I hadn't seen anything of Millie or even Summer, Kara or her little arse chums. Pretty sure not bumping into them was a good thing though.

I picked up the clock from the bedside table. Eleven PM, I seriously need to get some sleep tonight.

Climbing into the cool silk sheets, I pulled the fur comforter higher up to cover me, keeping me warm.

Switching off the light, I was plunged into darkness. The sound of the tapping on the window panes and my own hitched breathing were all that kept me company in the merciless night.

As I closed my eyes eagerly awaiting sleep to take me, I

heard what sounded like whispering. I pulled the sheets higher, directly under my neck. Shivers spread across my body. *I must be hearing things.*

Closing my eyes again, there it was, there was no mistaking it this time. It was clear as day, whispering coming from somewhere in the room.

Sitting up straight, I switched on the antique lamp, a warm, yellow glow filling the room.

Nothing. There was no one there and not a single thing out of place.

As I went to pull the switch to turn off the lamp, the whispering returned, except this time it didn't sound like it was coming from the room, it sounded like it was coming from the walls.

Carefully and silently, I stepped out of bed, my blue satin nightie grazing my thighs as I walked over to the wall. Gently I pressed my ear to the stone.

Whispering, so much of it. Like there was a conversation going on between dozens of people, all too muffled and quiet for me to understand.

Was it coming from another room? I had no idea but I knew one thing for sure, walls couldn't fucking talk. *I was going insane.*

There was no way I was going to get to sleep anytime soon, I knew that much. So jumping back into bed, I pulled out Theodora's rolled up journal, ready for a little bedtime story.

Theodora Alcott July 1911

Things have changed between Carlos and I. I can't explain when it began because I can't even really put a time on it myself, but he's become cold and distant with me, a shadow of the man I once knew.

He seems to like to hurt me. Mostly inside the bedroom. It started with the occasional crack of the belt on my bottom. A bite mark on my breast or rope burns on my wrists where he restrains me to my bed. I pretend to like it but I don't, I really don't. I want to go home but I'm not sure my letters are even reaching my parents or maybe they are and my confessions are too shameful for them. I fear I have been disowned by my own family. I don't know what to do.

To make things more difficult, I've just discovered that I'm carrying his child. It's early days and I haven't even told him yet. I'm terrified he'll do something to hurt me or my child. I'm so afraid and alone.

I've been keeping this journal hidden beneath the floorboards of my room. If he finds it, I don't know what he'll do.

I'm beginning to worry that the rumours are true, that he was involved in the disappearance of the mayor's daughter. I found her diamond ring in his pocket last night after I visited his bed. I knew it was hers as I'd seen her wear it at events I'd attended with my mother in Cedar Cross.

I know I need to get out of here, for the sake of myself and especially the sake of my unborn baby.

I can't confront Genevieve, she will kill me herself if she finds out about the baby. I must find my own way out and soon. The next few weeks I will plan my escape. If anything happens to me. He did it.

My blood runs cold at the last sentence. *What the fuck.* Theodora was an employee just like me, she'd even shared my room and she was involved with a Silvaro, with Ezra's great grandfather.

She was afraid. Afraid for her own safety and then that of her unborn baby. Fuck! I thought reading the journal would have helped me sleep but now all it had done was chill me to my very core.

Rolling the journal, I tossed it back into the drawer. There was no way I was reading that tonight. The wind howled, sounding like wild wolves were waiting outside the Knightchurch gates.

I switched off the lamp and buried myself under the covers, covering my ears with the furry throw.

Squeezing my eyes closed, I prayed for sleep to take me soon.

"BENNETT."

The voice echoing through the room. I stand from the bed. I'm in my room at Knightchurch except it doesn't look like my room. The curtains are shorter, the furniture older.

"Bennett." The voice is now behind me. I turn to see the silver haired girl in the corner. Her arms black and blue. Fingerprints tarring her skin like paint.

She's curled up, her arms wrapped tightly around her bent legs, forehead resting on her knees. Rocking back and forth. It seems like she's crying.

She lifts her head, blood pours from her nose and mouth, her eyes swollen and marked with tears. She stretches out a rail thin arm, almost as if she's trying to touch me. Her fingernails coated in mud.

My heart pounds in my throat as I take a step back. She slowly crawls towards me.

NO! NO! I feel the words lodged under my tongue but I can't get them out as she creeps further towards me. I can see the burst blood vessels in her eyes.

She's on her feet now, barely able to stand, her arms wrapped around her stomach.

"Look what he did to me." She whispers, lifting her head, her cold, hollow eyes meet mine.

"LOOK WHAT HE DID!!!!!!!!"

Her screams morph into mine dragging me from my sleep but I can't distinguish what is the dream and what is reality as I jump from the bed.

The room looks back to how I know it, but the walls look like they're closing in on me.

I stumble around the floor, loud whispers roaring into my ears. They just won't stop. Relentless and punishing.

Crashing into the bedside cabinet, I struggle to remain steady on my feet as my vision blurs and shadows appear to contort in front of my very eyes.

My lungs tighten and the ability to breathe gets more difficult by the second. I'm hyperventilating.

Am I asleep? Am I awake? I can hear screaming, it's coming from me.

All I can do at that moment is run.

Grabbing the door to my bedroom, I yank it open, darting down the long corridors, past all the portraits and down the winding staircase.

The house is pitch back, shadows move on the walls beside me but no one is there. *Oh god I can't breathe.*

I turn my head slightly, when my eyes are pulled to the figure standing by the entrance to the lounge in the darkness. Andreas Silvaro.

He's just standing there watching me. His penetrating gaze burns into me, suffocating me even more. He almost looks like he's smiling. The look on his face, stiff and sinister.

My fear has taken hold of me and I struggle to inhale. I force my feet to move as I charge towards the front door, ripping it open.

The force of the wind hits me like a hammer to the face. I'm only wearing my little blue nightie, but I don't care, I need to get out of here. I don't know where my legs are taking me but they're still moving.

I race out into the night, down the steps and past the fountain towards the dark wood.

My hair whips over my face, my skin slick with sweat from the nightmare that I can still feel chasing me. The nightmare that felt so real, that still feels so real.

It's so dark. I run into the forest. I have no idea where I'm going but I'm running as fast as my legs will possibly move.

Stones and debris bite into my bare feet, the sole of my foot still aching from my earlier injury.

I'm lost. Oh god I'm lost. I keep charging forward until I see it. The large iron gate to the cemetery. My feet don't stop as I push open the gate, running through the rows of ancient, decrepit gravestones.

I'm crying, sobbing, literally in hysterics and nothing I can do can ease the pounding on my chest, ease the pressure I can feel on my lungs like someone is sitting heavy on my chest. Just as I think my legs are about to give out I hear him...

"Bennett?"

I slam into a hard, stone-like chest. The smell of leather and smoke filling my nostrils.

"Bennett, hey... baby what's wrong?"

Ezra stands before me, his large hands gripping my shoulders, gently shaking me as if trying to coax me from my dream-like state.

My breathing slows as I look around me at my surroundings.

"Ezra?" His name comes out almost as a question.

He's looking me up and down, either to check if I'm hurt or to see how ridiculous I look in the freezing cold, in the middle of the night in just my flimsy nightie.

"Yeah baby I'm here." He whispers. My arms instinctively wrap around his waist as I slowly come back to reality, squeezing my eyes shut.

"What are you doing out here?" He asks

I stare up at him with tear stained eyes.

"I had a nightmare." *God I feel like such a child.* But this nightmare had felt so real.

However, instead of looking at me like I was crazy, he looks at me with concern, almost like he just wants to see if I'm okay.

I stand back slightly, looking back up at him. Those chips of ice dancing in his eyes.

"Wait, what the hell are *you* doing out here?" I ask.

Ezra just smiles. "I've been busy."

"In the middle of the night?" I'm confused and nothing this man ever says seems to make sense.

"Yes little bird," his mouth is so close to mine, I can smell the mint on his breath. "Got a problem with that?"

I shake my head. I do have a problem with that. A big fucking problem, as being in a graveyard in the middle of a freezing night is creepy as fuck. However I'm in a graveyard in the middle of a freezing night so I can hardly say anything right now.

His lips curl up into a smirk.

"You're cold."

I look down realising my arms are wrapped tightly around my body. I never even realised I was cold. However one thing I did realise was Ezra's heated gaze leaving my face and looking straight at my nipples. The sensitive buds, solid and straining behind my nightie like small bullets.

I suddenly become aware of everything I can feel, the cool wind on my arms, the goosebumps pebbling my pale skin and the slick feeling between my thighs as Ezra runs his tongue over his sharp teeth.

"Come on, you'll freeze out here."

He takes my hand, pulling me towards the back of the cemetery.

We arrive at a mausoleum, the grey stone starting to crack and deep, green vines entwining themselves in the crevices. The marble walls look like silver, illuminated in the moonlight. It's a beautiful yet unnecessarily elaborate piece of architecture. I'm not surprised to see it here.

Ezra pulls me into the tomb, closing the rigid door behind him. The relief of being out of the wind washes over me in an instant. My breathing begins to regulate as I slowly manage to regain composure and calm myself. *What the fuck! This really wasn't me.*

In the middle of the mausoleum sits a large, stone burial vault. I study the plaque on the surface.

"Jose Silvaro?"

"My grandfather." Ezra replies. "He always was a pretentious asshole, couldn't possibly settle for a normal headstone like the rest of them. Had to have his own fucking crypt."

I laugh, there didn't seem to be much love lost between Ezra and his grandfather judging by Ezras tone.

I looked around the small room. Candle holders were placed around the walls but looked as if they hadn't been used in a while. Cobwebs decorated every corner and the smell of damp and rot was pretty rancid and over-powering.

Turning towards Ezra, the yellow moonlight caressing his face, he looked even more beautiful than he did in the daylight. The glow through the crack in the wall only accentuating his sharp jawline and five o clock shadow.

Suddenly he begins to prowl towards me, alarm bells begin to ring through my head but fear, that is the last thing I'm feeling right now.

Chapter Twenty

Ezra

She stares at me with a defiance that makes my fingers twitch to wrap around her throat.

Her eyes glistening in the dark like precious emeralds and those lips, fucking soft, moist lips. *Fuck I'm hard.*

I want to hurt her, break her, make her bleed. The urge to force screams from her until her throat is raw is the most overwhelming thing I've ever felt in my entire life.

She stands still, her back against my grandfather's vault as I approach her. Her mouth is within inches of mine now. The sweet tang of cherries on her breath glazes my lips. I can't help but swipe my tongue across them to try and taste it.

I'd wanted to fuck her since the second she ran smack into my chest, running from her own nightmares in the middle of the wood. A wood I was currently walking through after disposing of Zacherys body, as far from Knightchurch as possible.

I glance at Bennett. Her nipples are hard, straining against the fabric of her blue nightdress. Fuck, that's one sexy piece of rag.

I reach out and yank both of the little pieces of string holding the dress up and watch them snap in my hands, exposing her tits. I grab the right one in my hand and squeeze hard as she leans back, a moan escaping her lips.

Leaning down, I take the nipple of the other breast and suck it into my mouth, circling around it with my tongue.

As I stand and meet her gaze face to face, I can see the heat flaring in her eyes the way it had in the stables.

Lifting her, my hands beneath her thighs, I sit her on top of the burial vault, right above where my fucking piece of shit grandfather is rotting away.

I feel no remorse, the bastard is dead and good riddance. Now he can watch me fuck my girl on his grave.

He thought he was powerful in life, that no one could stop his reign of terror, now he's powerless to do a goddamn thing.

I lean forward and press my lips to Bennett's, she moans into my mouth as I press my tongue against her teeth, forcing her to open to me.

Our tongues mingle in a lust driven dance and when I pull away, we're both panting and desperately wanting more.

My hand goes to her throat and I squeeze, applying just the right amount of pressure to cut off her air supply while leaving her begging for more.

"Ezra." She groans. *Fuck I love it when she moans my name.*

I push her backwards so she's laid out flat across the vault, as I slide her nightdress down, tossing it to the floor. She lays completely spread out in just tiny black panties. I stare at her goddess-like body, biting down on my fist, certain that I could probably blow my load by just looking at the girl.

Gripping the thin material at her hip, I tear off her panties in one swift tug. I consider stuffing them in her mouth but think better of it. I want to hear her scream for me.

A small yelp of surprise leaves Bennett's lips.

"How wet is my little bird?" I ask as I slide my fingers between the damp folds of her pussy.

"So wet." She purrs, writhing on the cold stone.

I lift my glistening fingers, bring them to my mouth and lick off her juices.

"Fuck Bennett you're soaking." I groan. She tastes like fucking heaven and hell combined. Sin dripping with syrup.

"Whose cock do you want?"

"Yours." Her panting is becoming more erratic.

I push a finger into her as she arches her back.

"Good girl, tell me who you belong to!"

She rolls her hips wanting more. *My filthy little whore.* I oblige by adding two more fingers into her begging pussy.

"You... Ezra... I belong to you."

The words are like fucking crack,

I pump my fingers in and out of her, while my free hand pinches her nipple. She looks sexy as fuck as she grinds on top of the gravestone as I finger-fuck her.

Her legs spread wider and with one final thrust, her cunt clamps down on my fingers, contracting around me as she comes. She cries out, her legs shaking from the aftershocks.

I remove my fingers as she moans in protest, but before she can say a word, I slap her pussy making her cry out again.

Her hips begin to buck and that's all the invitation I need as I rip off my leather jacket and shirt, unbuttoning my jeans and releasing my rock hard cock. Bennett props herself up on her elbows, staring at my length.

"I'll never get used to your size." She pants as she sits up and wraps her small hand around my dick, her fingers unable to touch.

"Oh you will." I smirk. My eyes rolling to the back of my head as she begins to pump my cock. Hard and tight. I feel like I'm balancing too close to the edge, walking the tight rope, so before she can continue working my dick, I push her back down onto the cold, hard stone, spreading her legs as wide as they will go.

Without warning and with one hard thrust, I bury myself inside her hot, tight cunt, not even giving her time to adjust before I begin my punishing thrusts.

She cries out, but I cover her mouth with mine, swallowing down her screams.

Angling her hips, I fuck her hard and deep. Almost as if this is the last fuck of my life and I'm desperately clawing for every second.

Her hands frantically search the cold grave below her for something to grip onto, finding nothing but smooth, cold, *dead* stone.

"You take my cock like such a good little slut."

"Yes." Her voice is desperate and needy and I fucking love it. Reaching down I press my thumb against her clit, massaging as I continue to drive into her with force.

Her moans slowly bleed into screams and I know she's close.

"Touch yourself little bird, let me see you pleasure yourself as you come."

Instantly she complies, her hand replacing where my thumb was, caressing the bundle of nerves.

While she's so focused on her pleasure, I use my other hand to pull out my pen knife from the back pocket of my jeans that are still sitting just below my ass.

Her hips buck.

"That's it Bennett, come for me baby."

I see her startled gaze as she notices the glint of my blade, just as her orgasm slams through her.

As I feel her inner walls squeeze the fucking life out of my cock, I press the cold steel into the flesh of her hip. She cries louder as I work quickly, carving the 'E and then the 'S' into her skin. The wound, not too deep but deep enough that it will leave a scar. Branding her as mine forever.

As I finish the final line, my body trembles as my cock swells inside her. The orgasm, so powerful I feel like I'm seconds from blacking out.

A carnal growl leaves my throat as I empty myself inside her, pushing as deep as my cock will physically go. That tight, little cunt milking every last drop out of me.

As I pull out, I feel my seed drip from her pussy, pooling on the top of granddaddy's grave. A big, old 'fuck you' to the man currently burning in hell.

As we come down from our high, Bennett scrambles up to inspect the damage done to her hip.

"Ezra, what the fuck?"

She runs her forefinger through the light trickle of blood oozing from the letters I've just carved.

Gently, I run my fingers through the smeared blood of the

wound and over the letters. Bennett hisses quietly through her teeth. Pulling my fingers back, I slip them into my mouth, tasting the coppery warmth of her blood on my tongue.

"You're mine little bird, and now the whole world will know it too."

Her eyes widened in shock. I can't determine if it's lust or pure horror in her expression, but when she jumps from the vault, her lips crashing onto mine in a punishing kiss, I somehow suspect that horror couldn't be further away from the truth right now.

Chapter Twenty One

Bennett

It's amazing how easily sleep finds you after an intense, body shattering orgasm. Even the ones you acquire in a dirty, old cemetery.

My body was so exhausted when Ezra brought me back to my room last night, dressed in a poorly repaired nightie and his leather jacket over my shoulders, that I slept without a single dream. Neither good nor bad.

When I eventually do plan on going back to see my father, I think I'm going to need to make an appointment to see the Cedar Cross doctor. My nightmares and sleep patterns were worse than ever.

I look to my hip to see Ezras initials carved into my flesh. The letters looked angry but no longer bleeding.

The shock when he had sliced his blade over me was instant but it had quickly been replaced with something else. Something carnal. I wanted the pain, I liked it. It was almost like I wanted him to hurt me more. *God I was fucked up!*

I wasn't in the mood for another day of whatever bullshit was assigned to me, however needs must and my dad was relying on the money I was making here, so I hauled my ass out of bed, showering quickly and heading downstairs.

Karas already waiting like a fucking drill sergeant as soon as I reach the bottom step. She was carrying a clipboard, *god knows who made her queen of the castle.*

"You're in the south wing today, the library staff need help sorting through some old junk." She barely looks at me as she barks out the orders.

"The south wing?" I've never been to the south wing before, come to think of it, I've never really been anywhere in the house that wasn't in the north wing, I didn't even know they had a library. Now I just felt ignorant.

"That's what I said, Andreas asked me to take you there, make sure you didn't get lost." Her words were laced with venom as if she was trying to insinuate that I was stupid. Anger fizzled slightly as I clenched my fists at my side.

"I can find it myself." I snapped. Kara looked at me for a split second before looking back down at her clipboard.

"Well they're Andreas' orders."

My mind went back to the incident last night. Where I fled down the stairs, catching sight of Andreas staring at me from the shadows. A shudder racked through me at the memory. It had been a hallucination, I was sure of it. I must have been still half asleep. That's the only explanation for why I saw him, why I fled the house into the night wearing just a thin piece of material.

Deciding not to fan the flames of the fire clearly brewing between Kara and I, I let her lead the way.

We walked down corridor after corridor, up and down staircase after staircase. Each one looking practically the same. We walked in silence, not speaking a word to each other, which to be honest I was pretty happy with.

Arriving at what I assumed was the library, Kara pushed open the heavy, dark mahogany, double doors.

My jaw dropped in awe. This place was incredible.

I'd seen the *Disney* film *Beauty and the Beast* numerous times as a kid, but I never imagined in my wildest dreams that a library like this actually existed inside someone's home. It looked like it'd jumped right out of the movie.

An elaborate, tarnished brass chandelier hangs in the centre of the embellished ceiling and a huge, dark mahogany fireplace housing pieces of thick, charred wood, rests as a centrepiece for row upon row of perfectly placed books. I don't think I've ever seen so many books in my entire life. This very room put the local Cedar Cross library to shame.

Kara turns now that her task of escorting me here is complete and begins to walk towards the door.

After taking two steps she turns back to face me.

"If you could avoid all the dramatics in the middle of the night again that would be great." Her sarcastic tone spiked with bitterness. "I heard all the screaming and banging last night. You're a freak show and you need sectioning. Don't think just because you ditched the goth look that you're anywhere near normal."

I raise an eyebrow in surprise. *What the fuck?!*

"I didn't mean to wake anyone. I'm just..."

"You're a science experiment Bennett, some weird, fucked up little girl that has the deluded idea that someone like Ezra Silvaro could ever be interested in her."

That was the final straw, it was like an elastic band snapping inside my head as I charged towards Kara, fists clenched, her eyes widening as she saw me coming.

"LADIES!" A gruff voice stopped me in my tracks and saved Kara from the pounding of her life.

We both turned towards the direction of the voice to see a short, round man with a snow white beard walking towards us. His perfectly round glasses, sitting on the edge of his nose. He watched us over the top of the frames.

"I won't tolerate behaviour of this sort in here."

Kara scoffed, not even stopping to apologise as she waltzed out of the library, letting the large doors swing closed with a loud bang behind her.

I turned towards the man. "I'm so sorry, I..."

"Am Bennett Keane. Yes I was told you were here to help me today."

I nodded, forcing a strained smile.

"My name is Winston, I'm the library manager here at

Knightchurch."

Winston gestures towards his small desk in the room by the corner of the library. A basic wooden table, holding a computer and a small, blue pen pot with nothing more than a pencil inside.

"The library is full, Mr Silvaro would like to donate a stack of special edition books to charity auctions and due to the volume of said books, it's going to take two of us to go through them."

Joy! This sounded about as exciting as polishing the fucking teaspoons.

I gave Winston another half smile.

"Sure, no problem."

Walking towards the pile of books already stacked by the desk, I began to sift through.

There were so many. Books of all kinds, Chaucer, Poe, the complete works of Shakespeare, so many.

"Make yourself comfortable at my desk Bennett, I need to go through the shelves and source all the editions on this list, so if you could record them all onto the computer system that would be amazing."

He potters off with his long piece of paper, leaving me to relax onto the little, old, worn computer stool and begin tapping away at the keys.

Thoughts of Ezra in the cemetery invade my mind and refuse to go away. *I wonder what he's doing today?*

I plan on finding Millie and Summer later and maybe going through a few plans for the Halloween ball.

The holiday is fast approaching and if I want to get this place in spooky shape I need to get a move on.

Six mundane hours later and my brain was frazzled from staring at a screen all day and my fingers aching. Some charities were certainly going to benefit from all the books the Silvaros were donating. Practically enough to build a second library.

"You can get off now Bennett, I'll finish up here." Winston gives my shoulder a gentle pat.

"Okay, if you're sure." I replied.

I wasn't going to hang around if I didn't have to, I had a

Halloween ball to plan.

Winston nodded, flicking through the pages of some battered old book, excusing me from the desk, so without another word I jumped to my feet.

"Well see ya later Winston."

He carried on turning the pages of his book, clearly mesmerised with whatever he was reading. I walked to the door and left without so much as a smile from him.

Heading back to the north wing, I bumped into Summer, her hair messy and a mop and bucket in her hands.

"You okay?" I asked as she looked up, giving me a worn out expression.

"Urgh! No, some chick who started working here a few days ago was suppose to be cleaning the toilets today but she got sick and has spent the whole day in her room, so lapdog here got the short straw."

I bite my lip, stifling the laugh that was brewing.

"Do you have any idea how many toilets are in this place?"

"A lot." I let out a small giggle as Summer returned my smile.

"Well fancy coming over to mine later? I'm hoping to go through some of the Halloween ball prep with Millie if you wanted to join in?"

Summer gave me a disappointed look. "I can't, I promised Kara I'd spend the night doing some shit with her, Riley and Elaine. Sorry B."

"It's fine, don't worry, I'm sure you'll have a great night."

Summer rolled her eyes. "I'd much rather be spending the evening with you and Millie, who I still need to get to know by the way."

I sometimes forget that Summer and Millie didn't know each other. It's strange how huge this place is.

"She's amazing, the three of us can get together soon."

"Sure thing." Summer smiles enthusiastically before picking up her mop and bucket and going about her duties.

If there's one thing I'll say about Millie, it's that she's bloody good at organising a party.

After finding her sitting on the embankment of the lake with a book, we headed back to my room and brainstormed all the ideas for the ball.

Hunting around the house, I managed to gather together some old bits and pieces that would help serve as decorations.

I was a little disappointed by the fact that I hadn't bumped into Ezra today but I knew he'd only be a distraction and right now if I was going to get the residents of Cedar Cross to see what a wonderful place Knightchurch was, I was going to need a goddamn miracle.

Millie agreed to stay in my room making some props to freak everyone out, while I decided to head back to the south wing and see if anyone had any bits and pieces over there that they could spare.

Heading in the direction of the library, I came across a small hallway leading to a white door at the end of it.
The door looked out of place compared to the rest of the house which made me even more curious about what was behind it.

Slowly walking towards it, I could hear light rustling inside. Swallowing hard I placed my palm onto the golden doorknob and grasped, turning slowly.

The door popped open and suddenly I was faced with what appeared to be a young girls bedroom. The walls were painted pale pink with long, white velvet curtains. A plush chaise in a deep cerise colour laid against the far wall and as with most of the other bedrooms in Knightchurch, a high four poster bed with a white duvet sat in the middle of the room.

The room itself was beautiful, so clean and fresh in contrast to the gothic manor.

But it was the person sitting on the bed that looked out of place. His dark hair and dark clothing clashing with the crystal white interior.

Ezra sat staring ahead, his elbows on his knees.
As he heard me enter the room, he turned to face me.

"Oh I'm sorry... I..."

"It's okay," he replied. "Come in, please."

I slowly entered, closing the door behind me. Taking in the beautiful decor and shabby chic white furniture, I sat down next to Ezra on the bed.

"This was Eleanor's room." A look of pain flashes across his eyes.

"Your sister?"

He nodded. "Dad always told her it looked like a child's room, that she was too old for pink but she wouldn't listen. She was a stubborn one, that one. Always was. But she was the kindest soul you'd ever meet, and she loved her family with all her heart. She was pure, she wasn't *tainted* like me."

Tainted?

His beautiful tan face brightens at the mention of his sister but then sorrow spreads across it once more.

"She's out there somewhere Ezra, she has to be."

He sits in silence for a minute. "I believed that at first but now, now I'm not so sure."

I look at his face to see for the very first time a single tear fall from his eye.

Leaning towards his face, I gently place a kiss to the tear, my lips wiping it away and hopefully wiping some of the pain away with it.

He leans his forehead against mine. His fingers travel down the outside of my bare arms and into the waistband of my leggings, gently tugging the fabric away to expose the letters 'E.S'

His dazzling eyes meet mine and I find myself getting lost in those deep whirlpools of blue all over again.

"Mine!" He says. Nothing more, nothing less.

I smile, my gaze focused solely on him. "Yours!"

Chapter Twenty Two

Bennett

The time leading up to the Halloween party had been spent putting together some amazing decorations and coming up with costume ideas for the staff.

Millie had finally decided to give up trying to coax any sign of life in her little garden patch and Ezra had hardly been at Knightchurch, as he and his father apparently had some business to attend to so I'd barely seen him at all.

I hadn't had a second to read anymore of Theodora's journal as I'd been so busy in the daytime and by the evening I was so exhausted that I fell straight to sleep.

The nightmares seemed to ease slightly and it was nice to feel more settled into life at Knightchurch. Things finally seemed to be on the up.

The night of the Halloween ball finally arrived and all my hard work decorating the house and sorting out the catering, with a little help from Summer and Estelle, seemed to be paying off.

The huge ballroom chandelier glittered with silver cobwebs that Summer and I had struggled to hang.

Skulls laden with black and pink flowers sat prominently on each side board and small synthetic spiders were mounted at different points on the wall.

My favourite part had to be the white pumpkins. Sourcing them from the gardens had been an experience, especially as

Summer and I had the pleasure of Riley and Elaine helping us. Kara was much too busy and important to help, doing other duties of course, which was more than fine by me. A day avoiding her sounded like ultimate bliss.

Riley had fallen over in the mud and Elaine had spent the whole day moaning about how her brand new suede boots were going to get wrecked, so they certainly weren't the people I would have chosen to help us with our task.

However now the pumpkins were carved into horrifying faces and were glowing with their orange flames, they made the perfect decor in this already haunting ballroom.

The residents of Cedar Cross came flocking in droves. I put this partly down to morbid curiosity, especially when the likes of Hunter Jackson and his little cop buddies arrived, but some, I could tell, genuinely wanted to see Knightchurch thrive.

They were mostly in the form of Mrs Potton and my dad who arrived at the doors arm in arm dressed as a Victorian couple. My dad, sporting his cane and walking with a slight limp.

I felt like I was about to burst into tears when I first set eyes on him. My emotions heightened due to the fact that it had been weeks since I'd seen him.

"Daddy!" I wrapped my arms around him tightly.

"Bennett. How are yer kid?" He smiled at me, his skin wrinkling at the sides of his gentle eyes.

The tears began to fall, as hard as I tried to stop them.

"Oh come on now sweetheart, you'll mess up that pretty makeup."

I giggled at his comment, knowing full well that my makeup was far from pretty.

I'd gone with a tight, black, floor length corset dress and white skull face paint. My dark hair in messy curls piled high on my head. I guess some might call it pretty but it certainly wasn't the look I was going for.

"I've just missed you dad."

My dad's grip tightens on my arm.

"I've missed you too darling."

Mrs Potton loops her arm through my fathers. He looks at her dainty hand and then back to my face.

"Bennett, we have something to tell you. Not now but we can…"

"I know dad." He doesn't need to say the words for me to already guess what's coming.

His eyes widened. "You do?"

I smile. "Of course, a phone call tells a million secrets." I wink at Mrs Potton. "I'm happy for you both."

Dad gives me a large grin before landing a kiss on Mrs Pottons cheek. She smiles coyly at him. It's the happiest I've seen him in a long time and he's been on his own for years, he deserved his happiness and I couldn't think of anyone better to have it with than this lovely woman.

Haunting classical music plays as dad and Mrs Potton head towards the giant punch bowl to the left of the dance floor.

Summer had told me this was her secret recipe, but after trying the toxic concoction, I was becoming slightly anxious that we were going to end up with several cases of alcohol poisoning before the night was through.

Ezra stood in the corner of the grand ballroom, illuminated by the candles I'd displayed all around the room.

His pitch black suit showed off every curve of his toned body, the memory of my hands gliding over his defined abs and up his chest sends shivers over my skin and heat collecting between my legs. *Jesus was it hot in here all of a sudden?*

His face was painted to match my own. A skull that portrayed the epitome of sex and evil. Just looking at it drove me wild and terrified me at the same time.

Estelle and Andreas sat at the back on throne like chairs. They weren't in costume, just dressed all in black but their very demeanour was unsettling and gave off a dark, gothic vibe. King and Queen of the manor.

Kara, Riley, Elaine and Summer were all dressed similarly. Floor length chiffon gowns in a rainbow of colours and their faces painted like cracked dolls.

I had to admit as much as I hated Kara for the bitch that she was, she really was beautiful. The fact Ezra apparently hadn't done anything with her was strange in itself. But then everything was strange about that man.

I'd only seen him vulnerable the one time in Eleanor's room and the memory stirred a feeling inside me that was alien. A feeling I hadn't experienced before but one that I had to admit I didn't want to let go of.

Whenever I looked in his direction, the letters on my thigh tingled despite being long healed, causing a surge of lust to spike inside me.

As I walked to the punch bowl to grab myself a drink, I noticed another tall, broad, suited man approach Ezra. The dark blonde buzz cut gave him away before I saw his face.

Caleb Fox, like Ezra, was a vision.

His pale blue eyes and light stubble would have any girl on her knees. I could see why Millie had set her sights on him.

"He's hot right?" Summer came up behind me. Her eyes trained on Caleb.

"Yeah I guess so." My instinct was telling her to back off due to Millie's confession, but we weren't in high school anymore and if Millie was going to hang around, someone like Caleb was going to get snapped up very soon.

Summer left my side and strode across the dance floor, her pink gown swaying as she approached Caleb. She whispered in his ear and he threw his head back in a thunderous laugh.

I walked to the pillar at the side of the room, leaning back with my drink and watching all the people who'd arrived tonight, dancing, drinking and being merry.

"Why is she talking to him?" I turned to see Millie behind me. She was glaring at Summer talking to Caleb, throwing daggers in their direction.

"Where's your costume?" I asked, avoiding her question. Instead of a typical Halloween costume, she was dressed in a white, knee length dress with little blue flowers all over it. It was pretty but it looked like something you'd wear to afternoon tea, not a Halloween ball.

Her face was her usual pale, tired complexion. Not a stitch of face paint to be seen.

"I didn't feel like wearing one." She replied, her eyes dropping to the floor and her feet shuffling.

I lifted an eyebrow, this girl was odd sometimes.

Deciding not to question whatever decision Millie had decided to make regarding her attire, I turned away from her to face Summer and Caleb, who were still deep in conversation.

Kara was standing to the side of the dance floor, her red dress glistening in the candlelight, her eyes trained on me. I gave her a sarcastic smile, turning my attention back to Summer and Caleb.

"You know I hate to sound obvious..." I begin to speak to Millie who's still standing behind me. "But if you don't tell him how you feel, then he's never gonna know."

Turning back to face her I'm greeted with an empty space. *What the fuck did I say?*

As I spin around, Kara is walking slowly to where I'm standing, champagne flute in hand.

"Freak!" She hisses the words as she continues to pass me. Her eyes locked on mine.

"You know you're a total bitch." I snap. The only response I receive is a cruel smirk.

"And you need to back the fuck away from Ezra." *Jesus not this again.*

The words were bubbling up inside me threatening to erupt in a stream of word vomit. I tried to push them down but my attempt was in vain.

"I FUCKED EZRA." The words escaped and there was no putting them back. I feel like I've just opened Pandora's box.

I thought I'd feel regret or shame or the tiniest bit bad for Kara but no, I fucking loved every second of it.

Kara's exasperated expression was worth every single word that had left my mouth. I expected a backlash. Some sharp words? Maybe a slap? But instead she stood, staring at me in silence.

Just as it looked as if she was about to say something, it seemed she thought better of it and spun around, storming from the hall. The heels of her stilettos clashing against the stone floor.

I exhaled a long breath I'd been holding since the confession left my mouth. Luckily despite my outburst, the only people who heard was Kara and by the looks of it, Riley and Elaine who were rushing out the doors after her. Both of them throwing disgusted looks my way.

I didn't want to hurt Kara, that was never my intention but I still couldn't get my head around why she hated me so much, yeah ok she had a thing for Ezra but this petty, schoolgirl behaviour was getting tiresome now. She needed to let it go.

I decided not to let it spoil the mood of the night. It didn't take long for the party to get into full swing.

Prisoner by *Raphael Lake* and *The Devil* by *BANKS* played one after the other, getting people onto the dance floor.

"Bennett."

I tried not to roll my eyes as I recognised the voice calling my name.

I turned to see Hunter standing there in a tight, black T-shirt and jeans, fake fangs moulded onto his teeth and some kind of cosmetic blood around his mouth.

"Hunter." I squeezed the smile onto my face, every fibre of my being wanting to run at that second.

"You look amazing." His eyes raked over my outfit, lingering a little too long on my cleavage.

"Thank you, so do you... werewolf?" The forced words tasted rotten in my mouth.

His mouth lifted into a wide smile, showing all his pearly white teeth. "Hilarious! No...sexy vampire babe."

Babe?

He took a swig of whatever liquid was inside his red solo cup.

"So it looks like the weirdos finally wanted to join society and open house." He chuckled as he scanned the room. "Must say, it's pretty impressive what they have up here. Jokers must be loaded." *God he was an arrogant prick!*

"Yeah well, I don't know about that, I'm just the maid." The fake smile was making my cheeks ache.

Hunter smirked. "So I was thinking we could have a dance, you know, as I never got to buy you that drink."

I could feel my forced smile begin to dissolve as I began to panic, looking for an excuse to leave.

"She's dancing with me."

His words washed over me like a cool breeze on a scorching summer's day. My eyes closed in relief.

Ezra held out his hand as he stood in front of Hunter face to face. The pair of them caught up in some dick sizing contest.

Hunter smirked. I half expected him to say something but instead his eyes scanned over Ezras tall, broad frame. He didn't look intimidated, but something told me that he was keeping it well hidden.

Hunter stood to the side, gesturing towards me as if giving his consent for Ezra to dance with me. The action forced a scoff from my throat.

Taking Ezras hand, he led me towards the dance floor. Music blared through the speakers and I could tell that everyone was starting to get a little tipsy as Miss Meehan, the Cedar Cross baker, was making out with Dario, the delivery guy and our postman Oliver was dancing, sandwiched between two girls that I'd noticed hoovering the bedrooms around Knightchurch.

Ezras hands slipped around my waist as my focus was pulled from the people around me and focused solely on him. He began to sway to the rhythm, guiding my hips as I moved in closer, sinking into his sensual touch.

Pressing his pelvis into mine, I could feel the rock hard bulge of his erection. The feel, setting fire to my insides and drawing a low groan from my mouth.

"See what you do to me." His voice, a whisper against my ear as I close my eyes and continue to sway, everything blurry and distorted apart from him. He's the only thing I can focus on. His lips brush against mine as the song ends and he stands back smiling at the melting mess I've become, just by being in his arms.

"I'll get us a drink." He runs his tongue across his plump bottom lip, my eyes transfixed on the motion.

I nod because, let's face it, I've lost the ability to string any fucking words together at this moment in time.

I continue dancing on the floor on my own, surrounded by the drunken townspeople.

Looking around I see Summer now chatting to Hunter as Caleb is giving his attention to some other girl.

Hunter is facing her, laughing at something she's said and the way she's touching his bicep is making me think that she's liking what she sees. I force down the rising vomit.

I should really go and look for Millie, I have no idea why she's not here right now but I'm being a
really shit friend by not at least checking if she's alright.

I wonder if it's something to do with Caleb?

Looking at the punch bowl, I can no longer see Ezra. I continue swaying to the music until suddenly a glass smashes just outside the ball room.

Walking towards the source of the noise, I see Ezra trying to walk away with Kara holding tightly onto his arm. I stand back, watching, careful not to let them see me.

"Please Ezra," Kara begs, "What is it about her? What does she have that you can't get from me?"

Ezra turns towards her, yanking his arm out of her grip, almost sending her tumbling to the floor. She stumbles back, regaining her composure.

"Stay the fuck away from me and stay the fuck away from Bennett, because if you don't, I will fucking kill you!"

With that he storms away, up the staircase. Kara fights to control the tears as she turns and sees me by the door.

She doesn't say a word before running off, a sob escaping her throat as she leaves.

I push out a long sigh. Think I've had enough drama for one night.

Heading back to the dance floor, I spend time with dad and Mrs Potton until they decide they've had enough 'at their age' as they put it and I give both of them the biggest hugs before they leave.

The night is coming to an end and Andreas and Estelle were nowhere to be seen. I'd hoped for their sake that they'd at least made an effort with the townspeople tonight, but I was pretty confident the ball had gone down well.

I still hadn't seen anything of Millie, so I planned to find out what the hell was going on with her tomorrow but tonight I was well and truly done in.

Summer hobbles over to me, her eyes half closed and her face looking a rather unattractive shade of green.

"You okay?"

She shakes her head, slapping her hand over her mouth.

"I don't feel so good, think it was the punch."

I giggle. "Well I did tell you to go easier on the rum."

An unladylike burp leaves her mouth, forcing me to laugh out loud.

"Come on, let's get you to bed."

She closes her eyes, shaking her head rapidly.

"No it's fine, I'm gonna go get some fresh air." She points towards the front door.

I look her over, she's going to feel like death in the morning.

"Want me to come with you?" I ask.

Summer shakes her head again. "No it's fine, you go find your lover boy, I'll be okay."

Finding Ezra was the last thing on my mind tonight. After witnessing what happened with Kara, it seemed like everyone just needed some space to cool off.

I hugged Summer and she waddled off towards the door.

Checking with a few of the kitchen staff, they assured me they would be there to clean up and that I should go up to bed.

Everyone else was already gone it seemed, so I didn't take much convincing to call it a night.

I went to bed satisfied in the fact that despite a couple of hiccups, the Knightchurch Halloween ball had been a success. I felt good about this, as I took myself off to bed, confident in the knowledge that Cedar Cross would be talking about this night for a long time to come.

Chapter Twenty Three

Bennett

The screams could be heard throughout the whole house. The sound, pulling me from the best night's sleep I'd had in years.

I jolted upright as the piercing wails echoed through the house as if someone was being tortured.

Grabbing my cream, satin robe, I pulled it over my nightie before running out of my bedroom door.

A few staff members flocked down the stairs in their sleepwear, some I'd never even seen before. Most looked worse for wear after the Halloween ball last night. All of them, like me, were eager to find out where the screaming was coming from.

"THE LAKE, SHE'S IN THE LAKE!"

Reaching the reception area, Andreas was already standing, staring blankly at the mess on the floor as a devastated Riley had dropped to her knees at Estelles feet, sobbing and screaming hysterically.

Ezra and Caleb came running down the stairs, a look of horror on both of their faces.

Estelle quickly dropped to Riley's level, clutching her other hand and trying to calm her.

"Riley please, stay calm, now tell me, what's happened?"

I stood, frozen to the spot as Riley gripped Estelle's hand with desperate force, her body trembling violently.

"SHE'S IN THE LAKE, KARAS IN THE LAKE."

Without a second thought, I ran, my body in fight or flight

mode as my legs moved at their own accord and I was practically flying from the house, down the path into the dark wood and towards the lake.

"BENNETT!"

I could hear Ezra and Caleb behind me but I couldn't think about anything except getting to the lake. My head, a murky whirlpool of grey fog.

As I reached the embankment, nothing could prepare me for the horror that was waiting.

Kara floated, face up in the cold, unforgiving, dark water. Her eyes open, bloodshot and vacant of all life. Still in her beautiful red gown and the cracked doll makeup from the night before, smeared and melted from her flawless face.

I gasped in terror as I felt strong arms wrap around my body pulling me in close. Turning, I buried my head in Ezra's chest, trying to block out the view of Kara's lifeless body but even with my eyes closed, the image of her face was clear as day, burned into my mind.

She was dead. Kara was dead. She hadn't even made it back to her room last night. While we all continued to party and sleep, she was here, alone, floating in a freezing grave.

It didn't take long for the police to arrive at Knightchurch. Summer and I sat together, huddled in the lounge with hot coffee, waiting for any information on what the fuck was going on.

Kara's body had been pulled from the lake and removed in a black body bag, the embankment closed off with tape, while the police conducted their investigation.

My blood ran cold as I saw Hunter's face emerge from one of the cop cars and walk inside the house to where we were all congregated.

"Bennett." Hunter nodded his head towards me in acknowledgment.

Gone was the playful womaniser and in its place a ruthless cop, fire burned in his eyes as he glanced over at Ezra who was standing protectively at my side, one hand on my shoulder.

Peeking into the hallway, I could see Andreas and Estelle talking to two other cops. One of them with a small notebook that I recognised as Cedar Cross' sheriff and the other, someone standing with a stern look upon his face. A detective maybe?

Anxiety swirled in my gut as Andreas looked up, his cold eyes meeting mine for a split second and then looking back to the detective. I couldn't help but notice the tight grip he had on Estelles arm. Almost like he was sending her a warning. Her face pale and gaunt.

"We're going to need to ask some questions regarding what happened in the last minutes before Kara Valance went missing from the party," said Hunter, breaking me out of my trance. "Who she was with, what kind of state she was in, that kind of thing."

I nodded. "I... erm..."

"I'll need to speak to you especially." Hunter's attention broke away from me and focused solely on Ezra. Accusation laced his tone.

"Be my guest." Ezras response was also filled with venom as he and Hunter stared at each other, neither one wanting to back down.

"I've already spoken to some guests who attended last night. Apparently there was an altercation with Miss Valance where you stated you were going to kill her."

Ezra scoffed, almost like the idea was unbelievable.

"It's a figure of speech, deputy Jackson or whatever your name is. I'm sure you've said it a few times in your life. Maybe to the women who've spurned your advances."

Hunter snarled, baring his teeth at the jibe. "I've heard about you... and Caleb Fox. Reputation gets around. Watch yourself, Silvaro. I know you had something to do with this and I'll be watching you until you slip up...and when you do, I'm gonna enjoy busting your ass."

Ezra smiled, the sharp points of his canines glinting in the daylight.

"Oh I'll be waiting, deputy."

The two men stood within inches of each other. The testosterone simmered between them as neither one wanted to back down. Like two pit bulls ready for the fight.

"Hunter." My voice broke the locked stare between them as Hunter turned to face me. "Until there's any proof that anyone was involved in what happened to Kara, then please just back the fuck off. This little pissing contest between the two of you isn't helping anyone."

Hunter shook his head. "I'm here for you Bennett, give me a call if you need anything at all."

I smiled.

"She won't." *Fuck sake.* Ezra stood by my side, his cold eyes trained on Hunter, a smirk on his face.

Hunter looked at me before turning and heading out of the door. *Fucking dick sizing contest.*

I turned back to Ezra, his hand landing on my shoulder, giving it a reassuring squeeze. His eyes, still cold as stone.

Estelle walked into the room, coming over and sitting on the small sofa, next to where Ezra and I were standing. Her face pale and her eyes sporting dark circles. She seemed to have the bags under her eyes frequently these last few weeks.

"Have they said anymore about what happened?"
I asked.

Estelle turned to look at me. "Erm... they think she drowned. They're looking for any evidence of foul play but it's obvious the girl had had too much to drink and fell in the lake."

I nodded, narrowing my eyes towards Ezra. Flashbacks of the argument between him and Kara are still fresh in my mind.

Luckily someone like Hunter didn't see what had gone on or this could be a lot fucking worse. But from what I remember, Kara didn't seem that drunk. At least not enough to fall into a freezing lake and not be able to swim to safety.

It didn't make sense. Ezra wouldn't hurt Kara, would he? I didn't want to believe it.

The Ezra I'd grown to know while I was here wouldn't just

murder a girl in cold blood but realistically how well did I know this man?

He sliced into my hip without a second thought in the graveyard and even though it was one of the hottest things I've ever experienced, it was still... out of the ordinary.

A chill brushed the back of my skull. He couldn't have hurt her, surely.

Riley sat nursing a cup of coffee, rocking slightly back and forth, Elaine at her side with a supportive arm around her.

She was wearing her gym gear so must have stumbled across Kara's body on her morning run, the girl looked traumatised. She'd literally just discovered her best friend's body, drowned in a lake. I can't imagine what must be going through her head right now.

Her face was as white as a sheet. Her hands trembled so hard she could barely retain the mug in them. It didn't seem like the cops had managed to get much out of her. The girl looked catatonic right now.

The sheriff was still standing outside the lounge, discussing something with Andreas. The man was shady as fuck.

I hadn't seen him at the end of the night when I was leaving. I assumed he and Estelle had headed up to bed, but I wouldn't be surprised if he knew something about what had happened last night.

He looked vacant, bored even, like none of this was affecting him at all. A young girl was found dead on his land. How the hell was he looking so calm?

Estelle looked worried, like she couldn't believe this was happening in her home, but Andreas just seemed to lack any emotion whatsoever.

I headed to the kitchen and brought back a mug of coffee for Estelle, before heading down to sit with Summer.

I felt like I needed to find Millie, see if she'd heard anything else, but the staff in the other wing were still over there. Apparently the sheriff wanted them to stay where they were until he and Hunter had had a chance to question everyone.

Caleb returned to the lounge following his questioning with one of the officers. He headed over to Ezra, leaning back against the sofa, both hands in the pockets of his black jeans.

"Come on, we got stuff to do." Ezra directed his words at Caleb before leaning down, kissing his mother on the head and then me. Caleb followed him without a word.

"I'll be back later." He whispered, giving my shoulder another reassuring squeeze.

As he left, I turned back to Summer who was watching carefully as the two men exited the lounge.

"You think he has anything to do with any of this?" She asked, still watching them walk away.

Ezra began speaking to the sheriff who, it looked like, was trying to tell him not to go anywhere. I'm not sure what his reply was but soon Ezra and Caleb were heading out of the door, no one stopping them or even glancing in their direction.

I turned back to Summer. "No... I dunno... no of course not." I rubbed my palm against my face. "God, I don't know what to believe. I want to say he'd never do something like that but sometimes... sometimes he looks at me like somethings changed inside him... like he's..."

"A killer?"

I flinch at Summer's words. Was Ezra capable of actually *killing* someone? The thought made my stomach churn but it kept rearing its ugly head inside my mind.

He'd threatened her but that's all it was, just an empty threat and what he said to Hunter was true, we've all made those empty threats before. It didn't mean we would actually go through with it, actually harm someone.

"He didn't do it." The tremor in my words confirmed I wasn't even confident in what I was saying but until someone proved me otherwise, I wouldn't believe this had anything to do with Ezra Silvaro.

"What do you think is gonna happen now?" Summer asked.

"I dunno," I sighed, "I guess we just have to wait and see what the cops come up with."

The day went slowly. Almost too slowly, it was painful.

We spent most of it sitting around, waiting for any news of what had happened to Kara and taking it in turns to speak to the sheriff and his team.

No one admitted to knowing anything. No one even remembered seeing Kara leave after the Halloween ball. I was literally the last person to see her leave, possibly the last person to see her alive.

Ezra and Caleb didn't come back for the rest of the day and I felt like I was holding in some kind of secret by staying silent about Kara and Ezras fight, even though Hunter knew about some of it.

Rumours circulated amongst the staff as they always do. Everyone was speculating about the events of the previous night.

All I could think about was that a young girl was dead. A girl, I sure as hell didn't like but a girl that didn't deserve to die. Someone's daughter. A sadness washed over me as I thought of my dad. How he would have felt if the girl in the lake was me. I inhaled deeply, trying to push the thoughts out of my mind.

"Bennett." I heard my name before I saw him as I turned to face Hunter.

"Not now Hunter, I'm really not in the mood."

"I need you to come with me for questioning."

My eyebrows furrowed in confusion. "Sorry what?"

"I need you to come back to the sheriff's department with me, I need to ask you a few questions. I've been informed by Riley Parker and Elaine Bond of some trouble that had been occurring between yourself and Kara Valance. I'm sorry Bennett, but until we get to the bottom of this, everyone's a suspect and you've just climbed the ranks to our number one."

Chapter Twenty Four

Bennett

What the actual fuck?

How was I even here?

The sheriff's department was quiet when I arrived and only a handful of staff from the house had been brought in.

It felt surreal to be away from Knightchurch as this was the first time I'd left since I started working there.

Hunter had gone through the basics, taken my fingerprints, explained that I wasn't under arrest but that I was definitely a suspect in the case now if foul play was detected.

He seemed to be bending the rules a little to make sure I was kept in the know and wasn't feeling too much like a fucking criminal, but I was, it was all I was feeling right now

"I don't have an alibi as to where I was last night, I was in bed, alone. I'm pretty sure ninety percent of the people at that party last night don't have alibis. Everyone went to their rooms alone... I think."

Hunter gave me a sympathetic sigh.

"Look Bennett, do I believe you had anything to do with Kara's death? Absolutely not, but you didn't have the best relationship with her and right now we need to cover all bases."

"I never wanted her dead, Hunter. FUCK!" I slammed my hand onto the table.

"Look, at the minute it's looking highly likely that she drowned. However between you and me there was some bruising on her neck. I don't know if it was there before or if it was caused by someone holding her down. It's too hard to tell at the minute."

Shock spilled through me. "Bruising?"

"Yes," Hunter replied. "It was pretty dark, signifying that if someone did hold her down, it would have had to be with some force."

I couldn't believe what I was hearing. I know for a fact that Kara didn't have bruising on her neck before she ran after her argument with Ezra. I remembered clearly how stunning she looked with the beautiful red dress and the cracked doll makeup. If there was bruising there then it had to have been put there after she left. There was no way I was divulging that little nugget of information just yet.

A memory entered my mind of my encounter with Andreas in the kitchen that night after Kara had been her usual dick self to me.

"Oh come on Bennett, I saw the rage in your eyes, felt good didn't it? Hurting her, making her suffer for what she did to you? Seeing that bitch get exactly what she deserves?"

Did he think she deserved to suffer? Did *he* want to make her suffer?

Hunter finished up his last few questions before the door to the sheriff's office burst open with a loud bang.

Ezra stands in the doorway, a look of pure thunder and rage on his face as he sees me sat at the desk opposite Hunter.

Striding over to me, he grabs me by my wrist, pulling me to my feet. Hunter jumps up from his chair.

"What the fuck is she doing here?" He roars.

Hunter's expression turns just as icey. "She's a suspect and she's in for questioning."

Ezra snarls, standing inches from Hunter's face.

"She had nothing to do with this and unless she's under arrest, I'll be taking her back with me."

Relief washes over me.

"She isn't under arrest," replied Hunter, his voice assertive and proud. I had to hand it to him, Ezra was ridiculously intimidating but Hunter wasn't backing down.

"Good," snarled Ezra. "My father has spoken to the sheriff and there's no reason for you to come knocking at our door anymore. We know nothing."

He tugs me behind him, guiding me towards the exit as Hunter laughs behind us.

"A girl was found dead on your land, Silvaro, I won't be staying away until I find out what the fuck is going on up there. Your daddy may have enough money to make the sheriff turn a blind eye, but no amount of money in the world is enough to stop me hunting you like the dog that you are."

Before Ezra could retaliate, I stepped in front of him before pulling him through the door out into the open.

A black Aston Martin sat outside the sheriff's department.

"Get in, little bird." Ezra commanded, as I rounded the other side.

Caleb was sitting in the passenger seat as I jumped in the back and Ezra jumped in the driver's seat. We headed back to Knightchurch in silence. A million questions swimming all over my mind.

I needed answers about what the fuck was going on at Knightchurch and I needed them now.

Pulling up by the fountain at the house, I practically dove from Ezra's car.

"BENNETT."

I could hear his voice but all I could think about was finding out what the hell was going on here. I didn't know who to trust and I was exhausted with all that seemed wrong with this place.

Returning to Knightchurch was like that part in a horror movie where you're screaming at the dumb chick to get out and never come back, but she doesn't listen and ends up with her head impaled on the serial killers fence or something equally as gruesome. Yep, right now, I was that chick. Even I knew that I would be screaming at myself to leave.

I was suspicious of everyone and I couldn't help but feel uneasy about so many things.

What was Andreas hiding? There was something but I just couldn't put my finger on what it was.

Why was Estelle so terrified of her husband? She was keeping his secret, I just knew she was.

Where was Millie going when I couldn't find her around the house? Still to the lake in the freezing cold? To somewhere else?

The Silvaros made it clear that they didn't like us to leave, even on the weekends, which was weird in itself, but yet Millie seemed to be doing whatever she god damn wanted and Ezra, this man was a mystery I couldn't unravel. In the daytime he stirred feelings in me that I've never felt before but at night he was stalking my nightmares, almost like he was a predator waiting for the right moment to pounce.

Opening my door, my legs were heavy and my mind even heavier.

I dropped onto the soft, slippery bed sheets and closed my eyes inhaling deeply. I wonder if any of our families had tried to contact the house about what had happened?! I'd need to call my dad at some point, reassure him that everything was alright.

Cedar Cross loved a story and I was surprised this new scandal wasn't plastered all over the news. Guess money really did help with everything.

Rolling onto my side, I pulled open the drawer in the bedside table, pulling Theodora's journal from the depths and turning to what I noticed was her final entry.

Theodora Alcott September 1911

I need to get out of this house. Carlos won't let me leave. Last night he locked me inside my room while I screamed until my throat was raw. I need to protect my baby, this is my last entry and if anyone should find this then please know that Carlos Silvaro is a monster, he isn't the man everyone thinks he is. I've begged for my life. I thought he loved me. He watches me day and night, there's never any chance of escape. I need to ....

With that the wording ended. The ink splotches below indicating that the pen had been dropped mid sentence. But more shockingly was the reddy brown marking at the bottom of the page. I ran my fingers over the stain. Blood.

I swallowed the lump in my throat as I quickly rolled up the journal and tucked it into my back pocket.

Leaving my room, I jogged down the stairs, finding Summer casually strolling through to the kitchen.

"Hey Bennett, I was going to come and find you when Riley and Elaine said that you'd been taken down to the sheriff's department. What the hell? You've done nothing wrong. How are you?" She stared at me with a concerned look on her face.

"I'm fine." I don't know who I was trying to convince more at this point, Summer or myself.

"You don't look like you're fine." Summer may come across as though she has no idea what's going on but something tells me she's probably more switched on than I give her credit for.

"Sum, I need to find some information on the Silvaros past but I can't even get a connection on my phone up here. It's useless."

I was kicking myself that I hadn't taken the one chance I had while I was down at the sheriff's department to do some digging.

Telling the Silvaros I was leaving Knightchurch now would look way too suspicious. Plus I didn't want to leave Ezra, everything about him was calling to me. I felt almost like he needed me in some weird, fucked up way.

"Winston."

Summer's voice pulled me from my thoughts. "Sorry?"

"Winston," she repeated. "The library. He has a computer, it's the only internet connection in the whole building. We can sneak in there after he's locked up and take a look. I know where he puts the library keys. They're just in a little box in the kitchen. He should be finishing in about thirty mins. We can follow him, make sure that's where he leaves the key."

My eyes widened in anticipation. "Yess, Summer I love you."

I grabbed her sweet, little round face and planted a huge, sloppy kiss on her cheek.

Her face blushed a pretty shade of pink. "Well I am kinda awesome."

I smiled, "come on, let's go."

Hanging around the library for Winston to leave seemed like it was taking years.

Summer and I hid behind the huge, thick, floor length maroon curtains in the hallway as the little, old librarian hobbled out, locking the library doors behind him.

"Wait here, I'll get the key."

Something told me Summer had suddenly thought she was in some fucking ninja action movie as she tiptoed across the landing, following Winston to where he stashed the keys.

As she returned grasping the keys, she quickly threw them at me as I ran to the library doors, forcing the key into the awkward lock with trembling hands.

As the doors finally opened, we pushed through them, quickly locking them behind us so no one would suspect anyone had broken in.

The library looked creepy as shit in the dark. The large, grey gargoyles that sat above the pillar of each shelf began to look animated. Almost like they were staring right at us.

I shrugged off a shiver, heading into Winston's makeshift office and loading up the computer.

The password didn't take a rocket scientist to figure out. Someone needed to tell Winston that 'Knightchurch' was a pretty obvious choice.

Summer and I crouched down, staring at the screen.

"So you gonna tell me why you're digging the dirt on the Silvaros?" said Summer, tapping her little foot.

"I found a journal underneath the floorboards of my room."

"Seriously." Summer dropped to the office chair, her interest piqued.

"Yep, it sounds weird but I was led to it in some crazy nightmare I had when I first got here. Some girl called Theodora Alcott. She came to work here in Knightchurch in 1911 and had an affair with Carlos Silvaro, Ezras great grandfather. She fell in love with him, thought he loved her too and ended up getting pregnant with his baby."

"Jesus, what happened to her?" Summers' eyes were wide as saucers, sparkling with intrigue.

"See this is the thing, I don't actually know. Her journal writes off before she explains anything. But with all the horror stories about this place and everything that's happened with Kara, I need to find out what the hells going on because something is, that's for sure."

I type Silvaro into the computer, hoping to acquire even a slither of information but nothing.

They don't even come up as owners of Knightchurch. In fact, typing in Knightchurch, there appears to be no information past the fact that it's a historical building crafted around the fourteen hundreds.

"Great, now what do we do?" Summer sighed. "It's like the internet has wiped all traces of them."

"Or they've wiped all traces of themselves, for whatever reason. They have the money, they could buy the whole of Cedar Cross ten times over if they wanted to. Hiding their dirty secrets wouldn't be an issue for someone like them."

I type furiously at the keypad for another twenty minutes before finally giving up.

Summer is shuffling through stacks of old books that Winston has been sorting, god knows what she's looking for but she's making enough noise, clattering through the filing cabinets, that she's gonna get us caught if she doesn't shut the fuck up soon.

There's nothing online about this strange family. They've

hidden their scent and now all they are to the world is a ghost story used to frighten children.

Defeated, I switch off the computer. Standing to stretch my aching legs.

"Bennett, quick!"

I turn and hurry out of the office to see Summer holding up what looks like a battered, dusty old file.

"What is it?" I narrow my eyes at the moth eaten old thing.

"A compartment underneath the filing cabinet, I noticed the bottom drawer wasn't sitting level so I gave it a tug and look at all this crap in there. Looks like someone has been collecting and hiding shit."

She pulled out all the old, browning papers. Some of them looking extremely ancient.

"What is this?" I asked, taking the file from Summer's hand.

"Dunno, looks like all sorts, some kind of hospital records, birth certificates, random newspaper clippings?!"

Flicking through the file. I came across an old, torn hand designed copy of a family tree. Dating back to Leonardo and Annie Silvaro who in 1884 gave birth to their son Carlos, the family tree then shows how Carlos and Geniveve Silvaro gave birth to a son, Jose Silvaro. *The name in the mausoleum. Ezras grandfather.* Liquid heat coursed through my veins at the memory of Ezra's cock thrusting deep inside me on top of Jose's vault. *Not now Bennett, you slut.*

Shaking the memory, I continue down the page to find a line flowing down from Jose and his wife Kaleen to... nothing. The rest of the family tree had been ripped away, right where Andreas Silvaros' name should be.

Turning the page, there was some kind of old doctor's records dated around 1886, two years after Carlos was born, with Leonardo Silvaros name on them.

Admitted to the White Lane Insane Asylum due to episodes of hysteria following the convicted murder of five women. Other women suspected to be amongst the deceased, however no trace as of yet.

My heart jerks inside my chest. Fuck, Carlos Silvaros father murdered five women, possibly more and was sent to a mental institution.

The rest of the records indicated the various treatments used at White Lane on Leonardo Silvaro before he finally hung himself at the facility in 1889 when Carlos would only have been five years old. His death certificate ripped and partially burned before being stuffed inside the file.

As I flipped to the next page, several paper clippings from newspaper articles and a photograph fell to the ground.

Crouching down, I carefully lifted the old pieces of paper. A young man stared up from the picture. His blue eyes and dark hair, identical to Ezras. The photograph looked just like his portrait that was hanging in the corridor of the north wing. His name, *Carlos Silvaro,* scribbled on the bottom of the picture.

I lifted one of the newspaper articles that had fallen from the file.

Females missing. Carlos Silvaro, suspect in the disappearance of female workers at Knightchurch manor.

Looking to the next one, a different story was told.

Carlos Silvaro cleared of murder in case of missing women at Knightchurch manor following search.

Seems Ezra's great granddaddy got away scot free from the scandal.

As I carefully placed the newspaper clippings and photograph back into the dusty, old file, that's when I saw her.

I recognised her face instantly, clear as day. Even with the black and white tone, I could see that silver hair as if it was radiating from the paper.

The girl from my nightmares.

In the picture she was smiling, far from the tortured soul who'd haunted my dreams, with her bloodied features and bruised eyes.

A shiver raced up my spine. My heart, hammering so much that I could feel the blood throbbing inside my head.

Turning the picture, scrawled on the back, was a handwritten note. I wasn't sure who the author was, could it be the police? A family member? I had no idea but the words burned into my mind like a hot iron rod, branding me.

Theodora Alcott - 1911

Body of nineteen year old Theodora Alcott was discovered in a shallow grave in the forest area of Knightchurch manor.

Miss Alcott had been severely beaten and following post mortem had died due to blunt force trauma to her skull. The girl and her unborn child will be buried this weekend at Cedar Cross cathedral.

Miss Alcotts family ask for privacy while in mourning.

I couldn't move. Turning back to the photograph, the young woman's eyes were haunting. She looked so happy, unaware of what was to come.

The box contained other snippets of articles. One confirming that Carlos Silvaro had confessed to the murder of Theodora and her unborn baby and then a further one stating how he was released following a trial led by his 'close friend and confidant' judge Jonathan Barkley. *He paid his way out. Fuck!*

The book contained more information and records on Jose Silvaro, Ezras grandfather.

Just like his father Carlos and grandfather Leonardo, Jose had been under investigation for the disappearance of *fourteen* women and young girls, all of whom came to work at Knightchurch and just like Carlos, he got off unscathed, without so much as a mark against his name.

Three generations of Silvaro men, each one a suspected killer, and now Andreas and Ezra.

Theodora Alcott was dead. Her life ended in the dark woods, the very place I walked regularly when visiting the lake. The life of her baby, gone just like that.

Tears glazed my eyes. She'd come to me in my dreams, she guided me to the box under the floorboards containing her journal. She wanted her story told as she never got the justice she deserved. Was she trying to warn me? Tell me that I was caught up in a genetic line of psychopaths and that I was destined to the same fate with Andreas and Ezra?

When I closed my eyes, all I could see was Kara's blood shot eyes, staring up to the sky. I wondered what it was that those eyes had seen, minutes before the light was forced out of them.

Dropping to the floor, I closed the file, I'd read enough. Ezra Silvaro came from a long line of serial killers. Was he even aware?

On the floor by the filing cabinet was a pile of what looked like old, browning letters. They must have fallen when the file was taken out.

Grabbing the pile of paper, carefully held together by a fine piece of dirty string, I opened it slowly, pulling out the first letter. It was addressed to the parents of Theodora Alcott. She was trying to communicate with them. I lifted the next letter and then quickly flipped through each one, realising that they were all addressed to Theodora's parents. Not a single one opened.

These were the letters that she'd been sending and thinking that her parents were just refusing to talk to her.

Carlos Silvaro must have been intercepting all the letters. Isolating her slowly before ending her life. The thought caused nausea to erupt inside my gut. I slapped my hand over my mouth to keep from heaving.

"Okay," Summer dropped to my side, pushing the old file to the side and grabbing the pile of letters. "We're gonna put this shit away before someone realises the library key is missing and then you're going to tell me everything. Starting with what the fuck is going on here and what the fuck it has to do with Ezra."

Chapter Twenty Five

Bennett

My skin felt like a million insects were crawling all over it.

Sitting in my room, tucked under the duvet of my bed, I poured out everything that I'd discovered to a wide eyed Summer, who sat there with her jaw practically on the floor.

"Wow! What a fucked up past for just one family." Summer sat, flicking her slender fingers through the tiny, tattered journal of Theodora Alcott.

"Yep, you can say that again."

"Someone clearly didn't want all of the Silvaros skeletons leaking out of the closet if they were hiding that shit in a hidden compartment in the library."

I nodded. "I don't think any of them wanted the skeletons leaking out. Look at how they all literally got away with murder. No one stopped them, any of them. They used the fact that they were a rich and powerful family for... evil."

I still couldn't believe what we'd uncovered, as well as the fact that none of it was anywhere online.

"Imagine though, each generation of your family bore a serial killer. A psychopath. Talk about getting the shit end of the gene pool."

I sat in silence contemplating Summers' words.

"I mean, I guess it explains why Andreas is such a creep and then...Ezra."

"NO!" I wasn't ready for what Summer was about to say next.

"Ezra isn't a killer, he isn't bad. This whole thing is fucked up but... it isn't about genes. No one is born bad, it's taught."

Summer sighed. I could tell her opinion was the polar opposite of mine.

"So what now? You just gonna drop it?"

I inhaled deeply, trying to compress some of the growing frustration inside me.

"I just find it strange that Theodora would haunt my nightmares purely to tell me that Carlos was the one who killed her. Like that can't possibly be the only reason she's been visiting me, Carlos is dead. He's been dead almost a century. Something doesn't add up. I feel like she's trying to tell me that something else is going on here."

"You could be right, something doesn't add up here. Didn't you say that Ezra's sister is missing?"

As the last word left Summers' mouth there was a loud knock on the bedroom door. The sound echoing around the old room.

In a fright, I jumped to my feet, quickly opening the door.

"Hey." On the other side was Caleb, his tight, black t-shirt stretched over his toned pecs sitting perfectly at eye level.

"Hey." The choked reply raised a pinkish hue to my cheeks.

"Andreas and Estelle have called a staff meeting in the dining room. They wanted me to get you both."

I looked to Summer who shrugged, jumping from my bed.

I turned to Caleb, "we'll be right down."

Caleb smiled, flashing his pearly white, perfectly straight teeth before leaving. The twinkle in his eye, mischievous. I could certainly see why Millie had a thing for him. He was certainly hot as hell.

Worry fluttered in my chest as I thought of Millie. I hadn't seen her in a while and after what happened to Kara everyone was on edge. I wondered if I'd see her at the meeting.

As we reached the foyer, everyone was starting to slip into the dining room, I avoided eye contact with Riley and Elaine. Those bitches had it in for me and I wasn't going to give them the satisfaction of a reaction.

The dining room was packed with staff. I scanned the room, relief settling in my stomach as my eyes landed on Millie.

She was peering between the shoulders of the chef and a waiter to get a view of Andreas, who'd taken a seat at the top of the long, oak dining table.

I gave a small wave and she waves back. I made a mental note to spend more time with her when all this was over. Help her build a relationship with Summer. I was sure they'd be great friends.

I felt the eyes on me before I even saw his face as I turned to meet those deep pools of icy blue.

Ezra stood in the corner. The hood of his black hoodie pulled up over his head, casting a shadow over his beautiful face.

Andreas coughed, silencing the room.

"I'm sure you're probably all wondering why I've brought you here today and the reason is we have had information back about the untimely and tragic death of our beloved Kara. The sheriff has reported that, following a post mortem, Kara sadly drowned following alcohol consumption at our Halloween ball."

The whispers began to circulate around the room.

I knew people had heard that I'd been taken in for questioning. Beady eyes stared at me from all directions.

"Now I know that there has been speculation and what not about the incident, but unfortunately the whole thing was just one very tragic accident." He lowered his eyes, glancing at his closed fists before looking back to the team.

"I would appreciate it now if we could put this to bed and move on for the sake of ourselves and Kara. Let her rest in peace and let's get Knightchurch back to how it was before any of this happened. Now I won't keep any of you any longer but like I said, I would like this incident to be put to bed."

With that, Andreas rose from his seat, nodding towards the door where everyone began piling out one after the other. Gossip quietly erupting between them.

"Do you buy it?" Summer asked.

My eyes darted round the room to find Millie but she'd already gone

"I dunno." I shrugged.

Part of me wanted to believe it. The thought that someone had harmed Kara was unsettling and terrifying to say the least, so the fact that it was declared an accident was definitely the best thing to think, considering.

I glanced back at Ezra. His eyes still fixated on me and nothing else. I needed to speak with him. Tell him how I was feeling and what I'd discovered with Summer.

I felt like now I was the one keeping dark secrets and I needed to find out what exactly he knew about his family's history.

Leaving the dining room, the last person I expected to see when I reached the door was Hunter Jackson.

It looked like he was in some kind of heated discussion with Estelle who was trying hard to stand her ground. I had to help her out. The poor woman was going through enough.

"Hunter." I interrupted. He turned toward me, a frustrated expression on his face.

"Bennett." He smiled but I could see a mile away that it was the fakest smile I'd ever seen.

"What are you doing here?" I asked.

Hunter moved from Estelles side and stood face to face with me.

"I'm still looking into the incident involving Kara Valance. I don't buy that this was an accident and I won't be going anywhere until more investigations have been conducted."

I frowned. "Hunter, the sheriff has assured the Silvaros that this was an accident. I'm sure there's other things you could be getting on with."

"Agreed, deputy." His smooth voice slides over me like a stream of silk as I turn to see Ezra standing behind me.

Hunter laughed, his tone mocking. "I'm not going anywhere until I've proved a girl was murdered."

He stared deep into Ezra's eyes. A sinister grin slowly appearing on Ezra's lips.

"It's fine. We have the room." Estelle interrupted, her hand landing on Ezra's shoulder. "Deputy Jackson, if you'd like to follow me, I'll show you to your room. You're welcome to stay until you feel you've erased your concerns."

Hunter smirked. "Thank you Mrs Silvaro."

Hunter and Estelle walked up the stairs towards the north wing as I stood with Ezra.

For the first time, I actually felt like Hunter may be the one in the right. *Fuck what was happening to me?!*

I'd never feared Ezra, never needed to. Did I believe he would hurt me? No, never, but this uncertainty and the secrets surrounding his family was getting too much to ignore.

I turned to face him but before I could say anything, his lips were on mine. His tongue gliding rhythmically over mine before pulling my bottom lip into his mouth. As I pull away, I quickly scan the foyer to see if anyones watching. Ezra, on the other hand, doesn't seem to care at all.

"Let me stay with you tonight?" He asks. His lips caressing along the sensitive rim of my earlobe.

Alarm bells ring as my head tells me spending the night with this man would be madness, but at the same time every cell in my body is on fire with just his touch.

"Fine, but one condition…"

I feel Ezra chuckle against my skin as he presses gentle kisses to my throat.

"And that is?"

"We spend the night in the east wing. We stay in your room."

Ezras head lifts, his eyes meeting mine.

"What brought this on?" He asks, a suspicious glint in those pools of blue.

"I don't want there to be secrets between us. I've never been to the east wing, never seen your room. If whatever this is between us is to carry on… no secrets!"

Ezra hesitates for a while before nodding slowly.

"No secrets."

Tonight I'm going to find out just who the hell Ezra Silvaro really is.

Chapter Twenty Six

Bennett

I'd never stepped foot in the east wing and I didn't really know what I expected it to look like, however walking through the long corridors with Ezra, I realised it was pretty similar to the rest of the house, just more basic.

The walls were free of the garish paintings that decorated the halls of the north wing, and where the curtains framing the windows of the other wings were red, these ones were midnight black.

My mind wondered if Kara had known what Ezra's room was like. He claims nothing happened with her but she sure as hell was persistent, that was a fact.

As we reached his door, he turned the golden door handle, pushing open the door and letting me see inside. The room screamed masculine energy.

The scent was just the same as Ezra, brimstone and citrus. It was intoxicating.

The bed was a deep, navy blue velvet four poster with black posts and black, glossy sheets.

Each side of the bed was framed by black wooden bedside tables and silver orb shaped lamps, sitting neatly upon them.

This room was by far the most modern room I'd seen in the whole of Knightchurch.

A huge rug laid straight in the middle of the floor.

"Make yourself comfortable, little bird."

I perched on the end of the high bed, gliding my hands over the soft, cool silk of the sheets.

Ezra opened up a globe sitting in the corner of the room. Inside sat seven different whiskey bottles. My mouth salivated. A drink was much needed for the conversation that was pending.

As if sensing my anxiety, Ezra lifted the crystal decanter, pouring the amber liquid into the small tumbler and handing it to me.

Taking a large gulp, I savoured the feel of the warm liquid trailing down my throat and soothing the spark in my belly. I need the Dutch courage tonight.

My insides fluttered at the sight of the man before me. He oozed sex in his fitted black tee and dark grey joggers that did nothing to hide his impressive size. The thought brought a flush to my cheeks.

I glanced around the room. "Has anyone ever been in here before? you know, like…"

"Women?"

I smiled awkwardly. "Yes."

Ezra grinned, sitting down next to me on the bed. Leaning forward, elbows on his thighs, he stared down at the whiskey tumbler between his fingers before looking back to me.

"No. At least not by invitation." A look of irritation glazed over his face, making me question whether pushing on that comment was the right thing to do.

"If you're asking if I've ever fucked any of the staff, then the answer is yes…over the years"

A knot tightened in my stomach at his confession. I swallowed the lump of jealousy in my throat.

"However, since the first day I saw you, sitting in the graveyard like some wounded animal, I've never even so much as wanted to breathe in the direction of another woman."

Looking into his deep blue eyes, a rush of warmth flooded through my body, tingling between my legs.

I nodded, but something else flashed briefly over Ezra's face.

"Things haven't always been platonic with Caleb."

My eyes widened at his confession. He said it with such ease, it was definitely not something I was expecting to come from his mouth.

"Oh... okay... are you guys..."

"We're nothing. He's my closest friend. There's no label." Ezra took another gulp of his whiskey.

I nodded, fiddling with the tumbler in my hand.

I didn't feel like he wanted to progress with the subject of Caleb, but for some reason I didn't feel jealous like I assumed I would when he mentioned he'd been intimate with someone else. If anything the thought of Ezra and Caleb together made me feel rather... turned on. I mean they *were* both hot and nothing should surprise me with this man anymore.

"What about deputy Jackson?"

The words caught me off guard. "Sorry what?"

"Has anything ever happened between you and deputy Jackson?"

A laugh escaped my throat, I didn't mean for it to come out as harsh as what it did. "No, Hunter and I...well, we went to the same high school but... I wouldn't even say we were really friends. I think he's just not used to a woman turning him down."

A dark glimmer reflects in Ezra's eyes. "It's lucky that you did turn him down... for his sake."

"And why's that?"

"Because you're mine, little bird, you've been mine since the day you stepped into this god forsaken house and no one touches what's mine. Deputy Jackson does well to understand that."

I swallow hard, not sure if now is the right time to bring up what's plaguing my mind.

"I found out some things. About your family." *This goddamn word vomit.*

Ezra nods, his eyes locked on his tumbler.

"I found a journal. It was hidden in a small box in the room I've been staying in. A woman, she came to me in my dream, showed me where it was." I sounded absolutely bat shit crazy, I knew I did. I expected Ezra to burst out laughing but he didn't, instead his eyes never left the glass.

"I've been hearing noises, coming from the walls, having nightmares, I just... pushed it away until what happened to Kara and... I wanted to find out what was going on here, especially as we were both in the frame for her death."

"Her death was an accident." His words were unyielding. "My father confirmed it with the sheriff. She drowned after the party."

"Your father is hiding something!" I couldn't stop the bitter frustration that was seeping from every pore in my body. "Tell me the truth Ezra, I know that you come from a long line of serial killers. That every generation has bore a... monster." The word lodged in my throat, expelling a taste of acid. "I found some old records, in the library."

He looked up from his glass for the first time.

"Why the fuck are you snooping round the library?"

Suddenly I could feel an intense anger radiating from him.

"I'm sorry but I need to know what's going on."

Ezra runs his large, calloused hands through his raven hair. Lifting the glass, he launches it at the wall.

I watched in horror as the glass shattered into hundreds of thick, shimmering shards. My body jumping involuntarily at the sound.

Suddenly without warning, Ezra pounced on top of me. His solid weight, holding me in place as he pinned my wrists with one of his hands, above my head.

"You want to know the truth, little bird? You want to know what dark and depraved secrets live inside my condemned soul." He trailed his other hand down the V of my neckline and over my breast.

My chest heaved with fear and adrenaline as the icy blue of his eyes morphed into something more sinister, something pitch black.

I nodded, unable to form the words.

"The truth is little bird that every generation of the Silvaros bears a killer. Someone with no control over their urges. Someone with a sickness enrooted into their soul. A sickness engraved into their very DNA."

I listened carefully as the feel of Ezra's breath tickled my lips. Fear and wanting, mixed together in a lethal cocktail inside of me.

"My grandfathers have always given in to their desire to kill. Women have been lured from the village under the guise of a better life at Knightchurch, only to have their life stolen from them to feed the sickness inside the Silvaros."

I close my eyes as Ezra confirms every detail of what Summer and I discovered in the library.

"My piece of shit grandfather Jose was one of the worst. He murdered so many women and used money to cover up his tracks. No one even knows where he hid the bodies. So many families out there with no closure. But it stopped with my father."

Confusion clouded my mind. "What do you mean?"

"My father and I have the sickness, an urge to kill just like the others but we've used our curse for good, at least that's what we told ourselves."

Ezra looks at me, our eyes locked as he prepares to bare his soul.

"I'm a killer Bennett."

I'm pretty sure in that moment that my heart stopped as the words raced through my mind, clouding every other sound.

"I've killed people, lots of people and I've enjoyed it. But the people I've killed, the people my father has killed, they're the stain of society. Paedophiles, child abusers, other killers, evil people. We hunt them out and end them. It ends their reign of terror but it also feeds the urge inside us."

My words are lost, my body numb from the words that are coming from his mouth. I feel like this is all a bad dream and I'm going to wake up at any minute.

"You kill... monsters?" It's the only thing coming from my mouth. I feel like I'm in some weird trance. Some twilight dream.

"We do. My father and I made the choice that no other innocents would ever be harmed by the Silvaro curse."

I scoffed. "Curse? This is not a curse, it's a choice. You don't have to do any of this." My voice, rising now.

Ezra's grip on my wrist tightens. "Oh but we do, little bird. This urge inside us, it's been passed down through the generations, ingrained into our genetic makeup. What more can I say? That I'm destined to remain in this house, a cage that's contained so many years of evil until the day I end up as ash in the cemetery in the forest, rotting with the rest of the damned?!"

"No one is born evil."

Ezra's eyes flash. It's only for a second but I see it.

"Are you so sure about that Bennett?"

With that his mouth was covering mine. Kissing me deeply and with desperation.

I responded, pushing my head up and tasting his tongue. An intoxicating mix of fresh cool mint and sin.

His subtle cologne drifted up my nostrils, forcing my eyelids to flutter in its delicious scent.

How can this feeling inside of me be anything other than utterly and consumingly good?!

His hand remains tightly grasped around my wrists, as the other slides back down over my chest and down to the hem of my knee length, floaty black skirt. He trails his fingers slowly up the inside of my thigh and over my panty covered pussy.

"Danger seems to excite my little whore." He smirks as he pulls my bottom lip into his mouth, biting down gently. "So fucking wet."

In an instant he tugs my panties, ripping them clean off my body. I groan into his mouth as he begins to draw lax circles over my clit, my hips bucking in response wanting… needing more.

He pulls down his joggers, his huge cock rubbing against the centre of my thighs. I want to taste him so badly it's all consuming.

His thoughts are clearly the same as mine as he pushes up off me, standing at the edge of the bed between my thighs.

He pumps his thick, hard shaft twice before I lean forward without a word, placing my tongue on the bottom of his cock and licking up the base in one swift motion.

Circling my tongue around his tip, he lets out a deep groan, his hands tangling into my long, dark hair.

He pushes forward, his cock lodging deep into my throat as he lets out a sharp hiss.

"That's a good girl, take all my cock. Let me fuck that tight little throat."

With that, he begins to thrust himself into my mouth, harder and deeper until it breaks through my gag reflex, saliva dripping from my chin as he begins to relentlessly pick up pace.

"That's it baby, fuck! Just like that." His dirty words spur me on even more as I peer up at him from under my long eyelashes. Tears glazing my eyes at the force of his thrusts.

He gently wipes a strand of saliva from my chin.

"So fucking beautiful."

I continue bobbing my head through more thrusting before I bring my mouth to the tip of his cock, licking away the bead of pre-cum and then sliding my teeth back down the shaft.

"Fuck!" Ezra pants, before tightening his grip on my hair and dragging me up, spinning me around and pushing me down over the bed.

He quickly lifts my floaty skirt above my hips, exposing my firm, round ass, his thumb grazing the sight of his carved initials.

Lifting an arm, he brings the palm of his hand down onto my ass cheek with a loud crack. I cry out in pain, before he gently caresses my cheeks, soothing the sting with his greedy hands.

I desperately begin to grind my bare pussy against the bed as I pant, pushing my ass up begging for more punishment.

Ezra is only too happy to oblige as he slams his hand back down a second time onto my ass cheek. Another low groan escapes from my mouth, my pussy throbbing now with need.

I look over my shoulder to see Ezra stroking his long, hard cock before lining it up at my entrance, teasing the soaking flesh of my pussy.

With a hard thrust of his hips, he slams all the way inside me, bottoming out. I cry out, a heady mix of pain and pleasure making my eyes cross before rolling to the back of my head. I feel my walls tighten around his size.

"Fuck Bennett, your pussys strangling my cock! Fuck that feels amazing."

"Oh my god." The words come out choked as Ezra begins to move, thrusting into me ruthlessly, building my orgasm with every slam of his hips against my ass.

He grips my hair again, pulling my head towards him until my body bows from the bed. With his other hand he reaches around, into my shirt, caressing my breast and pinching the tight, pink nipple.

Our combined panting and carnal moans fill the room. The large gothic windows begin to gloss over with steam.

"Rub your pussy baby." Ezra pants, still fucking me like it's the last thing he'll ever get to do.

I reach down, shamelessly rubbing the tight bundle of nerves between my legs, combining it with Ezra's thrusting until my stomach tightens and my orgasm crests.

I whimper as he pinches and pulls on my erect nipples one last time before sucking his thumb into his mouth and reaching down, slowly working it into my ass. I love yet hate the way my body so easily accepts him.

As he pushes past the tight ring of muscle, the feeling of being completely filled is too much to bear as the most intense and savage orgasm tears through my body.

My pussy clenches fiercely around Ezras cock as a roar rips from his throat and he empties himself deep inside me. His cock throbbing hard as my pussy milks him for every drop.

He drops down on top of me, his chest to my back.
Sweat trickles down the back of my neck and my forehead as we both lay there panting and spent.

I feel the gentle caress of his warm lips as he kisses me softly on my cheek before standing, pulling up his joggers then dropping down next to me on the bed.

The only sound in the room is our collective breathing.

"Thank you."

The words surprise me as they leave Ezras mouth.

"For what?"

"For agreeing to stay with me tonight."

I stare at the intricate art work on the ceiling unsure of what to reply.

Staying with him is all I've ever wanted to do, even when every fibre of my being has told me to run, to get as far away from Ezra Silvaro as I possibly can.

"Did you kill Kara Valance?" I can hardly believe I'm saying the words. I don't know what kind of response I'm hoping for. That he admits it? Would a killer just come out and admit their crime? He's admitted everything else.

"What if I told you that I did? Would you run, little bird."

A chill brushes over my skin, goosebumps prickling, I swallow hard.

"No." My body stills as Ezra turns onto his side before his tongue grazes the edge of my ear.

"Are you afraid? Do you want to run right now?"

"No"

"Good," he whispers, his hot breath caressing my lobe. "Because I'd catch you."

I turn my head as our eyes meet. Electricity coursing through my veins.

Whatever this is between us, it's got a hold on me like nothing I've ever experienced. I don't know when it happened but I'm addicted to the mystery surrounding Ezra, to the danger and the fucking fear. I get off on that shit. Maybe I'm the fucking psychopath too.

"No" A single word left his mouth.

"What?" My eyebrows pinched together in confusion.

"No… I didn't kill her."

His hand gently touch's my cheek, caressing downwards until it meets the buttons of my shirt. In our desperation before, we hadn't even removed our clothes before we had sex.

"Do you believe me?"

His fingers continue to work the buttons of my shirt undone as I reach my arm around the back of his neck and entangle my fingers into his jet black hair.

"I do."

With those two simple words, his mouth was back on mine, hands roaming and lips exploring as we made love over and over again, deep into the night.

After a night free of the horror of my nightmares, I woke to the sight of a peaceful room. The strobe of the morning golden light landing straight on the beautiful sleeping man beside me.

I felt my lips tug into a smile as I watched him sleep peacefully, his lips slightly parted and his chest gently rising and falling ever so softly.

The sheet had dropped down to his waist giving me a perfect view of his gorgeously chiselled six pack.

I'd lost count of the amount of times we'd fucked through the night, in all the positions, yet I still wanted to run my tongue over the hard ridges of his chest and stomach. *Fuck!* He left me with an insatiable appetite, it drove me crazy. I couldn't get enough.

Sitting up and swinging my legs out of the high bed, I pulled one of the light sheets from the bed, wrapping it around my body as I prepared to head to the bathroom for a shower.

The sticky feel of Ezra's cum on my thighs stirs a heat inside me once again. I smile, pushing down the butterflies that start to wriggle low in my stomach and continue to the bathroom.

Just as I reached the door before the en suite, a photograph caught my eye. It sat perfectly placed in the centre of the wall mounted shelf, in a vintage looking silver frame.

Walking closer, I lifted the frame from its placement, staring at the two people in the picture. Ezra and... Millie?

Nausea rolled in my stomach as I swallowed the bile threatening to rise in my throat.

He'd never mentioned her before, I'd never even seen them speak to each other and he had her picture in his fucking room?!

I heard the rustle of bed covers behind me as I turned to see Ezra walking towards me, his eyes focused on the picture in front of me.

"What is this about?" I can feel my voice shake as I ask the question, terrified of the answer.

"That..." suddenly his whole face changes. A sadness glassing his blue eyes and his face paling slightly, "...is my sister... Eleanor."

The pulse in my ear was so loud, it sounded like an earthquake inside my head. My body, frozen to the spot.

"I'm sorry... what." I shook my head, hoping to clear some of the noise and growing fog.

Underneath the picture, engraved into the intricate, silver frame were the initials 'E.A.S' and 'E.M.S.'

"This picture was me and my sister, taken about a month before she disappeared." He pointed to the initials. "E.A.S Ezra Andreas Silvaro and E.M.S... Eleanor Millie Silvaro."

My eyes widened as I wondered if what I was hearing was reality.

"She always called herself Millie, hated Eleanor. Although Millie never really caught on, at least not in the family." A saddened smile touched his lips. "Beautiful isn't she?"

Chilling Goosebumps flared all over my body, from my head to my toes as I tried desperately to process the words that were being said. Acid clawing up my throat.

"Yes." I replied. "She is."

Chapter Twenty Seven

Bennett

No, no, this person is Millie. My friend Millie, nothing more than a worker here, not Eleanor Silvaro. What the fuck?!

None of this was making any sense. Eleanor Silvaro was missing. Had been missing for two years. Millie was right here in this house! Wasn't she?

"You okay?" Ezras voice sounded like it was coming from far away, not right beside me where he was actually standing.

"Yeah I... erm... I'm just not really feeling very well." Running my fingers through my bed knotted hair, I suddenly began to feel extremely lightheaded.

"Here, sit down." He gestures back to the bed, but dark spots were beginning to form in front of my eyes and I was finding it more difficult to breathe by the second.

"I can't, I... I need to go."

Grabbing my clothes from the floor, I quickly threw on my shirt and skirt and fled the room, leaving Ezra standing in just his dark grey joggers.

Running through the corridors, back to the north wing, voices whispered, laughing heckled from the walls. *No, no, no, I wasn't crazy, Millie was real. She was my friend. I saw her!*

Sweat dripped from my forehead as shadows moved across every surface. *No, there wasn't anything there. I'm hallucinating. I must be.*

I didn't even know where Millie's room was, I'd assumed it

was over in the west wing with some of the other staff. Why hadn't I ever bothered to see where she was fucking staying?!

Continuing to run, I collided, head on, into a firm grip.

"Caleb?"

"Hey princess, what's the rush?" He chuckled as I pulled from his hold.

"Millie... Millie, the girl who works here, you know her, she... she had a thing for you! You know... Millie?"

The look on his face confirmed that he thought I'd well and truly lost it.

He shakes his head. "I don't know any Millie babe, I've never met anyone here by that name. The Silvaros had a daughter, Millie was her middle name I think?! That's the only time I've ever heard that name."

Without another thought, I continued to run back to the north wing, dashing inside my room and slamming the door closed.

As I turned, my back hitting the hard wood of the door, I slid down onto the floor, pulling my knees into my chest and desperately trying to calm my breathing.

None of this made sense. Eleanor Silvaro was missing. *For two years.* If Millie was her, then that would mean that she was fucking invisible or some shit and that couldn't be true because people had seen her, hadn't they?

Thinking back, I couldn't remember a time when anyone had had a conversation with both Millie and I when we had been together.

Estelle had seen us in the mud patch in the garden when I was helping Millie, but looking back at it now, she'd only actually spoken to me. I just didn't give it a second thought at the time and then at the Halloween ball, I stood at the back talking to Millie.

My mind flashes back to Kara walking past me at the ball, looking at me like I was crazy, like I was...talking to myself.

"*Freak.*" Her words hadn't phased me at the time but now, just the very thought of it made my blood run cold.

If no one but me could see her, then what the fuck was I seeing? A fucking ghost?

Resting my head in my hands, I had to get a grip on this and think logically. Millie... Eleanor or whatever the hell she was called, was missing. No one had a clue where she was. Ezra and his family seemed to think she was dead. Why would they think that? And if she was really dead and I was seeing some *ghost* then where the hell was she?

This was all just a massive misunderstanding. I didn't believe in horror stories and I sure as hell didn't believe in ghosts.

I'd see Millie and she can confirm I'm not fucking insane and that she's not some spirit or god knows what else and then I can pack my bags and leave this fucking hell hole, once and for all before I end up in a padded cell.

After a night of fucking, I was clearly way past exhausted and in desperate need of a shower.

Entering the bathroom, the free standing bathtub looked more than appealing as I turned on the golden taps and watched the smooth, clear water trail over the marble waterfall feature and into the tub. The steam filling the room and calming me slowly as I inhale deeply.

Dipping my toe into the warm water, I remove my clothes and sink into the liquid bliss.

The water rises up as I lay back, immersing myself into the heat.

I begin to relax straight away. As soon as I'm finished getting my shit together, I'm finding Summer and then the two of us are going to the west wing to find Millie and sort out all this crazy shit.

One thing I was sure of now was that my time at Knightchurch had to come to an end. I was packing my bag and heading back to Cedar Cross. It was something I should have done a long time ago but for some reason I couldn't bring myself to do it. Why?

The answer was too painfully obvious. Ezra Silvaro was my captor.

He might not be holding me prisoner physically but

emotionally he had my heart in a reinforced steel cage and there was no penetrating that shit.

My feelings for him are deeper than physical. It's an urge burrowed within me. Maybe I have a sickness too, just like him, a curse, a desperation and urgency that I'm enslaved to and it fucking terrifies me.

Exhaling, I close my eyes, letting the gentle swish of the water lull me into a sleepy state.

One minute I was laying in calming silence and the next I was dragged under the surface of the water. Liquid rushing into my ears, muffling every sound.

I try to scream but the water felt like it was locking my airways.

Thrashing around, I thrust my arms up to the surface of the water but all of a sudden it was as if the surface had been covered with a sheet of glass.

I could see the blurry light of the bathroom chandelier straight above me but there was no one there yet I couldn't sit up, I was trapped.

My heart is beating erratically as my lungs burn for oxygen but every movement only succeeds in drowning myself faster as water begins to seep inside me.

Just as my vision is about to blacken, a searing pain blasts through my head and I see it, clear as day. A flashback.

Millie. She's thrashing in water, I'm under there with her, she's drowning, her pretty eyes bulging from her beautiful face.

Someone is holding her under as I feel her fight with every fibre of her being. Fighting in vain for her life.

Her hands grappled, clawing at the water as her face contorted in pain. Blood dying the water a deep scarlet. She was hurt.

Suddenly I'm dragged from the vision to other flashbacks, this time of the happy memories of Millie and I, trying to make the roses grow in the flowerbed, spending time laughing and making fun of eachother in my room.

"If you're looking for somewhere to explore, Knightchurch lake is

just through the clearing."

"You had a chance to visit the lake yet?"

"If you ever can't find me, I'll be at the lake."

The lake, the lake, the lake, THE LAKE!

My head crashed through the surface of the bath water as I heaved in oxygen. My throat released a gargled scream as I choked on the air, coughing violently and retching up water.

"SHE'S IN THE LAKE!" The words came out like a bellowing cry as I pulled myself out of the bath.

I fell to the floor, the water pouring over the sides, my legs completely giving up on me as I crawled and finally managed to pull myself up with the towel rail.

Shivering with cold, I didn't even bother to dry as I darted into my room, pulling a loose, navy blue smock dress over my head and running for the bedroom door.

The draft in the hallway chilled me to my bones as I ran, still dripping wet. My teeth clattered together so violently it felt like they were going to break. *Keep it together Bennett, come on.*

I ran past gawking staff members in the corridors who all looked as though I was utterly insane as I fled towards the east wing.

Ezra and Caleb were walking out of his room, heading down the corridor as I ran towards them.

"Bennett?" Ezras arms were outstretched as he saw me running along the hallway.

"She's in the lake... she's in the... outside... in the woods... Millie..." I wasn't making a shred of sense as I gripped Ezras arms, desperate for him to understand. Oh Jesus I was going to throw up. I hunched over as Ezra held me tightly, a look of growing concern on his face.

"Bennett, please, come on baby, breathe. Now tell me what's wrong."

I inhaled deeply, closing my eyes, trying to collect my

composure as I struggled to shift the haunting visions of Millie being forced beneath the surface of the freezing lake. I couldn't see who was pushing her down but I could feel them. I could feel her terror. God they were so strong.

"It's Millie... Eleanor... she's in the lake... Ezra she's in the lake."

My voice broke out into a sob as I dropped to the floor, Ezra gently releasing my arms, his face, a vacant, white sheet of despair.

Caleb knelt down beside me. "Bennett, what are you talking about babe?" His brows knitted in confusion.

I struggled to breathe and calm myself as I inhaled through the rapidly flowing tears.

"Eleanor, I saw her, I've been seeing her... god I know this sounds crazy," I wasn't even sure I was believing the words that were coming out of my own mouth. "She's in this house, at least I thought she was, I don't know what I've been seeing but your sister, she's in the lake."

Ezra's face, now hardened, was turned towards me, his eyes searing into me like lasers.

"She can't be in the fucking lake." His voice sounded pained.

Fear took over me. Did he not believe me? I wasn't even sure what I'd seen, what I was saying at this point.

"What's going on?"

The voice came from behind me as I turned and looked up to see Hunter approaching. He dropped down onto the floor beside me and Caleb.

"Bennett, babe what's going on? Did he hurt you?"

His gaze shot upwards to Ezra, standing above us, a look of accusation in his eyes. Ezra returned the threat with a snarl.

"What? No, no he hasn't done anything. Hunter, please, Mil... Eleanor Silvaro is in the lake. She came to me Hunter, her body's in the lake."

It was the first time I'd said the word *body* out loud. It was like by saying it, I was confirming she was dead. That there was no chance she'd be coming home to her family. There was no more hope left.

Hunter nodded. "Ok Bennett, it's all going to be okay. I'm gonna call in the team, we'll get the lake trolled. See what we can find." He rubbed my back and in that moment all I wanted was for Ezra to be the one sitting beside me. Not Hunter or Caleb.

Ezra stood, running his hand through his messed up hair. All of a sudden he grabbed me by the wrist, yanking me onto my feet, his grasp almost painful, bruising my pale skin.

"Are you sure about this?" His eyes searched mine, almost like he hoped what I was saying really was a fabrication.

I nodded, a single tear escaping my eye. "Yes."

That one word. A basic whisper.

Ezra turned to Hunter. "Call your team. Now!"

It wasn't long before the whole forest was flashing with the sight of cop cars. Investigators and divers worked tirelessly to find traces of Eleanor Silvaro in the lake.

I stood, shaking on the embankment. Ezra by my side. I leaned into his frame in the hope of stealing some of his heat.

I needed something right now. I'd never felt so broken in my entire life. But he remained stoic. His walls firmly up as he stared at what I assumed was a homicide team, raking through the dirt and debris of the great Silvaro lake.

"Sir, over here. We've found something." I heard the words but I wasn't prepared for what was to follow.

We were too far back to see what they were looking at, but I knew what it was without even having to see it up close.

A body was pulled from the water. The police acted quickly, sorting body bags and taping off the area, the way they had with Kara. Within days, two girls had been found. Within metres of each other.

I heard the roar of pure grief before I saw her as Estelle broke down into Andreas' arms as they stood on the embankment. The raw pain was almost tangible. I couldn't hold back my own sobs.

Hunter walked towards Ezra and I.

"A body has been found. A woman. We have reason to believe that is that of Eleanor Silvaro, though we're yet to officially confirm."

Ezra nodded, not saying a word. Turning, he began to walk back to the house.

Hunter looked to me but before he had a chance to say a word, I ran towards the direction that Ezra had left.

"Ezra, please I'm sorry."

He stopped dead in his tracks. "Did you really see her?"

The words take me aback. "Yes."

He runs his large hand over his face. "Fuck! Why didn't she come to me?"

My eyes dropped to my battered *Doc Martens*. "I don't know." Guilt washed over me. "I'm so sorry Ezra."

He nodded. A defeated look on his face. "I knew she was dead. We all did. It was only a matter of time before they found her. I guess you just live with this stupid, fucking hope that it won't be true. That she'll just rock up one day, being the pain in the ass she always was."

I bite down hard on my bottom lip. "Ezra…"

He places his hand against his face as the tears fall.
In that moment, the cold, terrifying, angry Ezra Silvaro is gone and in its place is this vulnerable, beautiful man.

Ezra may think his soul is damned. That he's sick. Cursed. A stain on society. But what I see before me is not a psychopath. It's a misunderstood man. A man in heartbreaking pain. Seeing someone so powerful, a wall of steel crumble, makes me ache to my very core. He was no Carlos Silvaro, no matter how much he believed he was.

Wrapping my arms around his neck, he leans into me as I let him literally cry on my shoulder.

His warm lips find my neck, kissing gently, his lips smearing his tears against my skin. I turn to face him, my lips meeting his. I taste the salt of his tears on my tongue as it collides with his in gentle strokes. This kiss is not like the hungry, selfish kisses we've shared before. This one is delicate, loving and real.

"Bennett…"

"It's okay," I say. "You don't need to say it."

He stares into my tear glazed eyes for what feels like forever. I'm in love with this man, I know that now for certain, but the thought of him saying it to me terrifies me. I don't know what the fuck is wrong with me.

Gripping my hand, he squeezes gently as he leads me through the woods, back to the house.

Chapter Twenty Eight

Bennett

Things changed in the days that followed. After a formal identification, the body was confirmed to be that of Ezra's sister, Eleanor Silvaro.

Detectives swarmed the dark wood, searching for anything that would point to how and why Eleanor died.

Talk of digging up more of the Silvaros land yet again, circulated amongst the cops and the staff at the old Manor House.

Whispers about officers planning to scour the cemetery and open up old homicide cases were rife within the air, and my quiet, perfect little job at Knightchurch was morphing into my very own horror movie.

Millie had been found with several stab wounds but the cause of death had been confirmed as drowning.

This in itself took a horrifying toll on the Silvaros, but it was the way she was discovered that really affected Ezra.

Eleanor's body had been weighed down by large bags of rocks. Her body bound tightly to them. The weight had pulled her to the bottom of the lake and over time, she had become entangled in thick vines beneath the surface.

Hunter seemed to be working tirelessly between Cedar Cross and Knightchurch and suggested that Kara's case may also be reopened due to the discovery of Eleanor's body.

The days were excruciating for Ezra as the cops trolled the

lake, day and night, until it was concluded that there were no more bodies or evidence left in the lake.

Andreas had desperately tried to conceal what had happened from the press down in the village, claiming his family were experiencing enough grief following the death of Eleanor, but Hunter was becoming more ruthless by the day, refusing to leave the house and adamant that this would be the final piece of the puzzle that would put the Silvaros away for good.

All I wanted was to be there for Ezra. Speculation was mounting as to whether or not the Silvaros were involved in Eleanor's death but I knew in my heart that he wasn't responsible for any of this.

He may think he's a monster and most would say he was, but I could see the love he bore for his sister every time he said her name. There was no way he could be responsible for this.

Estelle was inconsolable for the following days. Andreas called for a doctor to come to the house who was keen to prescribe even more medication.

She refused to leave her room as Riley, Elaine and I took her food and supplies every day.

Some days she'd scream and throw things at the wall and only Andreas could calm her.

Ezra avoided visiting her, he was facing too many of his own demons.

After searching for Summer following the trolling of the lake, I was surprised when Andreas informed me that her mother had taken sick and she'd returned to her home village of Briar, several miles away.

She'd never said anything, never mentioned that her mother was even ill at all. I would have thought that she would have at least let me know that she was leaving, left a contact number or anything but there was nothing.

Thick snow hammered against the window panes as I lay in Ezra's bed. He'd asked if I'd stay with him in his wing following what had happened and to be honest the last thing I wanted was to be on my own.

I never saw anything more of Eleanor, or Millie as I will always know her, following the discovery of her body.

I suppose it made sense that she had come to me to help show me where she was and find peace finally, and now I was no longer needed.

I hoped with everything inside of me that she'd finally found the peace that she deserved but my heart ached for the friend I'd lost.

Ezra and Caleb had left for some kind of business they had to attend to. I knew it was bad. That it would involve things I never even wanted to think about, but I pushed down the feeling of dread inside me to remind myself that they were out there ending the lives of people who were evil and needed to be stopped.

I'd spoken to Ezra about giving up this life but he claimed it was the only thing that would help keep control of this sickness as he called it.

Pulling on my large, grey padded jacket and red scarf, I headed out to the gardens.

The large open spaces looked even more striking in the winter than what they did in the sunlight.

A film of crystal white covered the once plush, green land and tiny, thin icicles danced on the trees like delicate wind chimes.

It was a beauty you could never capture. Not in a picture or a postcard or anything. Pure perfection.

The chill from the still falling snow bit at my face as I pulled my bright red scarf higher over my mouth.

Down the steps. I glanced at the flowerbed that Millie had loved so much. The patch of old, decrepit soil that refused to birth anything, hidden under a layer of sparkling white. Until suddenly I saw it.

Breaking through the soft, fluffy snow, was a red rose bush. A rose bush growing so strong, even in the punishing winter conditions.

My breath hitched as a single tear left my eye, leaving a freezing trail down my cheek in its wake.

A smile tugged at my lips as I stared at the beautiful flowers, glowing blood red amongst the white.

"Goodbye Millie. I'll miss you."

And with that, I pulled the hood of my jacket over my head and walked back inside the house.

Hunter was storming through the foyer as I arrived back inside, cursing under his breath at his cell phone.

"How is it, that in the whole of this god damn house, the only connection to the outside world is one lousy landline phone from about seventy years ago?!"

I stayed silent. I wanted Hunter to leave Knightchurch, although now Eleanor had been found, on her own land, it wasn't looking good for the Silvaros.

Andreas had brought in one of the most expensive lawyers in the country, and of course a family friend, to help keep the cops off his back but by this point, everyone had him down as the number one suspect in Eleanor's death and now potentially Karas, which was looking less and less like an accident everyday.

"Bennett." *Fuck!*

"Hunter." I force a smile.

"I'm heading down to the sheriff's department later today, I just wanted to make sure you're going to be okay, up here by yourself... with him."

I already knew he was referring to Ezra. I struggled to contain my pent up sigh of frustration. Instead I settled on an eye roll.

"Hunter, I'm fine. Seriously you go do your job, you must be stressed right now."

Hunter scoffed. "Two young girls have been found dead. One was murdered years ago and hidden away. I just want to get to the bottom of what the fucks going on in this place."

I nod. *Likewise.*

"Look Bennett, please keep this to yourself but there's a witness that has come forward."

My eyes widened in surprise. "A witness?"

"Yes, she wouldn't come forward at first. She's been hiding

away in a nearby village, not far from Cedar Cross. Her mother says she's been a complete recluse. Refusing to see or speak to anyone until now."

My heart battered against my chest. "Who is she?"

"A former employee of Knightchurch, Madeline Korrman." Hunter's expression darkens as a shiver races up my spine. "She says while she was working for the Silvaros, she was attacked."

Chapter Twenty Nine

Bennett

Hunter left promptly after telling me about Madeline Korrman, the woman who claims she was attacked while working at Knightchurch, just over a year ago.

He promised he'd be back as soon as he could, but my head was spinning and the only person I wanted to be near was Ezra.

The whole day seemed to glide by in slow motion but there was no sign of Ezra whatsoever.

This particular job must have been a messy one and with the torment he was going through, the thought of what he was up to terrified me to my bones. Whoever they were after wouldn't be getting an easy ride that was for sure.

Laying in the cool silk sheets of Ezra's bed, I began to wonder just what I was getting myself involved in. Could I be happy in the arms of a killer? Even if it was a killer trying to make the world a better place.

Eventually I slept after tossing and turning for hours. The net was closing in on Andreas and anxiety was racking my bones. My dreams were haunting and unsettling but luckily by the next day, the dreams were no longer remembered.

Hunter hadn't returned to Knightchurch either. I realised that he must have been more tied up with the new witness in the case than he first expected, as after knocking for a good ten minutes on his bedroom door, there was no answer.

By midday, Ezra walked into the house. Caleb was nowhere to

be seen but Ezra looked exhausted, like he hadn't slept the whole night.

I jogged down the staircase to meet him.

His strong arms gripped me in a tight bear hug.

"You okay?" I didn't want to ask about what had taken so long, his life was new to me and I didn't yet know how to react to everything he had told me.

"I'm fine, but I'd feel even better between your thighs."

Heat pooled in my core as my thighs involuntarily clenched.

He kissed me deeply, inhaling as though he was trying to consume me completely. A deep need zapped through me.

"Come on, let's go, I need to take a shower."

He takes my hand and slowly leads me up the staircase and down the corridor towards the east wing.

His mind and body look drained and I can't decide if it's after a night of killing or the grief he still carries so heavily on his shoulders. I settled on a combination of the two.

I haven't even got through the door fully before Ezra is keen to resume what we started down stairs. His hands tangle in my hair as his mouth joins mine, tongues exploring.

He takes my hand in his rough, calloused palm without a word and leads me into his en suite, turning on the shower faucet and gripping the back of his shirt before tugging it over his head.

As steam begins to fill the room, I stare into Ezra's heated gaze. Those blades of ice melting before me.

Slowly, he grabs the hem of my black, loose T-shirt and pulls it over my head, before kneeling in front of me and slowly sliding down my leggings and panties.

Then his mouth is back on mine, kissing me with even more urgency before gliding this tongue down the side of my throat and onto my chest.

His hands drift over the top of my lacy, red bra as he squeezes my breast, his fingers sipping inside the cup and teasing my sensitive nipple. I moan louder than expected, which only spurs him on more as he pulls the material of my bra down and takes my small pink bud into his warm, wet mouth. The sensation driving me wild.

I grab the belt of his jeans, tugging it free, and pushing the jeans downwards, followed by his boxers revealing his straining cock already glistening with his pre- cum on the tip.

My hand wraps around his hard length and I pump him a few times as I feel his fingers unclip my bra and toss it to the side.

Once we've shedded all our clothes, he pushes me into the force of the spray, steam encasing both of us.

I force a deep breath as I stare at his god-like body, all hard lines and ridges. All I can think about in that moment is telling him to take me, hard and fast against these very tiles.

My breath hitches and I notice a grimace on his face as his fingers brush over his initials on my hip.

He presses into the healing wound, opening it slightly as I hiss through my teeth, a small trickle of blood mixing with the flowing water and swirling down the drain.

The sting forces tears to build behind my eyes but the pain only succeeds in turning me on even more, my pussy now throbbing under the gentle assault of the spray.

Ezra drops to his knees and glides his tongue over the wound, lapping up the droplets of blood as his fingers gently work their way up my inner thigh and between the delicate folds of my begging pussy. My thighs tighten around his palm.

Standing again he presses his knee between my legs, opening them wider to gain better access. I whimper as he suddenly slams two fingers deep into my core, adding in a third before finger fucking me wildly.

I slump against the cold tiles as he presses himself against my body, his mouth pressing against my ear.

"Fuck Bennett, I've needed you so fucking badly today."

He continues to ram his fingers inside me at a rapid rate, my slick wet heat coating his digits.

My head drops back as my hips grind into his palm. As my orgasm crests, he gently retracts his fingers, sliding them between his lips.

"I can't get enough of you little bird, you stir a thirst in me that I can't fucking quench."

"More!" my words come out breathy and desperate as my body begs for his touch. I need him like I need oxygen in my fucking lungs.

I've never felt an addiction like this, more potent than any shitty drug I ever got my hands on at Delilah's. This was one high that I couldn't stop chasing, no matter how far the drop would be.

Ezra reaches round grabbing my ass and squeezing, his tongue lapping the droplets of water racing down the skin of my throat. He spins me around, pressing his solid form into my back, his cock hard and ready.

My tits press against the tiles, the slick feel against my nipples, provoking a low groan from my throat.

Lifting my leg, Ezra lines himself up at my entrance and begins pushing into me. I gasp at the intrusion as I begin to stretch around him. Desire building up in the pit of my stomach. The sweet pain of being filled by him, all consuming.

He lets out a loud groan as he forces his cock all the way inside me, making me cry out.

I feel myself clench around him as he grunts in satisfaction before starting to jackhammer into me.

The water pours down between us as the cubicle is filled with the sounds of wet skin slapping against skin and our collective moans of ecstasy.

As he reaches round and begins circling my clit, I slowly begin to lose my mind.

His gentle touch becomes more vigorous and soon he's bucking up into me like his life depends on it. My name leaving his mouth in a mix of primal grunts and erotic hisses.

Finally I begin to reach the edge as I bite down on my lower lip, breaking the skin and tasting the coppery tang of my blood on my tongue mixing with the water.

With one hard thrust, I'm screaming as my orgasm tears through my body, shattering my heart and soul. Ezra quickly follows, slamming his hips against my ass as he growls, emptying his seed deep inside me, leaving me exhausted and dazed.

I stay plastered against the tiles, panting as Ezra begins to trail gentle kisses down my cheek and the side of my neck.

As he pulls his semi hard cock from my swollen pussy, his cum trails down the inside of my thighs, the water rising it clean away.

Ezra turns grabbing the shampoo bottle as he slowly begins to wash my hair while I pick up the shower gel and glide my hands over his smooth, inked skin.

The feel of him, helping me bathe, more sensual than any fuck I've ever had in my life. This man is fucking unreal.

When we've finished up, Ezra turns off the faucet and we both step out of the cubicle, drying off and slipping into fresh clothes. I'd left some in Ezra's room in the following days after Eleanor's body had been discovered.

The rest of the day we spent laying on the bed, talking about Eleanor and what she was like as a child. Having known her for a short while, it was heartwarming to hear of how she loved gardening and wildlife and how she enchanted everyone around her.

I could believe every word. Millie - as she was to me - was a true diamond in the short time she'd been around.

I told Ezra about her crush on Caleb, giggling to myself at how Millie would have killed me for telling her brother about her little secret.

He laughed, saying she was out of Caleb's league and there was no way he'd have allowed her to date him. I knew she would have wrapped him around her little finger though. That was the kind of charm Millie seemed to have.

We lay together, staring up at the black, crystal chandelier above Ezras bed in silence until I couldn't hold the words in any longer.

"Ezra, she was found on Knightchurch grounds."

Ezra sat up, his piercing eyes directly on mine.

"Yes, I know."

I follow him, sitting upright and tucking my knees into my chest.

"I know you don't want to hear this but after what you told me about your... urges!"

His glare darkened, rage coating his pupils. "I didn't hurt my own sister."

"I know... but your dad..."

"My dad would never harm his own daughter. She was his life."

I sighed, nothing made sense.

"Bennett, I told you about the long line of killers that I'm descended from, I trusted you enough to admit that I was the one with the sickness, I was the one who needed to kill. But I also told you that myself and my father would never harm innocents. That's not who we are. We wanted to use the Silvaro curse for some kind of good. Here look at this..."

He jumped to his feet, pulling back the giant rug on the floor, revealing what looked like a trapped door.

"Down there, at the end of all the grimy tunnels beneath, lies a soundproof room. That's where all my kills are held until it's their time, then I take them far away to be disposed of."

I stare in horror at the sealed entrance.

"You know all my secrets now. I don't know why the fuck my sisters body was in our lake but I do know that when I find out who did it, I'm going to fucking destroy them!"

His neck flushed with the rage he was trying to contain. Being within metres of a confessed serial killer should be terrifying to most, but I knew, I knew he'd never hurt me.

"A girl has come forward, to speak to Hunter and the other officers on the case. She claims she was attacked at Knightchurch, her name is Madeline Korrman."

I knew I'd said too much already, broken Hunters trust but I was in love with Ezra and I wanted to help him as much as I could.

"Madeline Korrman? She was a compulsive liar. She only

worked here briefly and accused one of the waiters of sexual harassment. We all believed her until she confessed that she'd made it all up because he'd spurned her advances. The man was gay, in love with one of our other waiters. She almost ruined his life."

My lips parted in shock. I'd need to give all this information to Hunter, when he eventually decided to come back to the house, although I was in no hurry for him to return.

"If you say your dad had nothing to do with Kara or Eleanor's death then I believe you. But please Ezra, something just doesn't add up. We need to know for sure, he wasn't involved."

"Fine, then we search his room. Tonight. Him and my mother are going out. They've been invited to one of the charity balls they've been donating to and wouldn't usually go except now he thinks after everything that's happened, he should show his face. Strange really if you ask me. So we go tonight and put an end to this."

I swallow the lump in my throat. I pray to god that I'm right about this because if I'm not, I'm staring straight at the only alternative killer, and the thought of that truth, kills me more painfully than he ever could.

Chapter Thirty

Ezra

There was always going to come the day when the Silvaro secret was revealed.

I made it my goal in life that the curse would end with me. I had always had no intention of marrying, of reproducing and carrying on this line of poison.

My father and I were different. We didn't kill on impulse the way our ancestors had. We were always in control and we never, ever murdered innocents. That was just an unspoken rule.

I always cleaned up my shit away from the house. I'm guessing so did my ancestors as the missing victims were apparently never found.

I was finally in a position where this line of insanity was coming to an end and now someone had taken my sister from me and worse still, she had been on our land the whole goddamn time.

I remembered the weekend she went missing all those years ago. I was away with Caleb. Eleanor never knew about the family history, the secret. She was untainted, pure, and myself and my father wanted to keep it that way.

She didn't have the sickness. She didn't have a single bad bone inside her body.

I'll never forget as kids, the day she found a stray cat lingering in the woods. God knows how the fucking thing even got there but it was cut up badly, probably from being attacked by a fox or some shit, but Eleanor wouldn't let it go alone.

She brought it back to the house and hid it in the stables. I was the only one she told, she begged me not to tell our parents. She could have got a fucking disease or anything from that rabid thing but she didn't care, as long as the cat got better. That was the kind of person she was.

Bennett was like that fucking stray cat, the day I found her in the cemetery. Now I know why Eleanor got so attached to the damn thing.

The day I returned after tying up some loose ends with Caleb, dad had told me she was missing. The cops were informed but told to keep it on the downlow incase it was some fucking ransom shit that was going on.

After a few months, I started to give in and admit to myself that she probably wasn't coming back.

The cops always tell you that the longer someone is missing, the less chance they have of coming back alive. Now it was confirmed. I just couldn't work out how the fuck she was found in our lake.

Bennett has suspicions. She always had about my father. But I know he wouldn't harm Eleanor.

My family line cleared all traces of their crimes, paying their way out of the consequences.

I felt for the families of the countless innocents that had suffered and lost their lives at the hands of the Silvaros but I would put an end to it. An end to the reign of terror. That's why I agreed, with my parents, to hide away all the reports that have been stashed in our library over the generations.

Medical records, newspaper articles, all the shit my family has collected and hidden away over the years so no one knew what we were. Demons in fucking human form.

I still couldn't belive Bennett had found the fucking hidden drawer compartment in the library. My little bird was a fucking snoop and I'd punish her with my cock for that later, but right now I need to find out what happened to my sister.

I know I won't rest until her killer is six feet under with

some of their limbs missing, and even though I think Bennett is barking up the wrong tree with her obsession with my father, I'm willing to help her and get to the bottom of this fucking nightmare.

My parents had finally left the house. I was glad that my dad had managed to persuade my mom to go to the charity gala. 'Save face' he'd said. He was a fucking recluse, I had no idea why he agreed to go but my mother was suffering. She was popping pills from dusk till dawn and then some, so the fact she was getting out actually made me hopeful that things might improve. It was doubtful, following the discovery of her murdered daughters body, but god I clung onto that hope.

I'm assuming the fact that Madeline Korrman has come crawling out of the woodwork is impacting my fathers decision to show his face more. Who knows why she's come from under her rock now. Probably for financial gain. I sense some shitty blackmail letter coming our way very soon.

Opening the door to my parents room, I was hit with the overwhelming stench of my mothers expensive perfume. The room was as immaculate as I remembered it.

I lived in the same house, yet I never came in here. Not since I was a small boy. Nightmares would cause me to run from my room in the east wing, and snuggle under the covers in my mothers arms.

I used to dream that the walls were whispering. *Fucking insane I know!* Sometimes it would get so loud that I'd force the pillow over my ears and sing one of my favourite songs until it went away. It never did. Not until I ran to my mothers bed and she held me tight, stroking my hair and telling me it was just a silly nightmare.

I don't hear the whispering anymore, my nightmares are of a different kind now. I'm the monster under your bed. I'm the demon haunting your dreams.

"We need to check everywhere." Bennett is frantically searching through my parents' drawers.

"What exactly are we hoping to find? We'd have more luck

heading to Cedar Cross and letting them know that if any of them is harbouring a murderer, they're about to face their worst fears. Someone knows who did this."

Bennett doesn't look up from the rummaging she continues to do as if she's completely disregarding what I've said.

I turn to the drawers on the other side of the room and start to sift through the contents. Clothing, old anniversary cards from my father to my mother, more fucking pills that my mother has been stashing, probably for a rainy day.

That's when I noticed it. A thin piece of material sticking out of the back of the drawer. It's so slight that I almost miss it but when I pull it, I notice it's coming from behind the drawer itself.

Pulling out the drawer, I tore, what looked like a white dress, from the back.

As the material slowly slid out of the darkness of the back of the drawer, I heard a gasp from behind me, Bennett was at my side in a flash.

"That's...that's Millie's dress... the one she wore at Halloween."

I didn't understand her words but the dress was white, decorated with tiny blue flowers. I recognised it instantly as one of Eleanor's favourite dresses. She'd worn it so many times, it was a present from my father for her birthday...and it was covered in deep, dark red blood. *Old blood.*

Slash marks destroyed the fabric, dirt staining the white along with the blood.

My heart pounded in my chest. My lungs restricting. An intense burning, forming deep inside my stomach. Pure unadulterated rage. Why the fuck was Eleanor's dress hidden at the back of my parents drawer?

"He did it, didn't he?" Bennett was starting to breathe heavily like she was starting to hyperventilate. She backed away from the drawer.

"Calm down, we need to find out how the fuck this got here."

Suddenly Bennett started screaming, her hands covering her ears as if she's in pain.

I drop the dress, running to her. "Bennett, baby what's wrong?"

She continued gripping her ears. "The noise. Ezra, the walls. The whispers are so loud. Pleeeease Ezra, make it stop."

Chills erupted over my body for the first time in years. *The whispers.*

I couldn't hear a thing as she thrashed out of my hold and stumbled towards the door.

I grabbed Eleanor's blood stained dress from the floor and followed Bennett, through the door, from the room.

She'd let go of her ears now but she was running, charging down the halls.

"BENNETT, WHAT THE FUCK ARE YOU DOING?"

I shouted to her but she continued to recklessly run, now as if she was trying to catch something.

"The voices, Ezra, they're moving." She sounded like a raving lunatic but I'd heard the whispers in the walls before. I knew them all too well.

Chasing after her, she headed through the corridors and down the stairs. The foyer was empty of staff, most had been given the night off, as she raced into the kitchen and through a small, wooden back door.

No one ever used the rickety, old door. It only opened to broken stairs that led to an empty basement. A basement that hasn't been used in years due to the fact the flooring on the ancient staircase wasn't safe to use.

Bennett didn't seem to care as she raced down the stairs, the wood groaning beneath her feet as I followed closely behind.

Reaching the bottom, I tugged on the string to switch on the old, yellow bulb, illuminating the room.

Bennett gasped and pure fucking horror rushed through my veins as we came face to face with a small cramped cage, one so rancid it wasn't even suitable for an animal...and there in the middle, bound and gagged was Hunter Jackson and Summer Edwards.

"Hunter, Summer." Dashing to the bars, Bennett stuck her

tiny hand through them as I ran to help.

Hunter's wide eyes were trained on me as he strained to get his mouth close to Bennett's hand so she could rip off the duct tape that covered his lips.

In one swift pull, he cried out as she tore the tape away, the skin of his lips almost going with it.

Panting frantically, Hunter tried desperately to pull against his restraints. Both hands tied behind his back with cable ties and his feet bound together, the same as Summer.

"Bennett, you have to get out of here, go, get the cops and you..." he looked at me with venom in his stare. "Stay the fuck away from her."

"Hunter, no, we know what's been happening here. Ezras here to help, we're going to get you both out and then we're going to make sure the cops know that Andreas..."

"Bennett, no! Madeline Korrman, she came to the sheriff's department, she told us about her attack. It wasn't a man who attacked her... Bennett it was a woman."

I froze, my feet rooted to the spot. Bennett shaking her head in confusion.

"So pleased you both could join the party."

The chilling voice came from behind me, the familiar silvery tone ringing in my ears. A voice I'd known my whole life.

Turning, I come face to face with the barrel of a .357 magnum caliber revolver.

Her eyes bore into my soul. Cold and calculated, like nothing I've ever seen before.

"Mother?"

Chapter Thirty One

<u>Bennett</u>

Everything suddenly seemed like it was moving in slow motion in some parallel universe. The air is so thick you could slice it.

Estelle stands before Ezra, the end of a gun pointing straight at his head.

I stare into her cold, emotionless face. Her once kind eyes, now black as asphalt.

I'd seen guns before, at Delilah's. A lot of the customers there were shady as fuck so guns were just a given a lot of the time. But I'd never been face to face with one. This was a whole different ball game.

"What the fuck?!" Ezra's face looked pained and confused as he stared at his mother. Not a single shred of fear breached his features, only complete and utter betrayal.

"You know, I wondered how long it would take you to figure things out Bennett." Estelles words were venomous, calculated, gone was the silvery voice with the sweet, timid undertones. It was like I was staring at a completely different human being as she looked over at me briefly.

I swallowed hard, my breathing shallow as I stared at her, my mouth refusing to form a single word, feeling more dry than the Sahara desert.

"You were always sticking your nose in where it didn't belong. Trying to see if I was being abused by my husband. Searching in my library. You just couldn't drop it could you?! Of course, *you* weren't supposed to be involved, my beautiful boy." She turned her gaze back to Ezra. "But what can I say, you just couldn't stay away from the little witch could you?!"

Ezra snarled. "What the fuck is this about?"

Estelle smirked, tilting her head sinisterly to the side. Andreas appeared behind her and with him three more men.

They were all dressed in suits, their large frames intimidating and the look in their eyes told me that they definitely weren't here to help us out.

Estelle motioned the gun towards the door of the basement. "The ballroom. Now. All of you. And if you make a single sound to alert anyone, you're all dead."

Ezra led the way, as I followed, keeping my eyes trained firmly on the gun.

I could hear the clicking of keys and the lock on the rusty cage as Andreas freed Hunter and Summer. The binds on their feet severed, but the ones on their wrist remained fastened tightly in place.

Hunter was torn from the cage with the collar of his shirt by one of the men who stood by Andreas and Summer was dragged by her bound wrists by one of the others.

She squealed as he gripped her wrist so tightly her hand began to turn purple.

"Get your fucking hands off her." Hunter roared at Summers' captor.

A brutal punch to the jaw from the man holding on to his coller silenced him, causing him to hunch over, spitting bright red blood onto the basement floor.

"Fuck sake Zora, we have to clean that," snarled Andreas in annoyance.

The man, Zora, didn't seem to give a shit as he yanked Hunter back up and proceeded to drag him up the broken, creaky stairwell and out of the basement.

The short walk to the ballroom was probably one of the most terrifying walks of my life.

Estelle had hidden Summer in the decaying basement, made everyone believe that she had gone home, and Hunter? He'd obviously come back to Knightchurch after the interview with Madeline Korrman. What the fuck happened?

The hallways of the house were shrouded in darkness. The only light was the gentle glow of candles sitting in dusty, antique candelabras. Now I had an idea how inmates on death row felt when they walked towards their fate on execution day. Except I didn't have a fucking clue what my fate held at all.

Arriving at the dark, empty ballroom. Summer and Hunter were pushed towards Ezra and I as we stood in the middle of the vast, open dance floor.

Two of the guys, Zora and the one who had held Summer stood by the exit blocking us in as Andreas and the final suited asshole stood next to Estelle.

Ezra grabbed my hand, squeezing, trying to reassure me that everything was going to be alright, but the pounding in my chest and the dizziness swirling in my skull were telling me that couldn't be further from the truth.

"Is someone going to tell me what the fuck is going on?" Ezra bellowed. His rage was burning as he hissed through his tightly clenched teeth.

"Well darling, let's just say you and that nosey little cunt ruined our lovely evening." Estelle threw me an evil smile, cruelty radiating from her face.
How did I never see it before? Was I really that naive to believe someone was something so different to what they actually were?

"What's wrong? Didn't have a good night at the charity gala mother?" Ezra sneers with sarcasm.

Estelle laughs, the very sound sending chills down the back of my skull. "Do you really think your father and I would be seen dead at a charity gala? You're more stupid than I give you credit for Ezra... no, me and your father were at a business liaison with Henrik here." She points to the greying, broad chested man standing next to Andreas. "Henrik here owns an exclusive and very expensive elite torture club with Zora and Niall over there.

He was hoping to get his hands on some 'disposable property' that he could chain up for clients, and is willing to pay a hefty sum. It's amazing how far people will go when they have so much money that nothing can satisfy them, and our little Summer here was the perfect candidate." She smiles at Summer, who winces under the duct tape still covering her mouth.

Henrik smiles, his yellowing teeth now on display. I swallow hard to contain the roll of nausea passing through me.

He runs his disgusting, wet tongue over his decaying upper teeth as he stares at Summer.

"She'll fetch a fine price. Our men always like to go for the pretty, young girls. Hearing their screams just hits differently."

I could see Summer trembling in the corner of my eye as Henrik stared at her like a ravenous hyena. Anger coursed through my blood.

"Why the fuck would you be at somewhere like that?" Barked Ezra, confusion and fury tarnishing his face.

"Because that's what the Silvaros do, it's who we are. You know that better than anyone. We have an urge. A deep tarnish within our DNA. A killer in each generation. There's no escaping our destiny."

This woman was literally insane.

"But dad and I were putting an end to all that madness. We were killing to rid society of evil. We were…"

"What would he know?" Estelle interrupts, looking in disgust at Andreas, who, for the first time, had a look of pleading in his eyes. "He isn't even a Silvaro."

Ezra's brows furrow in confusion. "Yes he is, he's the son of Jose Silvaro."

Estelles laughter is like thunder throughout the whole ballroom. "No he isn't!…" Her face turned murderous, dark shadows enveloping the cold glassiness of her eyes. "I'm Jose Silvaros … daughter."

What the absolute fuck?!

Ezra's eyes widen. "His *daughter?*"

"Yep, the one and only."

My heart races as my mind scans back to the time in the library. The family tree. Torn at the point where the child of Jose and his wife should be.

All this time I'd assumed it was Andreas... and by the looks of it, so did Ezra!

"But dad is Jose's son... I don't understand?"

Estelle smiles, shaking her head. "No, actually your father was the product of some whore who worked here when your grandfather Jose was alive. She became a victim of the Silvaro curse, murdered, hidden away. God knows who his real father is, but when my father Jose murdered Andreas' mother, he took in this helpless young child." She looks to Andreas, who is as still as a statue. "An act of pure love if you ask me. However, I came along soon after and we grew up together and well, the rest is history."

Ezra began breathing heavily, he runs his palm over his face, trying to process everything.

"Anyway, everything seemed to be in place tonight with Henrik here, until I saw the two of you in my room foraging through my things."

Her eye catches the white dress, still in Ezra's grip. Eleanor's white dress.

"You came across something that I didn't want uncovered. So it's fair to say that we came home early, our plans changed slightly."

"How did you know we were in your room?" My voice comes out as a whisper as I struggle to contain my fear. Right now showing fear to this woman would be like showing blood to a shark.

"Cameras my dear, you know modern technology. Fascinating really. I saw it all."

I reach around the back of my neck feeling the beads of sweat already forming and clinging to the fine hairs of my hairline.

"Why was my sister's dress hidden in the back of your drawers? And in this state?" Ezras fists clench around the dress, his knuckles turning white. "Did you do this?" He points accusingly at Andreas, who stands expressionless.

"No... I did." The words hit like bullets. Estelles face remains stoic like she doesn't have a care in the world as the ruthless words leave her lips.

"What?" Horror was etched deep on Ezra's face. "What do you mean you..."

"I. Killed. Her."

My head spun with the revelation. The horror on Ezra's face was slowly bleeding into desperation and pain.

"Did you kill Kara Valance?" Hunters voice almost feels like it's waking me from a deep trance. I'd almost forgotten he was in the room.

Estelle scoffs. "That little whore that wouldn't take no for an answer. She deserved everything that was coming to her. After that disgusting show with my son at the Halloween ball, I followed her out to the lake. She was crying, claiming she loved Ezra and he should be with her. Pathetic. I started to put the little bitch out of her misery, planned to dispose of the body afterwards, but I got disturbed...by you!" She points at Summer who's eyes widen in fear.

"I didn't have time to get rid of the body before I could hear you stumbling around in the bushes, throwing up, drunk out of your mind. I knew then that you were nothing more than just another worthless victim for my family."

Summer sobs, her sounds muffled by the tape.

I feel a need to pinch myself to wake up from this nightmare. Why the fuck am I not waking up?

Estelle continues her tirade with vengeance. Like we weren't just four innocent people standing before her but cockroaches needing to be trampled on.

"Things would have been fine until yet another spanner was thrown into the works when Madeline Korrman came crawling back into the daylight. She was a slut, a homewrecker. I was ready to end her until she managed to get away in the woods. I know she never saw my face so when she fled I wasn't really worried. I knew if I ever saw her again I'd finish the job, but then she had to speak to handsome deputy Jackson here." She flashes a toothy grin at Hunter.

"Of course I couldn't let him tell anyone the truth, so he was just, how do we say it? collateral!"

Inhaling sharply, I force the words from my throat.

"So you attack Madeline and Kara because you believe they were... whores? But then why..."

"WHY KILL MY SISTER?" Ezras rage flares. His silence finally broke from the chilling revelations, his voice like thunder. "She was no whore!"

Estelle pauses and for a minute I swear I see a smidgen of remorse, but then as quick as it arrives it disappears again leaving a demon in its wake.

"No... she wasn't. My beautiful Eleanor. Too beautiful for this world. Do you know, I was a pageant queen? One of the most beautiful women in the country? No I bet you don't. The Silvaro name tarnished everything in my life. People say money gives you freedom and many of my family, I'm sure would agree. But no, it never brought anything for me. Money can't change who you are on the inside. But Eleanor was different. From the moment she was born, I knew she didn't have the sickness. I mean, fuck I was the first woman in our bloodline to have it. What a curse that is. But Eleanor was loved and adored by everyone. By her brother Ezra, her father Andreas. Everyone thought she was amazing, a better version of me. She had everything."

"So you killed her out of... jealousy?" The word burns my tongue like acid.

"I killed her because I couldn't stand always being second best, always being looked at with disgust from my own husband because of the way I was. The way I *needed* to kill. Even the Xanax and endless drugs couldn't cure the insomnia, the nightmares. Andreas knew Ezra had the sickness, and when he knew his son didn't want to kill the innocents like we all had before, he helped him. Pretended he was part of the bloodline and the two of them went off like good little knights in shining armour with Caleb

Fox. The vigilante and the psychopath. What modern day heroes you are." She chuckled, the sound echoing through the walls.

"I suppose I snapped, I stabbed her, thought she was dead and then took her to the lake where I planned to hide her. Unfortunately she was still alive but I knew by now she'd lost too much blood, she was too weak to fight back now, so after stripping her and tying the rocks to her body, it was only going to be a matter of time until she drowned."

My stomach heaved and I began to retch as I felt the burn of bile hurtling from my stomach. A mother killed her own child in cold blood.

"Did you know about this?" Ezra whispered, turning to Andreas.

"Yes." He replied. "I wasn't there when it happened but yes, I knew."

Ezra's face and neck are now blood red, burning with rage. "And you did nothing? YOU DID NOTHING!"

My whole frame trembled at the violence in which the words were thrown out of Ezra's body.

Andreas never flinched, it was almost like he had become completely desensitised to everything. Like he couldn't even show any kind of emotion towards his own son who was standing in front of him, broken, destroyed.

"He loves me." Estelle had a cruel, narcissistic look of pride on her face as she held out the hand not holding the gun, grasping Andreas's palm. "He'll always be by my side."

"I was raised as a killer," Andreas begins to speak. "I may not be a Silvaro by blood but when you are raised in that world, it warps you and it's who you become."

I began to shake my head. How was he standing by her? She really did have him wrapped under some kind of twisted spell.

I think back to all the times I thought this man was abusing his wife. When I would see him grip her wrist tightly or scold her under his breath. He was trying to stop her from harming someone. Trying to stop her from giving in to these murderous, psychotic impulses that she had.

Behind me, I could hear the slight rustle of Hunter's binds as he struggled to get free. I wanted to get closer, see if I could help him loosen them but Estelle was too close to where I was standing. The gun sitting between Ezra and myself.

"Of course, now you have a choice," Estelle continued, her attention now aimed solely at Ezra. "Be who you are meant to be, come back to this family, kill the girl and her friends and take your rightful place with us or... die with her?"

Ezra visibly stiffened before baring his teeth in an animalistic snarl. "I would rather die than ever be near you again and I would never harm a single hair on her head unless she wanted me to."

Estelle laughs again. "Why? She means nothing."

"She means everything to me. I would never hurt her. I love her."

I think in that moment my heart temporarily stopped and restarted again as I took in Ezra's words.

Estelle turns the gun to me. "Do you love him? A monster? Could you love him now that you know who he is? What he's done? What he will *keep* doing?"

I close my eyes, the feeling that my ending is imminent, gnawing away at me, and knowing that if I die without telling Ezra the truth then everything we've been through since I arrived in this hell bound place has all been for nothing.

I open my eyes. "Yes." I reply, before looking towards Ezra, not giving Estelle the satisfaction of my reply. " I love you."

Ezras lips parted slightly, like he wanted to say something but the words were refusing to come out but it didn't matter to me anymore, I knew how I felt about this mysterious, tortured, absolutely fucked up man. I loved him. I loved him with all of my being and there was no way I was going to deny these feelings anymore.

"Well this is all super romantic and everything but we really don't have enough time for this. Things weren't really supposed to play out like this, and there isn't much time before someone from one of the wings comes snooping around, so let's get on with things. Henrik..." Estelle called to the man behind her, her eyes never leaving the four of us. "You've got two for one now. As well as the girl, you can take our lovely deputy Jackson here. I'm sure when your clients find out he's a cop, they will be wanting to get pretty...creative with their punishments."

"I'm not going fucking anywhere." Snarled Hunter.

"Oh but you are...Zora."

The burly fucker guarding the door stormed over to Hunter grabbing him by the throat.

Summer screamed under her gag as the other guy, Niall, began advancing towards her.

"WHY ARE YOU LETTING HER DO THIS?" Ezra roared, this time aiming his anger towards his father.

A sadness appeared to cloud the dark eyes of Andreas as he looked towards his son. "She's my wife."

"ELEANOR WAS YOUR DAUGHTER, JOSE KILLED YOUR MOTHER!"

"HIS MOTHER WAS A WORTHLESS WHORE." Estelle screamed, the angry veins in her neck protruding defiantly.

I stared between them in complete shock, unable to process the fact that Andreas, all this time, had been nothing more than a puppet on a string. Controlled and manipulated by his psychotic wife.

"You made your choice," said Estelle, pointing the gun directly at Ezra's forehead. "Now you'll die with her."

As if in slow motion, her fingers began squeezing against the trigger, I heard the faint whisper from Ezra as he looked, one final time at Andreas.

"and I'm your son."

My vision felt like it was closing in, shadows swirling as sheer terror filled my every cell. I wanted to scream, I wanted to dive in front of Ezra, I wanted to do something but my body all of a sudden felt like it was filled with lead but I pushed forward regardless, my only goal to save the man I loved.

Then, within a flash, before the bullet could leave the barrel, I heard the word, "STOP."

Andreas roared at Estelle. Before her fingers could release the fate of her son, Andreas pushed her arms with brutal force, the gun hurtling out of her grip and sliding across the ballroom floor.

"Urgh!" She bellowed in anger and that's when it caught my eye, the glint of a knife.

Hunter tore at his binds a final time as they broke free, releasing his hands. Turning, he threw his head back before smashing it forward, connecting with Zora's face. The oversized monster screamed as his nose made a sickening pop.

Adrenaline surged through my body all of a sudden as I dove across the floor, grabbing the gun, but it was too late.

Estelle pulled the blade from the waistband of her suit trousers before slamming it into the jugular of her husband and dragging it across his flesh, slitting his throat.

"NO!" Ezra ran to Andreas who collapsed to the floor, his eyes bulging as he choked and gurgled on his own blood. The liquid pooling at his feet like a slaughtered animal.

Before Estelle could swipe the knife at Ezra, he punched her hard in the face, she stumbled back, laughing as she spat blood onto the floor.

I pointed the end of the gun at Zora and Niall before Hunter grabbed Summer, tearing at her gag and bindings before pulling her into his chest.

Ezra crouched down, his hands glistening with his fathers blood but it was too late, Andreas was gone, the light in his eyes put out for good.

"Estelle, it's over." I cried. My hands were surprisingly steady as I held the gun towards her.

She began to laugh like a maniac, looking over my shoulder as I noticed Henrik running at Hunter with a candle stick he'd grabbed for the side unit.

"HUNTER!" I bellowed, turning towards Henrik, before my fingers instinctively pulled the trigger, a bullet piercing right between his eyes. Henrik dropped to the floor. An instant kill.

Zora ran at me, I closed my eyes, bracing for the impact but as he was about to slam straight into my body, he was knocked to the ground by another solid figure. Ezra pounced, his fists connecting with Zoras face over and over again.

Niall made a dash for the door but Hunter was on him.

As he pushed Summer to the side, Hunter dove towards Niall, blocking his escape and driving his fist into Nialls face.

I turned quickly to Estelle who was walking slowly towards me. My hands, still squeezing the gun.

"You know you're just like me now." She smiled, looking towards Henrik. "How did you find your first kill? Did you feel the euphoric high? Was it everything you imagined it would be? I remember my first kill...mmm...now thats something you never forget."

Cold sweat coated the back of my neck. "I'm nothing like you." I whispered.

"Hmmmm no, I suppose you're right, you're nothing but a WORTHLESS WHORE."

She ran towards me, screaming like a banshee as the blade of her blood soaked knife glinted above her head but I was ready, one pull of the trigger and the bullet flew through the air, piercing Estelle right in the stomach.

She doubled over and began to stumble, clutching at the wound before staring at me in disbelief.

Dropping the gun, I ran to Summer, who looked like she was one breath away from passing out. Her pretty eyes enlarged and her arms wrapped tightly around her small frame.

Hunter and Ezra had overpowered Niall and Zora and I wasn't entirely sure if the two men were dead or simply knocked out. I wasn't getting close enough to find out.

Estelle continued to stumble but instead of falling to the ground, she grabbed a large, lit candelabra from the side unit.

The four of us turned in horror as she smiled, a last evil smirk, before launching the flames at the floor as she fell, setting fire to the two large velvet-like curtains that hung near the exit to the ballroom.

Chapter Thirty Two

Bennett

Almost like they had been dipped in kerosene, the curtains set alight, the white hot flames raging up the thick, dark material.

"BENNETT." Summer screamed as I gripped her wrist, pulling her towards the exit, Hunter and Ezra following close behind. But the flames were unforgiving, spreading throughout the curtain frames and burning into the walls of the house.

As if like clay, the walls began to melt away.

"What the fuck?!" Ezra stared as the fire raged, reaping its deadly revenge. "OUT NOW!"

We ran to the doorway as thick clouds of smoke began to form, my eyes blurring as the fog hit me like a force field preventing me from taking a further step.

I felt Ezras strong hand take hold of my own as he pulled me through the exit.

"Bennett, take Summer and get outside, I need to alert the others throughout the house. Get them out." Ezra prepared to run up the staircase.

"No, I'm coming with you." There was no way I was leaving him in here alone.

"Go, we'll sort this," said Hunter, also heading in the direction of the staircase.

"No I'm staying, Summer leave, wait for the fire department, help people as we get them out."

Summer gave me a hesitant look before nodding and running

towards the door.

Hunter nodded at Ezra and I before the three of us charged up the stairs.

"You take that way." Ezra called to Hunter as we reached the corridors at the top of the landing.

Between the three of us, we fled through the house, banging on doors and shouting to alert everyone to get out.

People had already started fleeing their rooms following the sounds of the gunshots. Panic and desperation etched on their faces. Thick smoke was already clouding everything in sight.

Horror overtook me as I realised it was as if this whole house had been doused in gasoline, the way the flames were spreading like a plague.

Trying to keep so many people calm as they all fought to get out of the crumbling building was harder than I could ever have imagined.

Ezra had managed to set off alarms which would send a signal to the fire department, alerting them to what was happening.

Running back through the corridors, I couldn't stop myself from coughing violently, the smoke penetrating my lungs as the house began collapsing around us.

"The walls, Ezra, the walls." The wooden panels began crumbling into the flames as Hunter, Ezra and I watched the fire ravaging everything in its path, but it was what caught my eye next that truly made my heart feel like it had stopped dead inside my chest.

As the wooden panels fell away and the fire tore holes into the walls, small fragments began to fall out of the holes.

"What the fuck is that?" Hunter called as I continued to stare in horror at the objects dropping in piles from every hole forming from the raging flames.

The dirty brown tone and distinctive shape told me exactly what was pouring from the walls at that very moment. Bones. Human bones.

As if on cue, human skulls began falling from the holes. I screamed as one rolled right up to me and stopped just before my feet. *The missing victims of the Silvaros.*

All this time, the great secret of where all the bodies of the missing victims had been hidden had been right under my nose. They had been hidden inside the walls of Knightchurch.

Looking to Ezra, the shock on his face confirmed he had no idea that his home was nothing more than a giant tomb to all those who had fallen foul to his ancestors.

As the bones continued to pour out, Ezra began to walk slowly towards them. Hunter ran for the back door.

"We need to go NOW!"

As the final word left his lips, I heard the creak of the beam above his head.

"HUNTER!" I called to him in hopelessness as the beam broke away from the ceiling, but before it could hit him, Ezra charged toward him, knocking him out of the way, the beam barely missing both of them.

I ran towards the men as we crawled our way out of the exit, coughing and spluttering. Our faces tarred with black from the smoke.

The rush of fresh air felt like it was hitting me like a lorry as I inhaled deeply, trying painfully to draw in any oxygen I could get.

Standing back, the trees hiding our silhouettes, Ezra, Hunter and I watched, standing united, as Knightchurch manor burned to the ground, taking all its sinister secrets with it.

I watched as the fire continued to ravage before looking up to the window on the top floor. A face catching my eye.

At first I thought it was someone trapped inside, someone we'd missed until I looked closer and I realised... it was Millie.

She stood, her tiny palms pressed firmly on the window panes. A gentle smile on her lips. Slowly she removed a hand from the glass, her fingers curving into a small wave.

The feel of a hot tear leaving my eye and rolling down my cheek pulled me from my glare as I smiled back at her, nodding my head in acknowledgement.

As she gradually began to fade away, I swear for a second she was standing with the silver haired woman. Theodora Alcott. The woman who led me to the haunting truth of the Silvaro family.

But no sooner had I seen the image, it vanished again. The window, empty and in darkness.

Thick fog soared around the outside of the stone facades, engulfing the windows and doors as it climbed higher and tore into the sky.

By now sirens wailed in the distance, indicating that the fire department had arrived.

However, their efforts to save the magnificent Manor House would be in vain. Knightchurch would be no more.

Inside, my heart broke for the families of the victims hidden inside Knightchurch. So many people died without knowing what happened to their loved ones. A devastating secret kept hidden until now, and now the fire would destroy it all.

"Why the fuck are you still here?" Hunter looked at Ezra, the animosity of the past nowhere to be seen.

"Take me in." Ezra replied. "I'll tell them it was me that fired the bullets." His hand was on my shoulder squeezing reassuringly. *No!*

"No need. Leave. Now. A life for a life. You saved mine, I'm returning the favour. Get out of here, both of you and don't come back. That house holds enough human remains that after the fire, it's just going to look like Ezra Silvaro perished with his family."

I couldn't believe what I was hearing.

"But my dad." I couldn't leave him alone.

"He'll be fine. I'll make sure." Hunter threw his arms around me, hugging me tightly and for the first time, I sank into his embrace, holding him with all of me, including my heart.

"Thank you." Ezra held out his hand, grasping Hunter's palm in a firm hold before shaking.

"Go."

Gripping Ezras hand, we began to retreat into the woods.

"I'll contact my dad... when everything's died down. Please

just let him know I'm safe."

Hunter nodded, heading back around to the front of the house where Summer and everyone else were congregated.

I looked at Ezra, the chips of ice glowing in his beautiful eyes.

"I love you Bennett. I'll never stop loving you, and I'll never stop working to prove to you how much you mean to me."

Pushing up onto my tiptoes, my lips met his in a gentle kiss, the warmth of his tongue in my mouth creating a fire inside me enough to rival the destructive force that just ended the infamous Knightchurch Manor.

"I love you too."

With a smile, he tilts his head motioning towards the dark wood and together we begin to move, walking into the unknown beauty of our future.

Epilogue

∞∞∞

One year later

<u>Bennett</u>

If there's one thing I've learned in this life it's that you never really know what's going to happen next. The future is unknown to all of us.

This beautiful, frightening, inevitable thing that there's no escaping from.

You never know what you'll be doing, where you'll be or even who you'll be doing it with. Some people don't even realise their future isn't even written on the cards anymore and that the sands of time are slowly filtering to an end.

You can plan all you like, prepare all you like. But the truth is. The future cares for none of it. It's relentless in its forthcoming and we can pretend we have control over it as much as we want but at the end of the day, the power never really was ours to hold.

The delicate sound of the waves rustles in the distance. A cool breeze caresses my face as I clutch my notepad, the poem half finished in front of me. I toss it down on the warm sand and lean back on my elbows admiring the view, pushing my feet through the soft, fragile grains.

I've lived in the beautiful beach town of Reaves since the night I left Knightchurch with the man I love.

All we had were the clothes on our back as we walked through the dark wood into the unknown.

After reaching Caleb, he helped us acquire new passports and IDs as well as loaning us some money for our new lives.

Ezra had remembered my dream to live by the sea so we took the next flight out, arriving in Reaves and settling here from then on.

I began my life as a writer soon after arriving and I haven't looked back. I have a lot of words to share with the world, that's for sure.

My first book is set to be released soon under my pen name and I couldn't be more excited.

I contacted my father not long after the fire with the help of Hunter, who had become surprisingly close to Summer in the following months, and was over the moon to learn that he and Mrs Potton had filed for a marriage license.

I don't know if their wedding will be something we will be able to attend but I know for certain we can try.

According to dad, at their age you never knew what could happen so you just went for it. I didn't tell him that even in my lifetime I'd already discovered that for myself.

Knightchurch had taken so many innocent lives. Eleanor - my friend Millie - being one of them.

She had everything to live for, a bright and limitless future ahead of her that she should be grabbing with both hands, but instead it was ended before it had even begun. It just went to prove that no matter your age, nothing is guaranteed.

The house had a heart, it had a soul, but it was black. Black and rotting like the secrets encased within it.

After confiding in my dad about the things I'd been seeing at Knightchurch, I was shocked when he revealed my mother had always been 'sensitive to the other side' as he put it.

She'd seen things she couldn't explain and a lot of people thought she was psychic. He told me she was extremely quiet and had a very introverted personality which caused a lot of people to think she was strange. But he said he had always thought her gift was beautiful and unique and he wasn't surprised to hear I'd inherited it too.

Ezra never spoke about his mother again. He never told me how he really felt about the revelation, just that he intended to move on.

We spoke regularly about Eleanor and how she would have loved to be here on the beach with us now. We've even spoken about kids, although I feel like that's a little far into the distance right now.

Ezra continued his 'line of work' through contact with Caleb although they hadn't spoken to each other in a while.

I don't believe what he has is a 'sickness' as he has always called it. I believe in this case, nurture overtook nature and he was shaped in the life he lived with Andreas and Estelle.

I do believe one day he will stop killing but right now he's ridding the world of one evil after another and I can't say I'm against that. No matter how fucked up that probably makes me sound.

Maybe it isn't blood that runs through his veins, maybe it's poison, beautiful poison that consumes you so entirely that you never realise you're silently and benevolently dying.

I believe with Estelle, she did have deep rooted trauma going back to her life with Jose, but I think in the end she chose that as nothing more than an excuse for the evil she was committing. In the end she didn't want to be saved. She didn't want to stop what she was doing and unfortunately she had dragged Andreas down with her. Maybe he wasn't strong enough to stop her or maybe it really was that love clouded his vision. Either way he never stood a chance.

The cool breeze soothed me as I closed my eyes, tasting the rings of salt in the air.

I heard the gentle footsteps across the sand getting closer as I opened my eyes to see Ezra heading towards me.

He was dressed in brown cargo pants and a white linen shirt, similar to the white linen maxi dress I was wearing. His feet bare.

He looked far from the man I'd met just a year ago at a gothic mansion drowning in secrets and pain.

His face looked calm, his whole body at ease as he strode up to me, dropping down onto the sand by my side.

Pulling his knees into his chest and resting his elbows on them, he looked towards me. His inky black hair dishevelled and the sexiness doing something wicked to the area between my legs. Even after a year, he was still the most beautiful man I'd ever seen.

"Penny for your thoughts?"

I smiled. "I was actually thinking about how gorgeous our babies would be if they looked like their daddy."

He laughed. "Well I don't know about that, but I think they stand a pretty good chance with a mama like you."

He leans over, pressing a gentle kiss to my lips.

"Maybe we should head back, start practicing."

Ezra smiles, a glint of malice in his eyes. "The things I want to do to you right now, I'm not sure you're mentally ready for."

A laugh forces it way out of my throat. "Don't underestimate me Ezra, my mind likes to be fucked just as much as my pussy."

He raises an eyebrow, a delicious smirk on his sun kissed face and in that moment I know I've got everything I'll ever need.

Ezra

Life had certainly turned around in the last year. Sitting next to Bennett, feeling the sand beneath my feet and hearing nothing but the ocean and the gentle sound of her delicate breathing, I felt content for the very first time in my life.

Knightchurch was gone and with it, I hoped, the legends and horror stories used to scare kids into behaving for their parents. All of it lost and rotting with the embers.

Of course the monster remained. He was sitting next to a beautiful woman on the beach in the idyllic town of Reaves. But for now he was dormant, and I knew he would only ever destroy the evil of the world. The innocent no longer had anything to fear.

After discovering my whole life had been one big fucking lie, it was without a doubt difficult to process.

My sister had been murdered at the hands of our own mother. A truth I now had to live with for the rest of my life. She may be dead and fuck, was I glad she was burning in hell right now but still, I hated her for the fact that I would go on living now, knowing just what she had done.

I'd lived my whole life believing my father was the son of Jose Silvaro. Maybe I was blind, stupid even, god knows what else but my mother had the wool firmly over everyone's eyes.

Some would say I must have had a fraction of an idea what was going on with her but the truth is I didn't. A lot of that was probably being wrapped up in the fact I was trying to control my own dealings with the curse, not looking at how it was affecting anyone else.

However, I hadn't said a word about it since that day to Bennett. I left it burning in the past along with Knightchurch manor and there was no way I was going to let my mothers lies continue to destroy my life or the life of my little bird.

My sister Eleanor's death has changed me, of that I'm sure. What's the saying? Time is the greatest healer, some shit like that. But anyway, the fact is it's true. You never get over the loss of someone you love with all your heart, but over time that loss becomes more manageable. The pain never goes away, you just learn to live with it better. It becomes a part of you, stays with you like a stain on your soul.

That's the feeling I have now when I think about my beautiful sister.

Bennett and I share stories about her, it's strange yet comforting to hear that she sought out Bennett, almost like she knew my little bird and I were meant to be. That's how I like to think of it anyway so fuck it!

I do worry sometimes about another generation of the

Silvaros. It's the main reason I'm reluctant to have a child, but to be honest, Bennett wants to be a mother one day and we haven't exactly been careful in the past so I'm surprised it hasn't happened already. Bennett doesn't seem worried or even bothered though that she still isn't pregnant, maybe the universe has taken it upon itself to put an end to the Silvaro bloodline for us. I guess we can only hope.

Bennett leans her head on my shoulder.

"I love you, you know," she whispers.

I press a kiss to the top of her head.

"I love you too." As the words leave my mouth, my cell phone begins to ring in my pocket.

"How nice it is to finally be in a place that has a signal." She laughs.

I smirk as I pull the phone from my pocket, the number unknown.

Pressing it to my ear I listen as the familiar voice travels down the line, pulling a wicked smile from my lips.

I finish the call and hang up. Bennett, watching me with curious eyes.

"Who was that?" She asks.

"Caleb," I replied. "He's asked us if we'd like to return to Cedar Cross for a while... he has a little gift for us."

About The Author

Michelle Briddock

Michelle Briddock grew up in the glorious South Yorkshire city of Sheffield, before moving down south in hope of a bit more sun...it never happened.

She spends her days writing dark romance and being a slave to her 3 children, and her nights arguing with her husband about which Netflix series to binge.

As a little girl, she always loved the Disney villains more than the princesses, which she now channels into all her stories.

Join Michelle's world on instagram @wildflower_author for updates and all things bookish.

Also by Michelle Briddock...

The psychological, dark romantic thriller SIREN is available on Amazon now!
   Come and experience the world of Lexi & Alaric.

Aknowledgements

WOW! How surreal it feels that I've actually completed book number two. When I first started my debut novel over six months ago, I never thought that I would be sat here now writing the thank yous for my second novel.

I think my biggest thank you has got to go to you guys, the readers for taking a chance on an unknown indie author and helping me really get myself out there and share all the crazy stories that are whirling around in my head.
For showing support by buying/borrowing my books, sharing my posts and talking about my work to your friends and family, you will never realise how much this all means to me. Writing is my life and you all make the hard work so worthwhile.
Thank you to my family for your continued support and to my friends, who are probably sick of hearing about book covers and font sizes.
And last but not least, thank you to Jay Aheer at Simply Defined Art for the absolutely stunning cover for Beautiful Poison, you really are the book cover designing master

PSSSSTT...

WANT TO KNOW WHAT REALLY HAPPENED TO THE VICARS DAUGHTER?

Caleb And Rivers Story Is Coming Soon...

Hey You Lovely Lot...

Can I ask for a huge favour??????

WOULD YOU BE WILLING TO LEAVE ME A REVIEW?

One positive review on Amazon literally makes a huge difference to the world of an Indie author. Your support means everything to us. I literally read every single review and I am so grateful to everyone who takes the time to do this, so thank you so much in advance and hope you enjoy my books

Michelle xoxo

Printed in Great Britain
by Amazon